Brad pulled on the leath... rattles were just out of sight inside his shirt.

Abel spread his legs in a gunfighter's stance and held his arms out like a pair of parentheses, ready to draw.

"Snake," Brad shouted and looked down at Abel's feet.

He shook the rattles, and Abel jumped three inches off the floor. His face drained of blood as he looked around. The two men at the table scraped their chairs and lifted their boots off the floor. They, too, were looking for a rattlesnake crawling around somewhere.

Abel's right hand streaked for his gun.

Before Abel could clear leather, Brad snatched his pistol from its holster. He thumbed back the hammer on the rise as he brought the barrel up to bear on Abel's gut.

Brad held his breath and squeezed the trigger.

The .45 Colt bucked in his hands as its blue-black snout spewed lead, orange sparks, and white smoke.

The bullet smashed through Abel's belt buckle, cracked into his spine, and blew a hole the size of a small grapefruit in his back. His blood spattered the two men at the table, Curly and Nels.

Abel slumped to the floor, wild red blood gushing from the hole in his stomach. The stench from his ruptured intestines filled the air.

Berkley titles by Jory Sherman

The Vigilante Novels

THE VIGILANTE
SIX-GUN LAW
SANTA FE SHOWDOWN

John Savage Novels

THE SAVAGE GUN
THE SAVAGE TRAIL
THE SAVAGE CURSE
SAVAGE HELLFIRE
SAVAGE VENGEANCE

The Sidewinder Novels

SIDEWINDER
DEATH RATTLE
SNAKE EYES
NEST OF VIPERS

Other Novels

THE DARK LAND
SUNSET RIDER
TEXAS DUST
BLOOD RIVER
THE SUNDOWN MAN

NEST OF VIPERS

JORY SHERMAN

BERKLEY BOOKS, NEW YORK

THE BERKLEY PUBLISHING GROUP
Published by the Penguin Group
Penguin Group (USA) Inc.
375 Hudson Street, New York, New York 10014, USA

Penguin Group (Canada), 90 Eglinton Avenue East, Suite 700, Toronto, Ontario M4P 2Y3, Canada
(a division of Pearson Penguin Canada Inc.) • Penguin Books Ltd., 80 Strand, London WC2R 0RL,
England • Penguin Group Ireland, 25 St. Stephen's Green, Dublin 2, Ireland (a division of Penguin
Books Ltd.) • Penguin Group (Australia), 250 Camberwell Road, Camberwell, Victoria 3124, Australia
(a division of Pearson Australia Group Pty. Ltd.) • Penguin Books India Pvt. Ltd., 11 Community
Centre, Panchsheel Park, New Delhi—110 017, India • Penguin Group (NZ), 67 Apollo Drive,
Rosedale, Auckland 0632, New Zealand (a division of Pearson New Zealand Ltd.) • Penguin Books
(South Africa) (Pty.) Ltd., 24 Sturdee Avenue, Rosebank, Johannesburg 2196, South Africa

Penguin Books Ltd., Registered Offices: 80 Strand, London WC2R 0RL, England

NEST OF VIPERS

A Berkley Book / published by arrangement with the author

PUBLISHING HISTORY
Berkley edition / December 2012

ISBN: 978-0-425-25058-7

BERKLEY®
Berkley Books are published by The Berkley Publishing Group,
a division of Penguin Group (USA) Inc.,
375 Hudson Street, New York, New York 10014.
BERKLEY® is a registered trademark of Penguin Group (USA) Inc.
The "B" design is a trademark of Penguin Group (USA) Inc.

PRINTED IN THE UNITED STATES OF AMERICA

10 9 8 7 6 5 4 3 2 1

ALWAYS LEARNING   PEARSON

ONE

❧

The men rode out of a white fluffy cloud.

There were three of them. They all bore scruffy beards on their lean, hatchet-sharp faces. Their eyes burned like dark coals as they urged their horses to the edge of the precipice. Mist rose up around them. Their horses were festooned with ropes and quirts, extra pistols dangling from worn leather holsters. Rifle butts jutted from their saddle scabbards.

They halted their horses at the top of the sheer bluff and looked down at the lush valley below.

One of them lifted the pair of field glasses dangling from his grimy neck and adjusted the lenses after he put them to his eyes. He scanned the valley with the binoculars, from right to left and then back again.

"Most of the horses are in a corral just at the edge of the timber," Nels Canby said. "Some are grazin' over by the crick yonder. Maybe two or three."

"Let me take a look, Nelson," Abel Avery said. He reached an arm out.

Nels slipped the sling from his neck and handed over the binoculars.

Abel swept the magnifying glasses down at the house where a thin tendril of smoke spiraled from a brick chimney. Then he worked the glasses in a circular motion to take in the barn, a bunkhouse. He stopped as he stared at the bunkhouse for several moments. It, too, had a chimney, but there was no smoke rising from its metal stack. He lingered there for a few more minutes, then swept his gaze over to the far creek and down to the end of the valley and back up on the other side along the timberline. He paused when he saw a gap in the timber about a half mile down from the house.

"Well?" Canby said as Avery took the glasses away from his eyes.

"Pretty quiet, Nels, like you said it would be."

"What in hell are we waitin' for, then?" the man in the middle asked. They called him Curly, but his name was Dan Jimson, and he was as bald as a porcelain darning egg.

"You can see where Storm and his hired hand rode out. They left a pair of swaths right through that wet grass," Canby said.

"I see it," Jimson said, "and there, over yonder by the bunkhouse and barn you can see where some of the hands rode out to that cut in the timber."

"Yeah, that's where Storm ranges his cattle in the spring and summer," Canby said.

"So, the nighthawks will be comin' back to sleep," Jimson said. "We'd better get to it, if we're goin' to rustle them horses."

Canby turned his horse to the right. The two other men followed him. There was a talus slope where the bluff ran out, and it led right down to the valley. They rode down it, their horses braking with their hooves to keep from sliding or pitching forward. The ground was wet there and the iron horseshoes made little sound.

"Somebody must be in the house," Nels said. "Man wouldn't leave his fire a-burnin'."

"His woman," Canby said, his voice barely above a whisper.

"Well, we got to take care of her," Nels said. "She might come after us with a scattergun."

"Or a broom," Jimson said, a wicked smile on his face.

"Shut your traps," Canby said. "You boys get your ropes unlimbered at that corral while I check the house."

"We always get the shit jobs," Nels said.

"I'm takin' the dangerous one," Canby said. "If his woman's got a Greener a-settin' by the door, I might just get my balls blowed off."

"Likely she'll hit you with a fry pan," Avery said.

The other two men chuckled under their breaths.

"Shhhh," Canby warned as they reached the bottom of the wide slope. He turned his horse away from the other two men as they continued riding toward the corral. He kept his horse to a slow walk, straight toward the small porch and the rough-hewn front door. He kept his gaze fixed on the door as he let his horse creep up on the house. He dropped his right hand to his pistol and lightly grasped its butt.

The horses in the corral whickered softly as if murmuring among themselves as the two rustlers approached. Canby stiffened and halted his horse for several seconds. Then, he continued on, making his horse step out, one hoof at a time.

He looked over at Abel and Curly. Abel shook out a coil of rope he had detached from his saddle. He began to build a loop. Curly untied the thong that held one of his ropes and shook it out. It slithered on the ground like a galvanized snake.

Canby rode up to the porch and swung his leg over the saddle and dismounted. He tied his reins around a post that held up one corner of the slanted roof that shaded the porch. He stepped onto the porch from the side and walked to the door.

He stood there for several seconds, his head bent to hear any sound from inside.

He thought he heard something from the rear of the

house. Inside. Perhaps the kitchen. The sound was like a soft tinny clang. He touched the latch and lifted it with great care. The latch released, and the door eased open on leather hinges.

Canby tiptoed through the door. The front room was deserted. In the hearth, a fire blazed. The wood crackled as it released pockets of stored gases. He stepped into the center of the room and heard the clank of a pot from somewhere down the hall. In the dim light of the room, he could not see much beyond the doorway that led down a hallway.

He heard another clank and stepped into the hall. He drew his pistol and eased along the passageway. A floorboard creaked under the weight of his boot.

He stopped as he saw a ghostly figure in the room beyond the hallway.

"Brad, is that you?" Felicity called from the kitchen.

Canby held his breath and flattened himself against the wall.

"Brad?"

She held a coffeepot in her hand and stepped toward the hallway, her hazel eyes narrowed to pierce the dimness.

"This isn't funny, Brad," she said. Then, she entered the hallway.

"Julio? Is that you?" she said, her voice softer and this time, with a slight quaver to it.

She froze as she saw the shadowy figure of a man pressed against the wall.

Canby stepped away from the boards and the blued steel of his revolver flashed with a glimmer of light.

Felicity screamed when she saw that the man in the hallway was not her husband, Brad Storm.

She heard the click as the man hammered back his pistol to full cock. The sound was a snick that resonated in her brain like a knife blade jabbing into a bone in her skull.

She screamed again and there was rage in her voice, rage and a deep fear that she was going to die.

TWO

❧

Felicity's scream shattered the morning stillness. It froze Avery in his tracks. He had a horse roped, and Curly was about to slip a halter over its head when he, too, stiffened and his hands stopped in midair.

"What the hell was that?" Avery asked.

Then they heard a loud yell, followed by a banging of metal striking wood.

From the house, they heard the explosion of a pistol shot.

Both men dropped rope and halter and dashed to the corral fence. They clambered over it and heard a series of screams coming from the house.

"Sounds like Canby's tied into a wildcat," Avery said.

"A female wildcat," Curly puffed.

Sunlight gamboled in the pines and shot shadows in long lines from trees, bushes, and structures. The billowing clouds rising amid the high, snow-capped peaks turned pink and salmon as the clouds floated toward the valley.

Abel ran through the open door with Curly on his heels.

Muffled sounds of a struggle came from down the hall.

"Nels, what you got?" Abel asked as he saw two silhouettes tussling in the hall.

"A wild bitch," Nels replied and locked an arm around Felicity's neck.

He wrestled her down the hall as Curly and Abel backtracked to the front room. Felicity's blue flannel nightgown was ripped from the neckline to her belly and her pert breasts glared out from the torn opening in the fabric.

Curly's eyes bulged as Nels lifted her off her feet and she kicked with both of them. She twisted to free herself, but Nels held her fast.

"I'm going to put the boots to this little tigress," Nels said and threw her down on the divan.

Felicity screeched at him. "You filthy bastard," she spat.

Nels slapped her across the mouth. Blood seeped from cracks in her lips.

As Felicity moaned in pain, Nels drew his hunting knife from its scabbard and slit both of her sleeves. He jerked the remainder of her nightgown from her body, then grabbed her right arm and jerked her to the floor.

Felicity lay there on her back as naked as the day she was born.

Abel and Curly stared at the young woman with feral eyes, eyes that glistened with lust.

Nels unbuckled his gun belt, then his pants belt and dropped his trousers to a puddle around his boots.

Felicity opened her eyes and stared upward. She screamed and tried to scoot away from the savage standing above her ready to pounce.

Nels dropped to his knees and smashed her in the jaw with his fist. Felicity's head snapped backward and struck the hardwood floor. Her eyes went askew, then closed. She was unconscious.

Nels crawled over her and spread her legs wide. Then he plunged into her as Curly and Abel cheered him on.

"Give it to her, Nels," Abel gruffed, as he rubbed a hand up and down on his crotch.

"Stick her good," Curly growled in his throat, his eyes wide and bulging.

Nels finished quickly and rose to his feet. He pulled up his trousers and buckled his belt.

Abel dropped his pants and raped Felicity like some animal coupling in a frenzy.

Then, Curly took his turn and grunted and groaned until Felicity came to and lashed out at him with her open hands. Her fingernails ripped chevrons on his forearms and he grabbed both wrists and pinned her down until he had finished.

Felicity, with swollen lips, cursed the three men.

"My husband will kill you," she spat, and blood flew out with her spittle.

"You little whore," Nels said, then drew his knife.

Felicity sat up and scooted backward to get away from Nels.

An evil leer contorted his face and he strode over to her.

She lifted both arms to ward off the blow that she knew was coming. The knife blade flashed as a beam of sunlight streamed through the front window and caught its metal.

Nels slashed Felicity's arm, and it dropped like a tree limb in a windstorm. Then he stepped in close and slashed her throat in a wide sweep of his arm. The blade sliced her neck and opened her throat. Blood gushed from the gaping wound, and the knife ripped the other side of her neck in its lethal course.

Felicity's eyes opened wide and she sucked in a breath that went no farther than the gaping wound in her neck. The air formed bubbles of blood that dropped and fomented as she slumped over, her eyes glazed with the final frost of mortality.

She made no sound. Her heart stopped and pumped no more blood through her neck wound.

"That'll take care of the witness," Nels snarled.

"Let's get the hell out of here," Abel said.

"We got to get them horses and light a shuck," Curly said as he buckled on his gun belt.

The three men charged out the front door and left it open.

A deep silence settled in the empty house.

In the corral, a horse whickered.

Sunlight streamed through the front door and glazed Felicity's body with a sheen of golden light. Her dark hair, spread out like a fan, glistened like a raven's wing, and the blood on the floor began to congeal and turn a rusty black.

Flies zizzed in from the outside and landed on the fresh blood and peppered her slashed neck in a feeding frenzy.

Later, the three men drove the horses up the slash on the bluff and vanished into the thick timber of the Rocky Mountains.

THREE

❧

Shadows inched down the clapboard walls of the houses and buildings in Leadville as the sun cleared the eastern horizon. There was a chill in the air borne on the breeze that swept down from the high snow-mantled peaks to the west. Brad Storm and his foreman, Julio Aragon, rode down the dirt street, huddled in their sheepskin jackets, their horses blowing steamy mist through their rubbery nostrils.

"Why do we meet this man so early in the morning?" Julio asked.

"Because he sold his herd in Denver and offered to show me a few head before he goes back to Wyoming."

"I have never heard of this breed of cattle," Julio said.

"Hardly anybody has," Brad said. "But I've seen a few head, and I think we can do some mixed breeding and get a better price for bigger cattle."

"Our cattle are big enough," Julio said.

"The ones we're going to look at are bigger."

"So is the buffalo."

Brad laughed. "We might try that someday, too," he said. They rode through the small town to the edge where there were a few fenced stockyards. In one of the pens, they saw some gray cattle at the watering trough. Two men leaned against the fence watching the cattle drink. The cattle had humps on their backs and large floppy ears.

One of the men turned around when Brad and Julio rode up. He wore a battered felt hat, was short and lean, with a three-day beard shadow and a smile that was missing a couple of teeth.

"Howdy," he said. "You Storm?"

Brad swung out of the saddle.

"I'm Brad Storm. You must be Dale Gentry."

"I am. This is my *segundo*, Fred Nowicki."

Nowicki was a shade taller than his boss, with arms that bulged muscles, clear blue eyes and the same three-day beard that looked like embedded pieces of iron. He had a bulbous nose that appeared to have been broken at least twice in his lifetime. He had a stalk of hay in his mouth that left a green stain on the corners of his lips.

Julio stepped out of the saddle and walked over to the men.

"This is Julio Aragon, my ranch foreman," Brad said.

Julio shook hands with Gentry and Nowicki. He could not avert his gaze from the cattle in the pen.

Dale noticed Julio's fascination with the cattle. "Ever seen Brahman cattle before, Julio?" he asked.

Julio shook his head.

"They're from India," Dale said. "And over there, they are considered sacred, almost like gods. They are protected. But a few years ago, some people here in the United States had some shipped over here."

"I've seen 'em before," Brad said, "but never this close."

"The bulls can weigh anywhere from a thousand pounds to over a ton," Dale said. "That big one over there that I brought down weighs better'n fifteen hundred pounds and ain't yet fully growed. He'll make a fine breeder. I call him Caesar."

"You brought one bull and two cows," Brad said.

"The cows are Eloise and Minerva. In case you want to put your whitefaces with a cow or two."

Brad noticed a man standing on the other side of the corral. His horse's reins were wrapped around the bottom pole. He was staring at them but tried to appear to be just a casual observer.

"That man over there," Brad said, his voice pitched low, "is he one of your hands?"

Dale turned around to look at the man.

"No, but he rode down with us. He wants to talk to you as soon as our business is concluded."

Brad felt a wave of suspicion float like a small comber in his mind.

"Who is he?"

"Says his name is Joe Blaine. Ever hear of him?"

Brad shook his head. "Name don't ring no bell," he said. "What's he want with me?"

"He didn't say. I think he's with some detective outfit in Denver, though. I got that much out of him. I hope you're not in some kind of trouble."

Brad smiled.

"No, not that I know of. But I'm pretty sure I know who sent him. If he wants to talk to me, it'll be a real short conversation."

"Now, about that bull, Storm. You interested?"

"Sure," Brad said. "He's homely as a mud fence, but I think I can use him."

"What about the cows?" Dale asked.

"I'll take those, too. Anything I should know about them before I pay you?"

"Well, they're easy to raise. With that smooth hide they don't have no problem with ticks and flies so much. They can stand a lot of heat but not much cold. They'll eat grass and hay and whatever fodder you feed 'em."

"Julio and I will drive 'em up and put 'em to pasture."

Brad pulled out a roll of bills. He counted them as he placed them in Dale's palm as Fred looked on. Julio still stared at the ungainly cattle with the pale gray hides and the humps, the long droopy ears.

Fred pulled some folded papers from his pocket. He lifted one leg to write on and wrote the terms of the sale and signed it. He handed the paper to Dale, who signed it and handed it to Brad.

"Here's your bill of sale, Brad," Dale said. "You want to find a notary?"

"No, I'll have Julio sign as witness."

"Fair enough," Dale said. Fred put the other papers back in his pocket and spit out the hay stalk.

"Who bought your cattle, Dale?" Brad asked after Dale stuffed the role in his left front pocket.

"Ray Barnes. Owns the Lucky Day ranch north of Denver. Know him?"

"Met him once. He raises good horses and I bought a couple of geldings from him."

"He does have a fine string of horses, mixed Arabs and Morgans, I think."

"Yep. What's he going to do with Brahman?"

"They're callin' 'em Bramers, now. Ray is going to do what you aim to do, mix 'em in with Herefords and maybe Black Angus. He's got a large spread."

"I know. Besides his ranch near Denver he has another one up near the mountains west of town."

"Well, good luck, Brad," Dale said. "Fred and I got to be gettin' back. Stop by whenever you're up to Cheyenne. My spread is the Two Bar Six."

"I'll do that," Brad said.

The two men shook hands again. Dale and Fred walked over to another pen where their horses were tethered to a corner pole. They mounted up, waved, and set out for the road to Denver.

Brad looked at the cattle he had bought.

"I say rope that one cow and maybe the bull and the other cow will follow us back to the ranch."

"Or rope the bull," Julio said.

"Cow always leads the herd," Brad said.

"Whiteface cow."

"Maybe the Bramers do the same."

"All right."

"I want to get out of here," Brad said. "Quick as we can."

"What about that hombre over there who wants to talk to you?"

"I don't want to talk to him, Julio."

"It's too late," Julio said as he looked over Brad's shoulder. "He is walking this way."

Brad turned around.

"Hold on there, Mr. Storm," the man said. "I'd like a word with you."

"Not interested, stranger," Brad said.

"Only take a minute."

"Make it quick, then."

The man who approached them was almost as tall as Brad, with wide shoulders, a push-broom moustache with a rusty tint, sharp features, and pale blue eyes that were as cold and frosted as pond ice. He wore a pistol on his hip, a sheepskin-lined denim jacket, a neatly blocked Stetson, and shiny snakeskin boots.

"A minute's all I got," Brad said when the man was six feet away. "Less if you work for Harry Pendergast."

"I believe you work for Harry yourself," the man said.

"Not anymore. I quit some time ago."

The man stopped and looked Brad square in the eyes. "My name's Joe Blaine and I do work for the Denver Detective Agency. Harry sends his regards."

"All right. I send mine back."

"Hold on, Mr. Storm. I haven't used up my minute yet."

Brad studied Blaine's face. The man didn't blink. His stare was as hard as twenty-penny nails. He did not look like a man who would back down from anything. He didn't look much like a detective, either. He looked like a city slicker in a western outfit who summered at a dude ranch. Still, if you looked closer, there was something about him that belied his neat appearance. He looked like a man who could bulldog a steer and hogtie a yearling calf before you could say "Jack Robinson."

"I'll hear you out, but I just bought three head of Bramers and I'm headin' back into the mountains."

"Fair enough," Blaine said.

Then he reached into a shirt pocket and pulled out a sheaf of folded greenbacks.

Julio's eyes widened as he stared at the bills. The one that was on top was a hundred-dollar bill.

Blaine held the stack of greenbacks shoulder high and flashed Brad a wan smile.

"This," he said softly, "is a bribe, Mr. Storm."

The sun rose in the morning sky, and one of the Brahman moaned as it swung its head to look at the three men standing outside the stock pen. Its mournful eyes seemed full of a sadness that told a tale of long journeys and a longing for a lost homeland in India. Julio felt all this as he waited for Blaine to drop the other shoe.

FOUR

~

Brad looked at the money in Blaine's hand and felt something squirm in his stomach. Money was something he was often short of and now was no exception. But a bribe? A bribe for what? Or was this just one of Harry Pendergast's wicked jokes? Or Blaine's?

"A bribe," Brad said, "usually means there are a lot of strings attached. Are you really trying to bribe me for something?"

Blaine's hard stare never faltered.

"Harry told me you had a hard head and were stubborn as a Missouri mule, so I thought if I waved some greenbacks at you, you might be inclined to listen to what I have to say. Money talks."

"Well, you got my attention, Blaine, but unless I know why you're offering me money right upfront, I guess my attention span is about as short as a jackrabbit's tail."

"Harry also said you talked straight, so I'll get to the point."

"Make it short," Brad said.

Blaine continued to hold the money up in the air as if it were a temptation to hold Brad's interest.

"Harry wants you to come to Denver. He's got a case that's baffled him and me."

"That's his problem. I told Harry that I quit the detective business. I'm a cattle rancher, not a detective."

"He told me you might say that. He knows you no longer want to work for him, but he says this is urgent. And, it is."

"Well, he has you working for him. You take the case."

"Actually, I'm a horse breeder. I belong to an outfit called the Colorado Horse Breeders Association. I was hired by them to retrieve some stolen horses and capture the horse thieves. But the situation got worse and I took our case to Pendergast. He put me on retainer. So, I work for both my association and Harry's detective agency."

"A man can't serve two masters, Blaine."

"Which is similar to your situation, isn't it?"

"My situation?"

"You're a cattle rancher and have worked as a detective for Pendergast."

"Yeah, I did. But I quit the agency. Now I'm just a cattle rancher."

"Maybe I can appeal to your sympathy, if not your wallet," Blaine said.

"Sympathy?"

"We, and by that I mean myself and members of my association, are losing good horseflesh to a gang of organized thieves. And we don't know why. If your cattle were rustled, you'd want to catch the rustlers, right?"

"Sure," Brad said. "And horse thieving is a hanging offense anywhere in this country."

"If you'll come to Denver, I'll give you each five hundred dollars right now, on the spot. Just talk to Harry, that's all I ask. If you don't want to take on the job, the money's yours to keep. Now, how's that for an offer?"

There was a long silence among the three men. Julio stared at the money, and the figure of five hundred dollars loomed huge in his mind. It was more money than he had ever seen at one time. He swallowed hard and it was all he could do not to salivate.

Brad ran the amount over in his mind. He had just laid out cash for three head of Brahman cattle and that put him in some jeopardy. He had hands to feed and not enough cattle to sell in the Kansas markets. He was just starting out and had payrolls to meet. The cattle would pay off, eventually, but the honest truth was that he was short of cash. Still, he was afraid of being roped in by Harry and forced to do a job while his ranch went to pot. Besides, he had promised Felicity that he wouldn't leave her alone again.

"It's a mighty tempting offer, Blaine, but I can't leave my ranch right now. I just bought these cattle and have a lot to do, matching my cows with this Bramer bull and those cows with my Hereford bull. I got to find new pasture and build fences and grow hay for the winter. I have a lot of responsibility."

"I know that, Brad, and so does Harry. All I'm asking is that you come to Denver and talk to us. Harry is willing to pay for your time. You'd stay only a day or so and if you turn us down, you can come back and tend to your ranch with money in your pocket."

"Why do they want to hire me?" Julio asked.

"It's a big job. Fact is, Harry thinks it's going to take three of us to track down these horse thieves and shut them down."

"Three?" Brad asked.

"You, Julio, and me," Joe said.

Brad was struck dumb. For several seconds he was speechless.

"Harry's been drinking too much peach cordial," Brad said finally. "I work alone. He knows that."

"Not on this case. It's too big."

"How big?" Brad asked.

"These thieves aren't just stealing one or two or three horses. They're cleaning out entire stables."

"You check with the U.S. Army?" Brad asked. "They buy horses."

"Those horses aren't going to the military," Joe said.

"Where, then?"

Blaine shrugged. "We don't know. That's why Harry is making this offer. Five hundred apiece for you and Julio, just to listen to him for five minutes in Denver."

"I will go there, Brad," Julio said. "That is a lot of money."

"It is a lot of money," Brad agreed. "But it's money that stinks to high heaven. I know how persuasive Harry is, and I just don't want to do any more detective work for him."

"I will do any kind of work for five hundred dollars," Julio said.

"It has to be both you and Brad," Blaine said. "Look, gents, I'm not just the messenger here. I have a stake in finding these horse thieves. I had a dozen of my best horses stolen out of my stables. Fine horses. Horses I can't re-place."

"That may be so," Brad said. "But I don't have a stake in this. I'm a cowman. That's it."

"Do you own horses?" Blaine dropped his hand but held on to the money.

"A few. Enough for a remuda once we make our first trail drive up to Salina."

"If you have horses, then you're a target for these thieves."

"I doubt it," Brad said. "Look, Joe, I appreciate Harry's offer, but I'm turning it down. Julio and I are going to drive these Bramers up to the ranch and get to work breeding new stock. I wish you luck. Tell Harry I said howdy."

Blaine stuffed the bills back in his shirt pocket. It ap-peared to Brad that he had given up and was accepting the fact that he and Julio would not go to Denver to see Pend-ergast.

"All right," Blaine said. "I won't push you no more, Brad. Mind if I ride back to your ranch with you? I'd like to see your spread, maybe take a look at your horses."

Brad was taken aback by the offer.

"You're wasting your time. I'm not going to change my mind."

"I know. I promise I won't bring up the subject again. I'd just like to ride up with you and get to know you better."

Brad felt a worm of suspicion begin to crawl through his brain. But he shrugged and looked at Julio.

"I reckon you can ride up with us. Ain't much to see, but we can put you up and feed you."

"Good," Blaine said. "I'm tired of hardtack and jerky. It'll be a pleasure to meet your missus."

Brad looked at Julio again.

"I guess we can use some help driving these Bramers up, can't we, Julio?"

Julio frowned. "I would rather go to Denver and make five hundred dollars," he said.

"Joe, go get your horse," Brad said. "We'll see how good you are at driving cattle."

Blaine laughed.

"I'm better with horses," he said. "But, I'm ready to try my hand at wrangling cattle."

Fifteen minutes later, Julio was leading the roped cow while Brad and Joe drove the bull and other cow through the sunlit town and headed for the road to Brad's ranch.

It seemed to Brad that Julio was jerking on the rope more than was necessary.

Five hundred dollars was a lot of money, not only to Julio but to him as well.

But, with Harry Pendergast, it would be blood money. And a bribe was a bribe, no matter who was paying it out.

FIVE

❧

The sun rose in the sky and was near its zenith when Julio rode into the valley. Caesar looked around as he followed the other cow. He swung his head from side to side as he surveyed the pasture with its lush carpet of emerald grass shining in the golden rays of the sun. His stance and attitude were aggressive, but he saw no enemy, no bull to challenge him.

Brad looked toward the house and the corral. He stiffened in the saddle when he saw that the corral was empty and the gate open.

The door of the house was open, too, and there was no smoke rising from the chimney.

"Where do you want these cows?" Julio asked.

"Just let 'em graze," Brad said. "They won't go far."

"Nice spread," Blaine said. "That your house yonder?"

Brad didn't answer. He felt a crawling sensation on his back, and his stomach filled with a swarm of winged insects. He glanced over at the barn and the bunkhouse, then saw the silent cabin where Julio lived with his wife, Pilar.

Something was wrong. The air still held its morning

chill as the breeze blew down from the snow-capped mountains high on the skyline beyond the valley.

Julio rode up to the head of the cow and slipped the rope from around its neck. Caesar and the two cows began to graze.

"Boy, Brad's sure in a hurry to see his wife," Blaine said.

Julio looked in Brad's direction. A look of puzzlement etched itself in the lines of his face. He saw the empty corral, the open gate.

Then he looked toward his own cabin. It was beyond the barn and bunkhouse. Pilar should have opened the door and come out, but the door was closed. The door to Brad's house was open, but Felicity was nowhere to be seen.

"I think he has a worry," Julio said. "It is too quiet and there are no horses in the corral."

Julio turned his horse and galloped toward his log cabin.

Blaine sat his horse, bewildered. Then he put spurs to its flanks and rode toward Brad's log house. Something was surely amiss. He braced himself for whatever unknown events were yet to come.

Brad swung out of the saddle before his horse, Ginger, had come to a full stop. He hit the ground at a run and dashed through the open door of his home.

He stepped inside to glimpse an unimaginable horror. Coals glowed a pulsating orange-red in the fireplace. On the floor lay Felicity, sprawled on her back, a gaping wound in her neck. Brad rushed over to her and kneeled next to her naked body. He touched her bleached face and it was cold to his fingers. Tears welled up in his eyes and his body drained of energy as it went limp, as if all the muscles had suddenly vanished so that his body had become weak and useless.

He sobbed as he lifted her head to his chest and pressed her cold white face against his chest. A darkness flooded his brain as he rocked back and forth, squeezing his wife's lifeless body against his own as if he could infuse it with life.

"Oh, Felicity," he whispered. "What have they done to you?"

Blaine stood in the doorway, blocking the light. He saw Brad rock back and forth with a dead woman in his arms. He stepped inside and walked over to Brad. He put a hand on his shoulder but knew that it was little comfort to a man in the terrible grip of grief.

He lifted his hand and squatted next to Brad. He saw the slash in the woman's neck, the dull frost on one open eye. The sight tore at him, and his throat constricted as bile roiled in his stomach and tears stung his eyes.

"Joe," Brad said. "She's dead. My Felicity is dead."

Blaine could not bring himself to speak. His throat ached with every muscle in his neck taut and turning to cold iron.

"I—I can't let her go," Brad sobbed. "I just can't let her go."

Brad crumpled over, and Felicity's head touched the floor. Brad fell across her naked midriff and let the tears rush down his face. She was ice cold and her body was turning stiff, and his nostrils filled with the smell of blood. Filled with the terrible aroma of death.

Blaine saw the torn blue nightgown and the coagulating pool of blood on the floor. He could not look at the dead woman, nor at Brad. He was sick to his stomach and powerless to offer any comfort by either word or deed. So he stood there, like a mourner at a funeral. He did not know Brad's wife at all, and he had just begun to know something about Brad himself. It was not a good start to a friendship.

Brad got to his feet, bent over, and lifted the body of Felicity in his arms.

"I'm going to take her to our bedroom," Brad said huskily.

Blaine nodded. "If there is anything I can do?" he said.

"No. I'll take care of her. I'm going to wash and dress her."

"Brad, I'm sorry. So sorry."

Brad choked and couldn't speak. He carried Felicity down the hall. He saw the coffeepot and the spilled coffee that had stained the flooring.

She must have been in the kitchen when they came in on her, he thought. He entered the bedroom and laid his wife's body on the unmade bed. He closed her eyes with his fingers and began to weep softly as he looked at her frail naked body, the horrible gash in her throat.

As he stood there, his grief slid away and a slow anger began to boil in him. The anger was on the verge of developing into full-blown rage, but he calmed himself and turned away and walked out to the hallway. He picked up the coffeepot and walked into the kitchen.

He looked at the cupboard that was directly opposite the hallway.

There was a bullet hole in the cabinet door. He walked over, opened it, and saw the shattered plates. There was another hole at the back of the cupboard.

His heart chilled.

In his mind's eye he could picture Felicity in the kitchen, with a pot of coffee in her hand. She had walked down the hall and someone had fired a shot over her head. She must have been terrified. But she would have fought the man who attacked her. Man or men. She would have fought to the death, and that is probably what had happened.

His anger boiled up again and he had to take a deep breath to keep his rage in check.

He forced himself to pick up kindling next to the stove and open the iron door. There were coals inside, and he laid the sticks of wood over these, then bent down to blow on the embers.

A lick of flame appeared and he blew on it some more until the wood caught and flames ranged over the entire stack of kindling.

He found a pot in one of the lower cupboards and set it on the counter. He lifted the water pitcher and felt its weight. He poured some water into the kettle and set it on the stove.

Just then, he heard a commotion in the front room. He peered down the hall.

Julio stomped in with Pilar. Blaine rose to meet them, and Brad saw their shadowy silhouettes blend and separate. He heard Blaine speak in low tones to the couple.

Then, he heard Pilar let out a scream of anguish.

A moment later, she ran down the hall and stopped at the bedroom door.

She went inside and then screamed again. Louder this time. Brad went into the room and clasped her shoulders in his arms.

"I'm going to wash her up and dress her," he told Pilar.

She buried her face in her hands and deep sobs racked her small body.

"I will do it," she said. Then she dropped her hands and looked up at Brad. "Let me wash and dress her. Please."

"Yes, Pilar. She would like that."

"What happened?" She turned to look at him as he stepped back.

"I don't know. Horse thieves, I reckon."

"I have much sorrow," she said. "My heart is broken. I had much love for Felicity."

"I know, Pilar," he said and felt that his words were lame. He shook his head as she shooed him away.

"You go," she said. "I will make her look pretty again."

He began to sob then, and hung his head as he stumbled out through the door and walked down the hallway to the front room.

Julio stood there dumbstruck, his face a bronze mask that seemed rigid with the sadness of centuries. A young face suddenly turned old and hard. Yet his eyes swam with tears and teardrops coursed down over the faint vermilion embedded in his flesh, a reminder of his Indian heritage and the grief of a race that had been mixed and maltreated for hundreds of years.

"*Cuanto lament lo que ha pasado,*" Julio said in Spanish, in the tongue of his people, words that came from a deep place inside him. "I lament what has happened."

"Pilar is going to wash and dress Felicity," Brad said.

Julio rushed to him and threw his arms around him. He lay his head on Brad's chest.

"Yo tengo mucho dolor para ti y Felicity," he said, and there were tears in his voice and Brad felt the sadness of the man as he sobbed against his chest.

"Yo sé, Julio," Brad said. *"Estoy lleno de tristessa.* I know," he said. "I am filled with sadness."

"Pilar," Julio said as he broke off his embrace and stepped back, "was in the barn. She milked the Guernsey cow and heard the men. She heard the screams of Felicity. She heard a gunshot. She had much fear and hid in the stall. But she saw them. She saw the men."

"How many?" Brad asked.

"Three. There were three of them. When they came out of the house, they stole all the horses. They stole Felicity's mare, Rose. She saw them drive the horses up the mountain. She had much fear. She has much fear now."

"Did she get a good look at the men?" Brad asked. "Did she hear any of their names?"

"I do not know. She worried about Felicity and watched the house for a long time. She was afraid to go in the house. She ran to our house and locked the door and hid in the closet. When I shouted her name, she came out of the closet and unlocked the door."

Blaine cleared his throat, but did not say anything right away.

Julio and Brad heard the noise and turned to look at Blaine.

"Do you think . . ." Brad muttered to Blaine.

"Likely the same bunch I was tellin' you about, Brad," Blaine said. "It's just too bad that your wife was here, all alone. I'm deeply sorry."

Brad's jaw hardened. His eyes slitted and he took a deep breath, held it for a second or two.

"Joe," he said, finally, "when I've buried my wife, I will ride with you to Denver and talk to Harry. This changes everything for me."

"For me, too," Julio said.

Blaine stood up from the chair he had been sitting in and folded his arms across his chest.

"It's your decision," he said. "The offer still stands. And, I think you'd be a big help in solving these crimes."

"I will track down the bastards who killed my wife and stole my horses, if it takes me a lifetime," Brad said. "I want to see them all hang for this, if for nothing else."

Blaine dropped his arms to his side and raised his head slightly.

"I'm very sorry about the situation that has led to this. Though I know Harry will be pleased you're coming on board," he said. "And, so am I."

The three men stood there in silent communion, all feeling the grief that filled the house and thinking ahead to the time when they would confront the killers and send them all to the gallows.

SIX

⌇

Harry Pendergast, head of the Denver Detective Agency, sat behind his large cherrywood desk, toying with a lead pencil as he regarded the three men in his room. He had just finished listening to Brad's account of the death of his wife and a dozen horses stolen. He winced when he heard about Felicity and was concerned when he learned of the stolen horses.

"This could be a long trail, Brad. Have you made arrangements with the men tending your cattle herd?"

"I have a good man in charge," Brad said, "Pedro Alvarez. He found me a range for the Bramer bull and thirty head of Herefords. The two Bramer cows are quartered with one of my whiteface bulls. I gave him most of the money you sent down with Joe so he can buy feed and lumber if he needs it."

"Good," Pendergast said. He was now a portly man with graying hair and a jowly face that reflected years of good living with both spirits and fine food. "Have you had a chance to think of how you will go about catching these horse thieves? I wouldn't even know where to start. The horses seem to vanish into thin air. They don't show up at any local ranches or at auctions."

"I have," Brad said. "But first I want to meet the head of the Colorado Horse Breeders Association."

"Cliff Jameson should be here shortly. I've already sent for him. Lomax will bring him into the office the minute he arrives."

Byron Lomax, Brad knew, was Harry's office manager, a most proficient and efficient man who was also as fastidious as any diligent housewife.

"Joe told me something about the ground you covered before I came here," Brad said. "Anything turn up while Joe was gone?"

"No," Pendergast said. "Not a thing. We've gone to ranches from New Mexico to Cheyenne, and even into Nebraska. No stolen horses at any of the ranches, none at auctions or sale barns, none turned up in stockyards. It's a big mystery that frankly has me baffled."

"Maybe you've been looking in all the wrong places," Brad said.

"Oh? Maybe you have some fresh ideas you'd like to share with me and Joe."

"I have some ideas, but for the time being, I'm keeping them to myself. I want to know how much the breeders association is willing to pay, or how much you're willing to pay Julio and me to do your investigating."

"Oh, I think this job is well worth your time, Brad. Cliff is willing to pay my firm a substantial sum to find out who's stealing the horses, and more if we get them back. He's a tough bird and he wants justice. And, he wants this case solved right away."

"He doesn't want much, does he?" Brad said.

Julio kept silent.

Joe's brushy moustache moved up and down like a push broom, as if he were struggling to keep his mouth shut and not say anything.

Joe had been nervous on the long ride from Leadville to Denver as if afraid that Brad and Julio would change their minds and turn back. So he had held his cards close to his vest and didn't say much about the job. But Brad knew that

Joe had a stake in the outcome of the case. He was a member of the association of horse breeders, either as a member or a range detective. Joe had not been very clear about the way he made his living, but Brad figured he was somewhat at a loss to explain his own failure to find out anything about the horse thieves.

There was a knock on Pendergast's door.

"Yes?" Harry said.

"Mr. Jameson is here," Lomax called through the door.

"Show him in, Byron," Harry said.

The door opened and Lomax preceded a burly man with a barrel chest. He was wearing a woolen plaid shirt and a sheepskin-lined jacket that bulged at his middle. His face was florid from wind and weather, and when he took off his Stetson, he revealed a clumpy shock of curly blond hair. He wore a six-gun and a large knife on his gun belt. His boots were worn and made of sheepskin or antelope hide. His eyes were a clear blue that seemed to give off sparks. He carried a worn leather satchel that was bulging at the seams.

"Harry," Jameson bellowed, "I hope to hell you've got some good news for me. Or at least found someone more capable than Joe to help us out."

He glared at Joe when he said it. Then his eyes fixed on Julio, and Brad saw a cloud pass in front of his eyes. Finally, he looked at Brad, who was a head taller than he was, but twice as lean and wiry with muscles unlike Jameson's, which had turned partially to flab.

"Here's the man I spoke to you about, Cliff. Shake hands with Brad Storm."

Brad held up his hand, but Jameson didn't offer his. Instead, he shifted his gaze to Julio. And this time, Brad saw a look of contempt in his eyes and on his ruddy face.

Lomax walked backward through the open door and silently closed it as if he wanted no part of the dealings in that august room.

"And what's the Mex doin' here?" Jameson gruffed.

Harry started to tell him. He opened his mouth, but before he could say a word, Brad spoke.

"Julio Aragon works for me, Mr. Jameson," Brad said quietly. "And, he's not a Mex. He's a Mexican."

"What the hell?" Jameson bellowed. "Harry, you hired a Messican. What in the devil's name was on your mind?"

"I hired two men to help us, Cliff," Harry said. "Brad and Julio. If you don't like it, you can just turn around and go back to your ranch and we'll call it a day. Otherwise, sit down and shut up."

Jameson glared at Harry for a long moment. He seemed about to explode in a rage. He doubled up his fists, and his neck swelled under his collar like a bull in the rut. He huffed a breath in and out of his nostrils but clamped his lips tight and sat in a chair. He dropped his satchel and it clunked to the floor next to his chair.

"Fine," Harry said. "Brad, Joe, and Julio are going to be working on this case, and I would appreciate a little respect from you, Cliff."

"Something tells me you expect a lot more than respect, Harry," Cliff said.

Pendergast smiled. It was not a warm smile, but an indulgent, condescending smile that was from a man who knew he held all the right cards.

"This is a big, complicated job," Harry explained. "I'll have three detectives riding all over creation to find the culprits and bring them to justice. They will need food for themselves, food for their horses, and will probably have to spend a lot of time in the open, without shelter. If you want results, you must pay for the process."

"How much?" Jameson asked. He glanced down at his satchel.

"To start with, I'll ask you to tender an offer, Cliff."

"Then what?"

"Then," Pendergast said, "we haggle like a pair of fishwives in the marketplace."

Jameson swelled up as he drew a deep breath. His chest expanded to barrel proportions and his florid face reddened.

"I've already given you five thousand dollars as a retainer," Cliff said.

"Yes, and I've laid out more than half of that on expenditures necessary to the investigation. One thousand of that money was used to solicit the services of Brad and Julio. That's a nonrefundable expense, and distinct from the salary I must pay them."

"Costly," Cliff said. He glanced over at Brad for a moment.

"My agents must be paid and paid well. They will earn every penny I pay them since I envision they will travel many miles, possibly through mountainous country, to locate both the horses and the culprits. I need you to give me a figure that the horse breeders association is willing to pay for our investigative services."

Jameson squirmed in his chair. He glanced down at the satchel once again.

"I brought ten thousand in cash that I was able to collect from the members who have had their horses stolen. Some of the horses are very valuable, and years of breeding have been lost to these thieves."

"That's a start, Cliff," Harry said. "But you're going to need twice that much before we're through."

"Twice that much?" Cliff spluttered. "Twenty thousand? Why, that's outrageous. The members of our association won't stand for it."

Pendergast tapped the eraser end of his pencil on his desktop. A bemused smile curled his lips. He stroked one of his mutton chop sideburns with a single finger.

"The haggling is over, Cliff. I'll take that cash money as half of the payment, but if we are successful and solve this case, bring the horse thieves before the court, then you must agree to pay us another ten thousand dollars. I have an agreement already drawn up. All that's required is your signature and my countersignature."

"You've got it all figured out, haven't you, Harry?" Jameson drew himself up in his chair and clasped his hands together in his lap.

"I know what a case of this magnitude is going to cost," Harry said.

Jameson glanced again at Brad. This time he did not avert his gaze.

"I don't know nothin' about these men you've hired, Brad and the Mexican. What do they know about horses? Are they certified detectives? Joe is a damned fine range detective and he's a horse breeder as well. Brad looks like a country bumpkin who couldn't find his ass with both hands, and the Mexican looks about as reliable as a three-legged mule."

Brad stiffened but kept silent.

"Brad Storm is a cattle rancher. He just had a dozen head of horses stolen and the men who stole from him also raped and murdered his wife. And he has worked for me in the past and was successful in all those cases. Have you never heard of him before? He has quite a reputation."

"No, I never heard of him before."

Pendergast looked at Brad.

"Show him, Brad. Maybe that will jog his memory."

"Show me what?" Jameson boomed.

Brad slipped a hand inside his shirt. He lifted the set of rattles on the leather thong and shook them. They made a rattling sound.

Jameson jumped from his chair and looked all around him on the floor. "What the hell?" he said as he danced away from his chair.

Brad let the rattle fall back on his breastbone.

"Brad Storm," Harry said, "is better known around these parts as the Sidewinder. Those snake rattles are his trademark."

"You're the Sidewinder?" Jameson gasped in disbelief.

Brad said nothing. He just smiled. Julio grinned and Joe wore a smirk on his face.

"Well, I'll be damned," Jameson said.

He sat down again and lifted his satchel into his lap.

"I'll be damned," he said again. "The Sidewinder. Don't that beat all?"

Harry slid a sheet of paper over to the edge of his desk in Jameson's direction.

"Sign here, Cliff," he said, pointing to a line on the bottom of the agreement.

Jameson pulled stacks of bills from his satchel and set them on one side of the large desk. Then he stood up, leaned over and read the agreement. Harry handed him a pen.

Cliff signed the paper and slid it back to Harry. Harry signed it, then picked up a small bell and jiggled it. The door opened and Lomax entered the room.

"Yes, sir," he said.

"Count this money and put it in the safe. And file this agreement between me and Cliff Jameson."

"Right away, sir," Lomax said, his eyes bulging in wonder at the sight of the greenbacks. "Should I issue a receipt to Mr. Jameson?"

"That won't be necessary," Harry said.

Lomax left and closed the door.

Jameson started to rise from his chair.

"Hold on, Cliff. Brad has some questions for you."

"He can ask all the questions he wants as long as he don't make no more rattlin' sounds," Jameson said.

"If he ever does, Cliff," Joe said, "it'll probably be the last sound you hear before you hear his six-gun explode."

"I know. I've heard the stories," Jameson said. "I hear he's mighty fast with that Colt on his belt."

"He is fast," Julio said. "And he does not miss." He grinned at Jameson. The grin was more like a salacious leer.

Harry smiled. This has been a good meeting, he thought. He felt like rubbing his hands together in satisfaction. But that was not his way. He was, at bottom, a gentleman and he did not like to gloat.

Morning sun streamed through the windows of his office on the mezzanine of the Brown Palace Hotel. His new offices.

Business had been good and it was going to get better.

He had the utmost confidence in Brad Storm and knew that he had hired the most qualified man to solve the case of the stolen horses.

He had hired the Sidewinder.

SEVEN

～

Harry ushered the men into a large adjoining conference room and instructed one of the women who worked for him to provide them with fresh coffee and anything else they desired.

"As soon as you and Brad have discussed the case, he, Joe, and Julio will get right on it."

"Thank you, Harry," Jameson said. He set his satchel down on the floor and took a chair near the end of the table. Brad sat at the head. Julio and Joe took chairs on his left.

"I need some things from you, Mr. Jameson," Brad said.

"Call me Cliff," Jameson said. "May I call you Brad?"

"Sure. That's my name."

"That's one of your names," Jameson said with a smile.

"Let's get down to business," Brad said. "I need a list of brands from all the ranches that lost horses. And, I would like to know the breeds and colors, if possible, of all the missing horses. Would that be possible?"

Jameson reached down and picked up his satchel. He opened it atop the table.

"I have a list of the ranch brands," he said. "And, I know some of the breeds such as those I lost."

"Let's see what you have, Cliff. I may not need to know all the various breeds or markings from all the ranchers."

A young woman entered the room. She carried a tray with coffee cups, a small cream pitcher, a sugar bowl, spoons, and a pot of steaming coffee.

"Howdy, boys," she said airily as she set the tray down on the long polished walnut tabletop. "I'm Velma Fitzgerald, Mr. Pendergast's girl Friday. Now, if you wish. I can bring you sandwiches or bear claws, most anything you like while you all are talkin' here."

She had a slight Texas accent and wore a yellow taffeta dress with a small bustle that sported a large bow, patent leather shoes with silver buckles, and sheer silk stockings. Around her neck, she wore a choker with a small jade stone in the center. She had brown eyes and long black hair that was bunched up in a tight bun that nestled on her slender neck.

Every man in the room gaped at her, and she smiled becomingly at each one. She held her gaze on Brad, since he was at the head of the table.

"Uh, no, ma'am," he said. "Nothing for me, but maybe . . ."

Jameson butted in before Brad could finish his sentence.

"Sugar, when we finish up here, I'm goin' to take all these gentlemen to lunch downstairs. So, we don't need nothin' else right now. Buy your lunch, too, if you want to join us."

Velma blushed.

"Uh, no, sir. I brought my own lunch. But thank you very much."

"You're welcome," Jameson said. Velma scurried out of the room as if it were on fire.

"Nice little gal," Jameson said. He began to pour the coffee. He handed each man a cup and saucer. "Sugar? Cream?"

The men all shook their heads.

Jameson set some papers down that he had pulled from his satchel.

"Now, this is a list of all the ranches and you'll see their brands."

Brad picked up the papers and began to read.

There was the Rocking A, owned by Robert Anderson, the Slash D, owned by Felix Dunham, and so on.

"Bob Anderson raises Appaloosas," Jameson said. "Dunham breeds Missouri Trotters. Here's a pencil, Brad, case you want to write down any of this information."

Brad wrote down the breeds after each man's name.

Jameson leaned over and went down the list. Some ranchers raised roans, both blue and strawberry, while others raised quarter horses or Arabians, and some mixed breeds. Brad wrote them all down.

When they had finished going over the list, Jameson scooted back in his chair.

"Mind tellin' me how you're going to proceed with this case, Brad?" he asked.

"Right now, I want to keep my method to myself."

"But you do have a starting point, I reckon," Jameson said.

"Yes. Several," Brad said.

"As long as I'm payin' good money for your services, you should at least tell me your plans," Jameson said.

Brad folded the papers and put them in his jacket pocket.

"Cliff, I can't talk about my plans. Not to you, not to Harry. Not to Julio here, or Joe. If word leaks out what I aim to do, I'll fail. Now, to be blunt, you can take it or leave it."

Jameson drew himself up and swiped a hand across his mouth.

"Secretive, eh? All right. But, you'll surely give regular reports to Harry, won't you?"

"No, I won't do that, either," Brad said. "And, we're going to skip lunch. After I meet with Harry, we're going to set out to solve this case. Don't try to interfere or follow us. If you do, I'll drop the case right back in Harry's lap."

"Boy, you don't pussyfoot around, do you?" Jameson said.

"I have my own way of working, Cliff."

"Yeah, I'm sure you do. Okay. Let's just leave it at that. I wish you luck. All of you. I hope you get those bastards and bring 'em into court. I'd like nothin' better than to see their necks stretched at the end of a rope."

Jameson stood up. He picked up his satchel and touched a finger to the brim of his hat.

"So long, Cliff," Brad said.

"Be seein' you," Jameson said awkwardly and left the room.

"Now what?" Joe asked as he looked at Brad.

"Now, we go next door and see Byron and Harry. We'll draw money and buy the supplies we'll need."

"You don't waste much time, do you, Brad?" Joe said.

"Time wasted is time lost," Brad said. "You can't get time back once you've spent it."

"True," Joe said.

Brad rose from his chair. Julio and Joe got up, too. They followed him to Harry's office.

Lomax sat at his desk and looked up when the three men came in.

"Harry in?" Brad asked.

"He had to leave on an errand," Byron said. "But he wanted me to give you this, each of you." He opened a desk drawer and withdrew three envelopes.

"There's two hundred dollars for each of you. Mr. Pendergast wants you to keep track of expenses, which he will pay."

The three men took the envelopes.

"Is this expense money or salary?" Brad asked.

"Both," Byron said. "You are each to garner one hundred dollars a week in salary and the extra hundred is to pay your initial expenses."

"Harry seems pretty sure of himself," Brad said.

"Mr. Pendergast said to tell you that the money is just a

starting point. He feels you will be entitled to much more as the case develops."

"We may be gone for a month, maybe more," Brad said.

"You will be well compensated for your work, Mr. Storm," Byron said. "If you think you'll need more money before you leave, just let me know and Mr. Pendergast will advance what you need as well as pay any salary that is due."

"I don't like it much," Brad said. "But I can live with it, I reckon."

"Mr. Pendergast will be pleased to know that," Byron said.

"Let's go, boys," Brad said. He folded his envelope and tucked it into his back pocket.

"We goin' to eat?" Joe asked. "My stomach's growlin' like a bear."

"We'll eat on the trail," Brad said. "I want to get started on this case."

"And you do have a plan, I take it."

"I have a plan, Joe, and as soon as we're out of town, I'll tell you what it is. That good enough for you?"

"I reckon it'll have to be," Joe said.

"You must trust Brad," Julio told Joe.

Joe nodded.

Brad walked outside onto California Street and breathed in a gulp of air.

He couldn't wait to get out of Denver and ride into the mountains. He looked up at the Front Range of the Rockies. That's where all the secrets were, he thought. That's where all the horses were.

EIGHT

❧

Brad, along with Julio and Joe, rode into the foothills west of Denver late that same afternoon. Julio and Joe followed Brad, who headed straight for Lookout Mountain, taking the trail that would eventually lead them into the heart of the Rockies. They halted up on Lookout Mountain and gazed back at the sprawling town of Denver.

"Take a good look," Brad said. "It'll be a while before you see a town that big again."

Smoke rose from chimneys, and the prairie around Denver rippled with tall Kelly green grasses stirred by a bustling wind they could feel at their backs. The town seemed small and rustic at that distance, with no streets visible, only a jumble of nondescript buildings. It might as well have been a ghost town, except for the smoke rising from factories and houses.

"It don't look like much from here," Joe said.

"The mountains make everything look small," Brad said.

"There are wagons and riders on the roads," Julio said. "They look like little ants."

Joe chuckled.

"Maybe now's the time, while we blow the horses, for me to tell you both about my plan," Brad said.

"Yes, tell us," Julio said.

"I'm all ears," Joe said.

"I got to thinking, Joe, when you and Cliff and Harry told me about your search for the stolen horses. You couldn't find them."

"Yeah, and I think you said we might have been looking in the wrong places."

"Yes, that's right, Joe. You couldn't find any horses that had been stolen, even though you looked from New Mexico to Cheyenne. Why?"

"Damned if I know," Joe said.

"Well, I got to thinking about the mountains. What's the biggest industry in the mountains?"

"Hell, I don't know," Joe said. "Hunting, maybe."

"The mines," Julio said. "There are many mines far back in the mountains. Leadville is a town of much mining."

"Good for you, Julio," Brad said. "That's what I think. If you don't see stolen horses down on the prairie, they have to be selling them up in the mountains. Mine owners need horses for hauling, for pulling stumps, for prospecting."

"I think you're on to something, Brad," Joe said. "So, we have to go to the mines, sure as shootin'."

"Another thing I thought of," Brad said, "was where do you keep a lot of horses before you sell them to the miners? And I think I know of the perfect place."

Joe tilted his hat back away from his forehead and scratched a fingernail behind his ear.

"You'd have to have corrals or pens, I reckon. Someplace to keep the horses until you found buyers."

"Maybe not. Don't make it too complicated. If you had a big valley, you could hold horses there for quite a while. They'd be on grass and you wouldn't have any feed bills. They'd have water from the creeks."

Joe squared his hat, and he looked back over his shoulder at the snowcapped mountain peaks.

"You might ride forever in these mountains and never find such a place, Brad."

"You might," Brad said. "But I know a perfect place that's just like that. It'll take us a couple or three days to get there, but I've seen the place before, and it's a perfect hiding place for stolen horses. In fact, there were horses there when I first saw it."

"There were horses there? Stolen?"

"No, Joe, wild. It's even called Wild Horse Valley. I think the Utes used to go there and catch wild horses. The Arapahos, too. Or, maybe they kept the horses they stole there."

"I never heard of it," Joe said.

"I have heard of this place," Julio said. "The Indians did keep horses there, and when a horse went wild, it came to that place. Some of my people used to go there to look for wild horses they could catch and tame."

"That's right," Brad said. "Nobody's been there in a long while since the Utes and Arapahos were driven out. It's a big valley, and there are probably still a few wild horses from Indian times that go there. Elk and deer aplenty, last time I saw it."

"So, is that where we start?" Joe asked.

"That's where we start, Joe. Tighten your cinches and let's head into the mountains while there's still daylight."

Julio grinned.

"I wish to see this place," he said as he spurred his horse, Chato.

"You will, Julio, you will," Brad said and rode back to the trail leading into the massive mountains.

They rode with the sun in their faces and jumped mule deer and jackrabbits on the trail. They rode into the high, lonely mountains, leaving all traces of civilization behind them.

Far out on the prairie, a dust devil came into being. It arose from the earth and swirled across the landscape like a living being. Then it vanished over the horizon and left no trace of its path in the gama grass.

And the three riders vanished into the wilderness of the Rocky Mountains. Somewhere a mountain quail, perched on a yucca, piped a plaintive series of notes that might have issued from some ancient flute. Then, all was stillness under the jagged skyline of glistening mountain peaks flocked with snows that looked as if they were filled with tiny diamonds.

NINE

❧

Jack Trask was a wizard with the running iron. So was his partner, Wilbur Campbell. They took turns with the iron. While one brought up a haltered horse and steadied it, the other planted the hot iron onto the existing brand and created a new one.

Jack had a hot fire going and plenty of cherry-red coals. There were three running irons basking against the coals. He turned the shaft every so often to keep the irons glowing uniformly.

"Okay, Wil," he called to Campbell. "Bring up the next horse."

Campbell pulled on the rope attached to a tall sorrel gelding bearing the brand Bar S. The horse was one of those stolen from Brad Storm.

The other horses were confined in a rope corral built just for branding purposes. Once they bore new brands, they were turned loose to graze with the large herd in Wild Horse Valley.

The sorrel neighed as it approached the blazing fire. Campbell jerked its head down and pulled on the lead rope until he had brought it alongside the branding fire in the ring of stones.

"What're you makin' these, Jack?" Wilbur asked as he tightened down on the rope to hold the horse's head down close to its chest.

"I'm just goin' to make it easy for us. Thought about makin' it into a Box 8, but with one iron I'll have a 2 Bar 8."

"It's enough different, I reckon. Where are these new ones goin', do you know?"

"Some have been sold to a logger up above Estes Park. Others are goin' to a mine twixt there and Lyons, I reckon."

"Jordan sure knows his business," Wilbur said.

"Yeah, for a half-breed. Ever been to his saloon up in Cheyenne?"

"Nope. I met Killdeer a few times, once't when he come down with some new men he wanted me to break."

Jack laughed.

"Yeah, like you break horses, Wil," he said. He brought the end of the iron close to the sorrel's haunch and held it a few inches away from its hide.

"Hold him steady, Wil," Jack said.

He placed a hand on the horse's hip and pushed, then drove the hot branding iron into the "S." The curved iron turned the "S" into the figure "8." Then he added a "2" with another iron. Hair burned and flesh sizzled as the burning brands did their work. The horse jumped and kicked out both hind legs. But, the brand was set.

"He'll get over it," Jack said. "Go get another of them Bar S horses, Wil."

Wil slipped the halter off the sorrel's head and turned him out with a slap on the rump. The horse galloped off to join the other horses at the rope corral. But when it saw Wilbur walking back with the rope and halter in his hands, the horse turned in a tight circle and galloped off to join the horses grazing in the long wide valley. Sheer bluffs of sandstone rose around three sides of the valley and the other end was thick with timber. There was a road down through a pass in the bluffs and another emerging from the timber.

Wilbur caught up another horse, a bay mare. This was Felicity's horse, Rose, but he didn't know that. He didn't even know where the horses had come from since the three men who drove them into the valley never spoke of their deeds. They were under strict orders from Jordan Killdeer not to discuss where they had been to any of the other hands. He paid well and demanded loyalty. Someone always came down from Cheyenne once a month to pay Wilbur and Jack. They never knew his name and he never told them anything. He just gave the men cash money and then rode off to parts unknown.

But Jack knew that Killdeer had several men working for him in the mountains. They saw them only when they brought in horses or took out the ones with changed brands to either mining or lumber camps.

"Got you a mare, Jack," Wilbur said as he pulled the horse up to the fire ring. "Pretty thing, ain't she?"

"They're all pretty, Wil," Jack said.

"This was probably some woman's horse. Gentle as a kitten. Hell, I even crawled between her legs and she never lifted a foot nor bobbed her head."

"You ain't supposed to play with the stock, Wil. Just bring 'em up to the brandin' fire."

"Hell, there ain't that much to do way up here in the middle of nowhere. I'd like to ride this one."

"If Jordan ever found out, he'd have you draw your pay."

"Aw, he wouldn't do that. He ain't never fired nobody. Leastwise, I never heard such."

"Well, you ain't been with him as long as I have, Wilbur. They was one man what quit one day and just rode off. Next thing I knew was that he was shot dead up in Laramie."

"Bar fight?"

"No, he was back shot at night. And he wasn't the onliest one I heard who quit or got fired from Killdeer's outfit."

"Oh? Who else?"

"Well, there was a young feller who got in an argument with one of the bunch. He said he was goin' to quit, and they shot him to pieces before he could get on his horse."

"You're just tryin' to scare me, Jack."

"I'm just tellin' you like it is, Wil. Don't nobody work for Jordan Killdeer and quit on him. Or, if he fires you, you ain't goin' far."

"You are scarin' me, Jack. Hell, I didn't know it was that way. I mean I'm an outlaw, but there is such a thing as honor among thieves. Ain't there?"

Jack laughed and turned the iron before drawing it from the coals.

Wilbur pulled on the rope and Rose bowed her head as docile as a lamb.

"Not in Jordan Killdeer's book. He don't want nobody talkin' about his doin's. So he makes sure by killin' anybody who quits him."

Jack set the iron on the "S" of Rose's brand and made it into an "8." Rose snorted and whinnied but did not jump or kick out.

"Jordan believes in the old sayin' 'dead men tell no tales,' Wilbur. And, if he don't like you, you're gone in a heartbeat. And, I mean real gone. Forever."

Wilbur swallowed a trickle of spittle and felt a shiver crawl up his spine like spiders with icy feet.

He slipped the halter from Rose's head and turned her away from the rope corral.

He gulped in air and watched Jack put the iron back on the coals. Then he shrugged and walked back to get another horse.

Jack dug out the makings from his shirt pocket and started to roll a cigarette.

"Makes you think, don't it, Wil?" he said as he struck a match and touched it to the end of his cigarette.

Wilbur nodded but said nothing.

He looked out at the horses in the valley, then back at the ones in the rope corral.

"We're all prisoners up here," he muttered under his breath.

He suddenly felt more sorry for himself than for the horses. He kicked at a clump of grass and then crawled under a rope to catch up the next horse to be branded. *At least the horses are goin' somewhere,* he thought. "And I ain't."

The last was just a whisper, as if he were talking to himself. Which he was. He now realized that he could not expect any sympathy or understanding from Jack, who could work for a man like Jordan Killdeer because he was cut from the same bolt of cloth. Neither Jack nor Killdeer knew the meaning of the word "mercy."

Damn them, he thought.

But he, too, was an outlaw, and he drew his pay just like all the others.

He wondered how long the job, all their jobs, would last.

And he didn't have an answer.

TEN

◦⌒◦

Brad and his two companions rode deep into the forest. There was no longer any road into the mountains. They encountered only game trails and thick timber. Just before dusk began to darken the sky and deepen the shadows, they entered a region where many trees had been cut down. There were drag marks where large logs had been skidded uphill to some unknown destination. The ground was littered with broken pine branches, pinecones, and scattered pine needles.

"We'd better make camp," Brad said to Joe and Julio. "It gets dark real quick up here."

"Too open here," Joe said. "Too many trees gone."

"We can use the pine branches for shelter and cut some spruce boughs to put under our bedrolls."

"Good idea," Joe said. "We can make camp in that stand of timber over yonder to keep us out of the wind." He pointed to a thick stand of pine and spruce a hundred yards off to their left.

Brad nodded and turned Ginger in that direction. He had been pensive all afternoon and had not said much on the ride. He seemed to be in a world of his own and Joe attributed his quietness to the recent death of his wife, Felicity. Besides, the mountains had their own soft hum beneath the deep silence. They occasionally heard the sounds of deer and elk rising from their wallows and moving like shadows through the trees, sometimes cracking a downed branch or rustling brush. There had been a distinct solemnity to the afternoon and none of them had spoken much.

They found a small glade in the timber and halted their horses. They dismounted and unsaddled, tying their mounts to small trees until they had finished setting up their camp for the night. As Julio gathered rocks and cleared space for the campfire, Joe and Brad cut spruce bows and laid them on the ground before covering them with their bedrolls. Joe pulled squaw wood down from the pines to use as kindling, while Brad helped Julio gather downed limbs that they stacked next to the fire ring.

Joe and Brad looked for small forked limbs. They cut these from the trees and also cut straight limbs for braces. They each sharpened one end of the forked limbs, driving these into the ground on both sides of each bedroll. Then they laid the straight limbs in the crotch of the forked limbs, which gave them a framework for building a makeshift shelter. They cut thick spruce boughs and stacked them from the ground to the top of the frame. When they finished, they had three lean-tos that would protect them from rain and falling pinecones during the night.

Julio built a fire using squaw wood and small dry pieces of fallen limbs. When the fire blazed, he added larger logs that were dry. The smoke gave off the scent of pine. The fire and its smoke helped keep the insects from annoying them.

The night was deep and black and came on suddenly after the slow dusk and the brilliantly painted sunset that lingered long enough for them to hobble their horses and remove the bridles. Each of them set his rifle and case next to their bedrolls.

Julio set a pot filled with water from one of his canteens on the fire and added ground coffee. They chewed on jerky and hardtack bought in Denver, and Brad opened a can of peaches with his knife. Each of them forked the peaches with their knives and gobbled them down as an antidote to the dry food.

In the blow of the banked campfire, Brad looked up at the sky.

"Up here," he said, "you almost feel like you're a part of that Milky Way up there. The stars seem so close."

"Yeah, it's beautiful," Joe said. He sprawled out and looked upward through the pines. "Makes a man feel mighty small."

"The stars are far away," Julio said. "And a priest once told me that they are suns like the one that shines on us every day."

"He's right," Brad said. "They are suns, but so far away they look like silver stars."

"Hmm," Joe said. "Looks like we have a couple of astronomers in camp."

"Somehow," Brad said, "when I look up at the sky, I imagine that Felicity is looking down on me. I know it sounds crazy, but all afternoon I could feel her on the wind. I felt her all around me, somehow, as if her spirit had scattered in a billion places."

"I'm so sorry that she's gone," Joe said. "I hated to see the boys lower that pine box into the ground."

"I choked up when Pablo dropped that first shovelful of dirt on her coffin," Brad said. "That's when I really knew that she was gone from my life forever."

"Pilar was weeping, and I could not speak," Julio said.

"I'm just glad Luisa wasn't there when Felicity got killed. They would have killed her, too."

"Who's Luisa?" Joe asked.

"She's a kind of *criada*, a maid who helped Felicity with the household chores, helped Pilar milk the cow and feed the stock we kept in the corral."

"Why wasn't she there?" Joe asked.

"Felicity gave her a month off to visit her family in Pueblo. She'll be back in a couple of weeks, I reckon."

"She will cry, too," Joe said.

"Yes. She and Felicity were close."

The men went silent for a while. Brad continued to scan the sky. Julio put more wood on the fire.

"I wonder where she is," Brad said, after a few minutes. "She believed in heaven, but I never had much truck with it. I guess the Injuns believe we all go to a Happy Hunting Ground up there. They even call the Milky Way the Star Path, and I guess they believe their souls, or their spirits, follow that path to the hunting grounds."

"I don't much believe in heaven, either," Joe said. "My pa always said 'when you're dead, you're dead,' and I ain't never seen no evidence that he was wrong."

"I believe in heaven," Julio said. "I am Catholic, and we believe there is a heaven and a hell."

"I think," Brad said, "that ancient people, like the Egyptians and maybe the Greeks and Romans, thought we all had souls that went someplace, to some kind of paradise. Maybe in the sky, maybe someplace else. It's hard to imagine."

"I can't imagine it," Joe said.

Julio was silent. He poked the fire with a dry stick, and hundreds of sparks flowed upward with the blue tendrils of smoke.

"What gets me," Brad said, "is that if there isn't anything else when we die, then why in hell do we live? I think some part of who we are, or who we were, must go somewhere like those sparks that Julio stirred up. I think the Greeks thought that it was the breath that was the soul and that when a person took that last breath, it went on up into some kind of heaven. Egyptians buried their kings with all kinds of jewelry, food, and eating utensils. They wrapped them in bedsheets and sometimes put boats in their tombs so that they could sail up to the gods."

"People get funny notions, I reckon," Joe said.

"Yeah, and I feel lost without Felicity. I don't know where she is, but I hope some part of her is alive, her mind, her spirit, her breath, maybe just her sweet smile. It seems to me such a waste to be born and die and turn back to dust."

"I can't make no sense out of it," Joe said.

"In the church, the priest, he says you must have the faith," Julio said.

"Faith in what?" Joe asked.

Julio shrugged. "I don't know. Maybe you got to believe that there is a life after death, that we have souls that leave the body and go up to heaven like smoke. I do not think of these things much, but my mother and our priest talked much about them when I was a little boy."

Brad got up and stretched.

"I think we better change the subject," he said. "I'm thinking, also, about tomorrow and that I left something out of my plan today."

"What did you leave out, Brad?" Joe asked.

Brad brushed the dirt and bark off his trouser legs.

"I thought maybe the horse thieves were selling what they stole to mining camps. I didn't even think about lumberyards. There are probably more lumberjacks working in these mountains than hard-rock miners."

"Maybe they're sellin' to both," Joe said.

"Sure, they could be. The men who cut timber have to haul the logs to wagons. They have to pull the wagons and get the logs to the sawmills. They need horses even more than the miners, maybe."

Joe sat up and clasped his legs with both hands.

"I think you're right, Brad," he said.

"Let's follow one of those drag marks and see if there's a lumber camp close by. See if they have any horses they bought in the last few months from some wandering horse trader."

"That's a damned good idea," Joe said.

"It's another place to start," Brad said. "I still want to go to Wild Horse Valley and see if the horses are wild or broke and stolen."

"I think we will find out something," Julio said.

"Bound to," Joe said.

Brad walked to his bedroll and unbuckled his gun belt with its knife and pistol. He wrapped the holster and sheath in the cartridge belt and set it next to his bedroll. He rolled up his saddle blanket and put it down for a pillow at the head of his blanket. He sat down, pulled off his boots, and set them under his saddle.

Then he lay down and rested his head on his folded arms.

"Good night," he said to Joe and Julio. "See you at daybreak."

"Good night," Joe said. He walked to his bedroll and started his preparations for sleep.

"Buenas noches," Julio said and put more small logs on the fire.

Brad pulled his blanket up after he buttoned his denim jacket. He continued to stare up at the array of sparkling stars, those in clusters, and those that seemed to be all alone on that vast dark prairie of space. They looked like little campfires out on the plain, or the lights of houses in some lonesome prairie town.

He closed his eyes and began to dream of Felicity.

ELEVEN

∽

Just before Brad fell into slumber, his gaze fixed on a lone star. He wondered if it might be Felicity and if she was sparkling and winking at him as a way of saying good night. It was a foolish thought, he knew, but he dreamed of her that night and when he awoke before dawn, he thought she was lying next to him. He could feel a slight pressure on his blanket and it seemed that her spirit had somehow come to him and her ghostly hand had touched him.

He got up quietly and shivered in the morning chill. Joe and Julio were still asleep, and the fire had turned to ashes with a few tiny coals glimmering under the gray mounds of ash. He walked away from the camp to relieve himself and check the drag marks of trees that had been hauled away after being cut.

The star he had seen the night before was gone, moved to another place in the sky, or maybe, he thought, that had been a sign from Felicity that had disappeared as soon as he had fallen asleep.

He missed her. He missed her terribly, and he no longer thought about the way she had died but the way she had lived. Now, it was like a hole had been ripped out of the universe, leaving an empty hollow place in its fabric where she had once been, alive, breathing, and loving. He could hear her voice in his head, but everywhere he looked there was that empty hole where she should have been but was no longer. His thoughts twisted him up inside, and he had to summon his willpower to keep from sobbing. He wanted to talk to her. He wanted to hold her in his arms. He wanted to kiss her. He wanted to ride up over the bluffs and into the timber with a tablecloth, a basket of food, and a bottle of wine so that they could spend an afternoon away from the ranch and Leadville, all the cares and worries of the civilized world. As they had done more than once, he reflected. Moments remembered; moments gone. Forever.

He walked back to camp and put more wood on the ashes. He stirred the small coals with a stick and saw smoke rise from beneath the thin claws of the squaw wood. Some of the twig-like fingers caught fire and blossomed tiny flames. He blew on the coals and they flared up, heated the skinny limbs, and burst into flame. He added firewood once the flames were raging and this wood caught fire, too, and he felt the welcome warmth as he piled on more dry logs.

Julio woke up first and fixed coffee to set on the fire. Then he walked away to relieve himself. Joe sat up and threw his blanket aside, his features lit by the firelight, his face orange and shadowy, his clothes painted with the same dancing colors.

"Mornin', Brad, you sleep all right?"

"Fair enough. You?"

"Like a log," Joe said. He stood up, reached down, and picked up his gun belt. He strapped it on and walked to the fire. Steam began to spool out of the pot in a cloudy mist. "Mmm. Coffee smells good."

Julio walked up. "The coffee she is not yet cooked."

"I'll wait," Joe said as he gave the air another sniff.

"Let's saddle up," Brad said. "I think it's going to be a long day."

The three men bridled and saddled their horses, tucked the hobbles in their saddlebags. They ground-tied their horses while they drank coffee and warmed themselves by the fire.

They tore down their lean-tos and kicked dirt on the fire to put it out. When they rode away, there was little trace of their overnight presence.

Julio and Joe followed Brad as he tracked a log up the slope. Within fifteen minutes they began to hear the sounds of an ax striking a tree trunk, the buzzing sound of a cross-cut saw and the voices of men. All around them were fresh stumps and drag marks.

Men were trimming branches from fallen trees with hatchets and saws. Horses pulled on chains attached to logs. One man stood out when they rode into the logging camp. He was tall and muscled, wearing red long johns under his pants and no shirt. He wore suspenders and smoked a corncob pipe. He held an ax in his hand and barked orders to the men who used the horses to skid logs onto a loading ramp. A large wagon stood under the ramp and men were using picks to roll the logs on the platform down onto the wagon.

"Howdy," Brad said to the man with the ax.

"Hunters?" the man asked.

"Yeah, we're hunting," Brad said. "I'm Brad Storm. Can I talk to you for a minute?"

"Sure. I'm Claude Miller, boss of this worthless outfit."

"It looks like you've done some damage up here."

"We cut down only the biggest and tallest," Claude said.

Brad stepped out of the saddle. He held up a hand to keep Joe and Julio mounted.

"You got some fine horses here, Claude," Brad said.

"We go through horses like shit through a tin horn," Claude said. "We buy 'em, wear 'em out, and buy more. They're worth every penny."

"Where do you buy your horses, might I ask?" Brad said in his most polite tone of voice.

Out of the corner of his eye, he saw Joe drift away toward some of the skid horses. Julio held his ground, watching the loggers fell trees up on a ridge across from the loading ramp.

"Man out of Cheyenne come by one day and asked if we

needed horses. Offered to supply all we needed at fifty bucks a head."

"What's the man's name?"

Claude lifted a work boot and placed it on a stump in front of him. He wore no hat, but there was a red bandanna tied around his forehead. He had large hands that were callused and gnarled.

"Jordan Killdeer. He's a Cherokee half-breed. He made good on his offer, for sure."

"And does he bring the horses to you himself?" Brad asked.

"Nope. He sends some men with a string of horses, and I get to pick out the ones I want. I pay the men and they take the horses I don't buy someplace else."

"Do you know the names of the men who bring you the horses?" Brad asked.

"Say, feller, you interested in huntin' or horses?"

"Both," Brad said. "I'm just curious. I might want to buy some horses for myself."

"Well, sir." Claude puffed on his pipe and blew smoke from his nose and the corners of his mouth. "They's usually three or four men what brings the horses to me. One of 'em's called Curly, but I don't know his real name. He's as bald as a billiard ball. 'Nother one calls himself Nelson Canby. He seems to be kind of the boss. They call him Nels, and another one is Abel Avery. Tell you the truth, I never did get the name of another feller who sometimes comes with 'em. I think they called him Slim or Slick or somethin' like that. Don't none of 'em look much like horse traders. More like hard cases, you ask me."

"Mind if we look at some of your horses? I might be interested in meeting Killdeer or the men who bring you the horses you buy."

"Help yourself," Claude said. "Long as you don't hold up none of the work." He took his foot down from the stump and walked over to a tree that had been skidded there and began to trim the limbs. He worked fast and hit hard and made short work of the job.

"Jethro, you can skid this'n up to the loading ramp," he called to a man who was leading one of the skid horses.

Brad climbed back up in the saddle and motioned for Julio to follow him.

They rode up alongside, Joe who was looking at some horses tethered to a fallen tree. They were in harness and had blinders on their bridles.

"You checking the brands, Joe?" Brad asked, keeping his voice pitched low, just above a whisper.

"Yep," Joe said. "They're all wearin' different brands. And all the brands look like double stamps."

"What's that?" Brad asked.

"Like somebody used a running iron to change the brands. So it's hard to figure out right off just what the original brand was."

"Damn," Brad said. "I was hoping we could find original brands and maybe find out who the thieves are."

"Well, take a look at that horse closest to us," Joe said. "That brand on its hips looks smeared. It's got a slight shadow in the marking, which makes me think somebody took a hot iron and changed the brand."

Brad looked at the brand. It did appear to be slightly askew, as if it had been altered. The brand that showed was a Bar E. The bar was fat, and there was a tiny streak of hair showing at its center. The "E" was wavery, like something that could be seen in the bottom of a glass of water if the glass was jiggled a little.

Brad took the papers from his pocket that Cliff had given him. He looked down at the list of brands from the various ranchers who'd had horses stolen from them.

"I think," Joe said, "that the 'E' once was originally an 'F.' They just took a running iron and put a bottom on the 'F' to make it into an 'E.'"

"There's a Bar F listed here," Brad said.

"Yeah, that's Malcolm Foster. He lost twenty head."

"What about the other brands?" Brad asked.

There was a dun with a cropped mane and tail that had what appeared to be a fresh brand on its hip. The edges of the brand were scabbed over and Brad saw traces of red in the hide there, which might have been blood.

"That dun bears the brand of the Circle J," Joe said. "And it sure looks like somebody switched it with a running iron. Hair ain't growed back much and you can see meat showin' under the markings."

Brad studied the list of ranch brands.

"There's a Box I here," Brad said. "The letter I closed in by a square."

"That's Jerry Iverson's brand," Joe said. "You look real close and can see where the circle is fatter on the corners. Somebody turned that box into a circle and added a pigtail at the bottom to turn it into a 'J.'"

"Well, that's enough for me," Brad said. "I learned from the boss there who is head man in this horse-thieving business."

"Who would that be?" Joe asked.

"A half-breed name of Jordan Killdeer. Ever heard of him?"

"Nope. Name doesn't ring no bell."

"I also got the names of some of the men who are probably doing Killdeer's dirty work for him. I'm going to write them down on this paper before I forget them."

Brad pulled out a pencil and began to write down the names.

Claude walked over to them.

"See any you like?" he asked Brad.

"I was wondering if you know where this Killdeer has his headquarters. I might want to talk to him."

"Oh, he's from up in Cheyenne," Claude said. "I think he has a ranch up there and a saloon and gambling hall of some sort, and maybe owns a hotel."

"Thanks, Claude. I just might look in on Killdeer and look at some of his stock."

"You want horses for hunting?" Claude asked.

"I'm thinking of opening a guide operation to take hunters up here for deer and elk in the fall," Brad lied.

"Well, Jordan's got all kinds of horses. You just might find what you're lookin' for."

Claude drew smoke through the pipe stem and blew a cloud from his mouth. He snapped one of his suspenders and smiled with satisfaction.

"So long, Claude," Brad said. "Thanks for talking with me."

"Always glad to be of help to a stranger," he said.

They waved good-bye to Claude and rode out of the logging camp. They climbed ever higher, crossed a ridge, and went down another slope.

"Now what?" Joe asked.

"Now, we ride to Wild Horse Valley. We may not find anything there, but at least we know more than we did this morning when we woke up."

"Will we make it there today?" Joe asked.

Brad shook his head.

"Just look at all those hills and those mountain peaks, Joe," he said. "There's no end to them. We've got a ride ahead of us that's more than a stretch of the legs."

Joe sighed. "It burns me that we found some of the stolen horses and can't do a damned thing about it. Claude probably bought them in good faith and has no idea where they came from."

"I'm sure you're right, Joe. No, we can't do anything about those horses we just saw, but we just might find the thieves, and we can sure as hell go after Jordan Killdeer."

"When?" Joe asked.

"When the time comes," Brad said.

He looked out over the vast expanse of hills and mountains. The land seemed to roll on and on like some mighty ocean, all green and shining in the golden blaze of the sun. It was enough to fill up a man and make him never want to leave such a grand place.

For as far as he could see, the country seemed like a hidden and untouched Eden.

Virgin timber everywhere he looked, and if a man wasn't real careful, the land could swallow him up and none other would ever find him.

TWELVE

꩜

As he rode, Brad felt as if Felicity were riding with him. He could almost feel her arms around his waist and her breasts pressing against his back. He sensed her presence in the very air of the mountains, and he was gripped by a deep sadness that his feelings were just empty illusions.

He could even smell Felicity's perfume. The scent of lilacs was in the air.

Felicity's favorite perfume.

They stopped at a small spring-fed stream that coursed through a narrow valley, to water their horses and fill their canteens. As they let their horses drink and blow, Joe stepped up to Brad with a worried look on his face.

"You know, Brad," he said, "I been thinkin' that maybe we could have wrapped up this case this mornin'."

"Oh? How so?" Brad asked.

"Well, we could have hauled Claude Miller back down to Denver and had him testify in front of a judge about the whole shebang. The judge would've issued search and arrest warrants, sent U.S. marshals up to Cheyenne, arrested Jordan Killdeer, and maybe gone after his hired men."

"You think that would have wrapped up this case, Joe?" Brad said.

"Yeah, I do, kinda."

"Kinda is right," Brad said. "You think a judge would arrest Killdeer on the say-so of one man?"

"Well, we could've run the horses down to the stock-yards and penned 'em up as evidence. That would have cinched it, in my estimation."

Water gurgled into the mouth of Brad's uncorked canteen until it was full. Brad stood up and put the stopper back in the canteen.

"One man's testimony, Joe," he said. "A half-dozen horses that you might have to slaughter to check the brands under the hide for proof. I disagree with you. We don't have a case yet. Leastwise, no case we can prove."

"I think we do," Joe said stubbornly.

Brad hung his canteen on his saddle horn. His eyes glinted a savage blue in the sunlight.

"We have a small amount of evidence that we can't use just yet," Brad said. "A witness who may or may not testify."

"Miller seemed cooperative enough."

"Yeah, because he was in his own element, the logging camp. He probably wouldn't be too happy with us if we he took him away from his work and ran the horses he bought on good faith down to the stockyards and butchered them to see if the brands were changed. He might be right hostile even and tell us all to go to hell."

Julio sauntered over with both of his canteens filled as the argument between Joe and Brad heated up and their voices grew louder.

"You got somethin' to say, Julio?" Joe snapped.

"No," Julio said, "I got nothin' to say. I am not a real detective. I am only a poor vaquero. I do not know nothing about the law, but I think we do not have much to show a judge. A few horses maybe, and a man who bought them from some thieves."

"That's all we have, Joe, just as Julio laid it out."

"Hell, neither one of you is worth your salt as detectives in my book." Joe's anger rose as he faced both men who were disagreeing with him.

"No, we're not either of us bona fide detectives, Joe. We're cattlemen. But Harry hired me to solve this case and that's what I aim to do."

"I was hired, too, and I'm an experienced range detective." Joe was adamant.

"You want to ride back and ask Claude to go before a judge in Denver and drive those stolen horses down there, go right ahead, Joe."

Brad walked away to retrieve Ginger at the stream.

"You know I can't do that by myself," Joe yelled after him.

Brad pulled on the reins and Ginger lifted his head and turned around to follow him.

"Then, Joe," he said, "I guess you're stuck with me and Julio. If you don't like it, you can ride on back and turn in your chit."

"Is that your final decision, Brad?"

"No, it's not my final decision, Joe. It's just one I have to make right now. I expect I'll have to make a few more before we get what we're after."

"Damn you, Storm. You're a stubborn bastard."

"So, now you bring my parents into it, eh, Joe? Well, a desperate man who thinks he's in the right will just shave himself down to a nub and cuss at whoever doesn't agree with him."

"I, ah, I didn't really mean you were a bastard, Brad."

"Then don't call me one. Saddle up and ride with me, Joe, or ride off. I don't really give a damn which."

Brad hauled himself into the saddle. Julio got Chato and pulled himself into the saddle. Joe stood there, thinking for several moments. Finally, he jerked his horse's reins and mounted up.

"I'll ride a ways with you, Brad, but when we get back to town, I'm goin' to write a full report about this conversation. I think you're wrong and I mean to let Harry and Cliff know how you wasted expense money."

"Suit yourself, Joe," Brad said as Joe climbed into his saddle. "But you either go along with me willingly or I'll fire you from the case."

"You'd do that to me, Brad?"

"I would," Brad said. "Right now, Joe, you're on a mighty thin rope."

Joe opened his mouth to speak but changed his mind. Brad gave him one more searing look, then rode off down the valley.

Late in the afternoon they heard a distant boom from somewhere up ahead. They all stopped to listen. They were in thick timber on one of the ridges.

"What was that, I wonder?" Joe said.

"Sounded like a blast," Brad said. "Dynamite. There's a little river up yonder in a wide valley. We just might be heading for one of those mining camps."

There was another explosion and another loud boom that echoed, this time, until it faded out.

"Yes," Julio said, "that is dynamite."

"No mistake," Joe said.

Brad turned his horse and they rode upward onto another hill that gave him a view of the surrounding terrain. In the distance he saw the white shoulders of limestone bluffs.

"Yonder lies the mining camp," he said, pointing to the cliffs.

"I see the bare bones of some bluffs," Joe said. "Don't see no camp."

"There's a little creek runs under those bluffs," Brad said. "I've run across prospectors panning in that creek. One of 'em must've found some color in his pan."

"How far away is it?" Joe asked.

"As the crow flies, Joe, not far," Brad said. "But, we aren't crows and we can't fly, so it'll take us better than an hour or so to make it to those bluffs."

"I'm game. Let's see what's goin' on over there."

"That's just what we're going to do, Joe. Glad you agree with me."

Brad smiled at this small victory.

Joe tried to smile back, but it just wasn't in him. He snorted and put spurs to his horse's flanks.

Julio grinned like a Halloween jack-o'-lantern.

THIRTEEN

∾

Smoke and dust billowed out from a hole in the side of the limestone cliff. The third blast still echoed from the far hills and canyons of that region of the Rockies. The cloud of white smoke shredded in the fingerlings of wind that whipped through the long valley. Dust drifted down on the log shacks with their slanted roofs, the few clapboard buildings, the Wild Cat Saloon with its small false front, next to the Gulch Hardware store and the modest Canyon Grocery & Sundries, all scattered along a shelf with a rough road packed down by rock sleds carving a path.

"Hell, there's a damned town here," Joe said.

"A mining town," Brad said. "There are dozens of them sprung up in these mountains."

They rode up to a crudely painted sign that read ARAPAHO GULCH, and underneath, POP. 86. The 86 was crossed out with a slash of black paint and another number in red paint read 92.

Beyond the rudiments of the town, men lined a small creek while others stood behind log barricades in front of the bluff where a large hole still swirled with wisps of smoke and brownish puffs of grainy dust. Horses, some saddled, some unsaddled, lined the street in front of the stores and the saloon.

"They got a bar here," Joe said. "Anybody want a beer? I'm buyin'."

"First we check the brands on all those horses tied at the hitch rails," Brad said.

Julio licked his lips but said nothing.

"Get out your list, Brad," Joe said.

They rode up to the little café at the beginning of the street. The sign read MABEL'S EATS. There were two horses tied outside the eatery, an Appaloosa and a Trotter. The Trotter was at least sixteen hands high, a tall rangy, deep chestnut gelding.

The brand on its hip appeared fairly fresh and yet it was difficult to see if it had been altered.

"The brand reads Bar B," Joe said. "But, I'll bet that 'B' was once an 'E.'"

Brad looked down the list.

"The Bar E is owned by Edward Elliott," he said.

"Yep, that looks like one of Ed's horses. He raises Missouri Trotters."

"What about the 'Paloosa?" Brad asked.

Joe rode in closed and nudged the horse off its hipshot stance and looked down at the brand.

"This one's a Running R," Joe said.

"Legitimate?" Brad asked.

Joe leaned over and rubbed a finger across the brand. It was not a fresh brand. The hair was gone where the brand had been burned onto the hide, but the brand felt uneven to the touch. He felt the contours of the 'R' and then took his hand away.

"This brand is older than some of the others we've seen," Joe said. "But I'd say it's been altered from a Running K to a Running R. The top part of the 'R' is wider and a little uneven."

Brad checked his list.

"There is a Running K ranch listed here. Owner Ted Kilroy."

"Ted raises Appaloosas," Joe said. "That fits, then."

"It sure as hell does. Let's go inside the café and see if we can find out who owns these horses."

"Good idea," Joe said.

They all climbed out of their saddles and wrapped their reins around the hitch rail next to the two horses they had just checked.

The café was small, with a counter and stools, four tables, and one large booth.

Two men sat at the counter, while another sat at a table. A woman stood behind the counter with a wet glass in her hand, a drying towel in the other. The man at the table was a bearded man in his sixties, with a battered hat on his head, grimy, dusty jacket, soiled denim shirt, and work boots. He was eating a piece of lemon pie and drinking coffee. His eyes were tired and bloodshot. To Brad, he looked like a man at the end of his rope, out of luck, out of hope.

"Good morning, gents," the woman said brightly. "Menu's on the blackboard up there if you have a hankerin' for vittles. I make all my pies fresh, and we're fresh out of bear claws."

Joe sat down. Julio sat next to him. Brad looked at the two men sitting on stools before he, too, sat down.

"Coffee for the three of us," he said.

"I could sure gobble down a piece of that lemon pie," Joe said.

"We don't have time for you to feed your face," Brad said. "Just three coffees, ma'am."

"Comin' right up," she said and set the dried glass on a shelf behind the counter under the blackboard with its menu chalked in block letters along with the high prices of her fare.

"Ma'am," Brad said to the woman as she set out three porcelain cups in front of them, "do you happen to know who owns those two horses out front?"

She poured coffee from a steaming pot and looked out the window.

"I see five horses," she said.

"One's an Appaloosa, the other's a chestnut Trotter," Brad said.

"Al, isn't that colored horse yours?" the woman said to one of the men on a stool.

"The 'Paloosa's mine. Just bought him, matter of fact. Less than an hour ago."

"Trotter's mine," the other man said. "I bought him from the same men Al did. Why? You want to buy them?" he said to Brad.

"No, but I'd like to talk to the man who sold them to you. If they're still in town."

Al, a short, thin man in his thirties with a week's beard stubble on his face and chin, a small wet mouth and a crooked nose, said: "Likely you'll find them at the Wild Cat," he said. "They had cash money burnin' holes in their pockets when they left here."

"Men?" Brad asked.

"They was three of 'em. They brought a half-dozen horses. Sold four of 'em to Todd Sperling, who owns that hard-rock mine bein' blasted in the cliff yonder."

"Benji," the woman said to the man sitting with Al, "you cheated those men sure as I'm breathin'. You wouldn't pay his price until he come down a whole ten dollars."

Benji laughed. He was a chubby man in his forties with a rosy button nose, a full beard streaked with gray, and a doughy neck pleated with rolls of fat.

"Horse needed new shoes," he said. "So, he knocked ten dollars off his price."

"How much did you pay for the horse?" Joe asked.

"Thirty dollars. Man wanted forty. Said his name was Curly, but he was bald as a hen's egg."

"Yeah, I had to pay thirty-five for the Appaloosa," Al said. "Shoes warn't too worn."

Benji laughed again.

Brad blew on his coffee and sipped some of it.

"That'll be fifty cents apiece," the woman said.

"Fifty cents for a cup of coffee?" Joe said.

"That coffee has to be hauled up from Denver like everything else in this town," she said. "One dollar and four bits for the three of you."

Brad pulled some bills from his pocket and laid out two one-dollar bills.

"Keep the change," he said to her.

The woman smiled broadly and snatched up the bills in her flabby hand.

"Why, thank you, sir. You're a gentleman."

"Drink up, boys," Brad said. "I want to talk to Curly and the other men he's with before they ride out."

"Oh, they ain't goin' nowhere real fast," Al said. "Them three was wantin' to jine up with a couple of glitter gals what works at the saloon. I expect they'll stay the night in what some calls a hotel here. More like a bunkhouse with walls."

Benji laughed again.

"Well, I want to talk to them before they hit the feathers," Brad said. "Thanks for the information."

"They told me they could get us more horses if we needed 'em," Benji said. "Them three was real horse traders, I tell you."

"That's good to hear," Brad said as he drained his cup and stood up.

The old man at the table had finished his pie. He looked at Brad.

"You ask me," he said, "them three warn't no horse traders ner ranchers. They were hard cases and packed big pistols on their hips. I seen their kind before, you bet. Them was pistoleros like I seen in Taos."

"Gunmen, you say?" Joe said as he stood up.

"Yep. Mean faces, big guns. I bet they stole them horses they brung up here."

"Oh, Petey, you just shut up," the woman said to the old man. "You think everybody who comes to town is out to steal your poke."

The man shook a bony finger at her.

"Mabel, you don't know nothin'," he said. "Them were hard cases. Sellin' them horses so cheap, they had to have stole 'em."

"Thanks, old man," Brad said. "We'll sure watch out for them down at the saloon."

"You better," Petey said, wagging his finger at Brad. "Watch yore back, stranger."

Brad, Joe, and Julio left the café and walked out onto the street.

"We can walk to the saloon," Brad said. "Do you see a hotel anywhere?"

Joe looked down the street.

"Next to the saloon, there's what looks like a boarding-house."

"We'll see," Brad said.

"What do you aim to do, Brad?" Joe asked.

"Ask some questions," Brad said.

"You might not get the answers you're looking for," Joe said.

They walked toward the Wild Cat Saloon.

"Maybe they do not answer no questions," Julio said as they neared the saloon.

"No answer is the same as answering," Brad said.

"If that old man was right, there could be trouble," Joe said. "Gunplay even."

"That, too, is an answer, isn't it, Joe?"

"I reckon so," Joe said.

"I smell blood," Julio said.

They passed a number of wagons parked in between buildings. Down on the flat there was an arrastre with a mule hitched to it, walking around in a circle, the mechanism breaking rocks, ore carts next to it. Along the creek, men were shoveling dirt into dry rockers and squatting with gold pans that they dipped into the stream. Farther down, men were pouring shovelfuls of water and sand onto a placer rig.

And there were three saddled horses in front of the Wild Cat Saloon.

They all bore the same brand, a J Bar K.

Warning klaxons sounded in Brad's brain. These were not altered brands. These were the real McCoy.

The building next to the saloon had a small sign that said ARROWHEAD HOTEL, and underneath, ROOMS FOR RENT.

"Well, there's the saloon," Brad said. "With a hotel right next to it. Only one thing seems to be missing."

"What's that, Brad?" Joe asked.

"There should be an undertaking parlor right in between."

Joe loosened his pistol in his holster. So did Julio when he saw what Joe had done.

Brad fingered the thong around his neck, but he did not shake it. The rattles nested against his breastbone under his shirt.

He pushed on the bat-wing doors and entered the saloon.

Motes of dust danced in the beam of sunlight. The saloon was dark and quiet at that hour.

Three men sat at a table near the entrance.

They looked up at Brad, and their eyes gleamed in the sudden shaft of sunlight.

The bat-wings creaked and stopped swinging as Brad, Joe, and Julio stood there, adjusting their eyes to the gloomy inside.

The eyes of the three men at the table went dark, as if they had retreated into a cave, like feral creatures in hiding.

FOURTEEN

~

The upper torso of a man standing behind the bar appeared out of the dimness.

"Howdy, gents," he said. "Don't just stand there blockin' off all the air. Have a seat."

Joe headed for the bar. He blinked his eyes as if to wash out the sunlight that lingered there.

"Might as well," Brad said to Julio. "Come on and wet your whistle."

Julio followed him to the end of the bar. Brad pulled out two empty stools next to Joe, who was leaning over the bar.

"I'm Chet Macklin," the barkeep said. "What's your pleasure, gents?"

"A beer, if it ain't too hot," Joe said.

"Oh, we ain't had no snow here in a month of Sundays, but it keeps fairly cool in the keg."

"I'll have a beer, too," Brad said. "Julio, order whatever you want to drink."

Julio sat down next to Brad.

"You have any tequila?" he asked Macklin.

"Nope, you got to go south a ways for them spirits. Pueblo, maybe. Or Santa Fe."

"I will take a beer," Julio said.

Brad sat down, and Joe pulled out a stool and seated himself.

"Comin' right up," Macklin said. He was a man in his mid-thirties with a thin hatchet face, a crop of wiry red hair, and a scarred nose. He stood about five foot nine and was muscular under his pale chambray shirt that had seen many washings. He poured three glasses, heavy beer glasses, to the rim and scraped off the foam as he set them on a tray. He carried the tray to the end of the bar and set the glasses down in front of each man.

"That'll be six bucks," he said.

Joe groaned as he reached for his wallet.

"I'll get it, Joe. Goes on the expense account."

"Thanks, Brad."

"Don't thank me. Thank Harry and Cliff."

Joe chuckled as Brad pulled out some bills and laid out six ones on the bar top.

"You fellers some kind of agents, maybe minin' agents, or something?" Macklin asked as he shoveled the bills from one hand to another.

"Why do you ask that?" Brad said.

"Talkin' about an expense account and all. Ain't none of my business o' course."

"No, we're not mining agents," Brad said. "We're range detectives."

Joe nearly choked on his beer as some of it went down his windpipe.

Brad spoke loud enough for the three men at the table to hear and he looked at them with a sidelong glance. They seemed to stiffen in their chairs and one of them jerked his lit cigarette from his mouth and glared at Brad and his two companions.

"Well, there ain't no range hereabouts," Macklin said. "So what brings you to the Gulch? If you don't mind my askin'."

"Horses," Brad said in a loud voice.

Joe cringed. A flicker of a smile played on Julio's bronzed face. Macklin looked puzzled.

"Horses?" he said.

"Yeah, we want to buy some. Heard we could find some here in the Gulch that were pretty cheap."

One of the men at the table sat up straight as if he had been jolted by a cattle prod.

Able Avery rose from his chair and stood there for a moment. Curly and Nels scraped their chairs. Nels lifted a hand and stuck it in front of Avery to halt him.

"Stay out of it, Abel," Nels said.

"Hell, they want to buy horses, Nels. Let's see what they're willing to pay."

"I don't like the smell of it," Curly said.

Abel pushed Nels's hand aside and walked over to the bar. He stood at the corner for a moment.

Brad fixed the man with a searing look.

"Who wants to buy horses?" Abel asked.

"I'm looking for some good horses," Brad said.

"And who might you be?" Abel asked. He walked behind the three men and stood close to Brad. He looked Brad up and down with a look that was a mixture of scorn and curiosity.

"What's my name got to do with it, stranger?" Brad said. He reached into his back pocket and pulled out a long wallet. He opened it and flashed a stack of greenbacks. The bill on top was for one hundred dollars. Beneath the bills was a torn scrap of blue cloth.

"You said you was a range detective," Abel said. "For all I know you might be wantin' to buy horses what was stole. If you do, we can't help you none. But we're traders and it looks like you got the cash."

"What've you got?" Brad asked. "And how much are you asking?"

"Why, we got all kinds of horses, mister. You name it. And, we only want what's a fair price, dependin' on the breed and age of the horse."

Julio and Joe turned on their stools to look at Abel. Brad looked past him at the two other men still sitting at the table. They were all ears.

"How long would it take for you to bring me a half dozen head to look at?" Brad said. "I'm lookin' for some good cutting horses."

"Why, it wouldn't take more'n a half day," Abel said. "I got cuttin' horses, you bet."

"We'll go with you," Brad said. "No use you ridin' both ways."

A look of suspicion crept onto Abel's face.

"Ain't no trouble. We sold some horses we brought up today. We'll bring 'em to you." He looked at the open wallet again. "'Course you might want to give us a little earnest money."

"Oh, I don't think old Earnest would like that," Brad said. "He's tighter than a widder's purse."

"That ain't funny," Abel said.

"You want something funny," Brad said as he slipped the torn swatch of blue flannel cloth out from under the bills. "Take a look at this. It's still got a little blood on it."

Brad thrust the cloth at Abel. Abel jumped backward a half foot, his hands up as if to ward off something evil or untouchable. His eyes bulged like those of a besotted bullfrog as he stared at the piece of blue cloth.

"What in hell's that?" Abel barked.

"You might recognize it. It's a piece of my wife's nightgown. She was wearing it when three men cut it off her, then raped her and slit her throat."

"I don't know nothin' about that," Abel said.

"About what?" Brad asked, shaking the cloth at Abel.

"'Bout no woman gettin' jumped and kilt."

"You're a lying sonofabitch," Brad said in a soft, even tone of voice.

"Them's fightin' words where I come from," Abel said as he backed away another foot or two.

Brad slipped the cloth into his shirt and pulled on the leather thong around his neck until the rattles were just out of sight inside his shirt.

Abel spread his legs in a gunfighter's stance and held his arms out like a pair of parentheses, ready to draw.

"Snake," Brad shouted and looked down at Abel's feet.

He shook the rattles, and Abel jumped three inches off the floor. His face drained of blood as he looked around. The two men at the table scraped their chairs and lifted their boots off the floor. They, too, were looking for a rattlesnake crawling around somewhere.

Abel's right hand streaked for his gun.

Before he could clear leather, Brad snatched his pistol from its holster. He thumbed back the hammer on the rise as he brought the barrel up to bear on Abel's gut.

Brad held his breath and squeezed the trigger.

The .45 Colt bucked in his hands as its blue-black snout spewed lead, orange sparks, and white smoke.

The bullet smashed through Abel's belt buckle just as the barrel of his pistol was still an inch from being fully drawn. He doubled over as the bullet cracked into his spine and blew a hole the size of a small grapefruit in his back. His blood spattered the two men at the table, Curly and Nels. They scooted away from the table and jumped to their feet.

Abel crumpled up as his knees gave way and he slumped to the floor, wild red blood gushing from the hole in his stomach. The stench from his ruptured intestines filled the air.

Curly and Nels ran for the bat-wing doors.

"Hold on," Brad shouted.

Julio and Joe both drew their pistols.

Brad swung his pistol in a small arc as he hammered back for another shot.

But the two men were out the doors and climbing into their saddles.

They both drew their pistols and fired through the doors. The bullets splintered wood and plowed furrows in the wooden floor.

Brad ducked, then squatted, staring at the swinging doors.

He could not see the two men, so he did not shoot.

Julio fired a shot from his pistol that cleared the tops of

the doors and whined off into the air as it caromed off a post outside.

Abel croaked as blood spewed up into his mouth and gushed onto the floor. He was paralyzed and losing blood so fast it streaked across the floor and made dark little pools. He didn't even twitch because he could not move his legs. He gasped and struggled to draw air into a mouth filled with blood and whiskey.

Brad heard a sound and turned toward the bar.

Macklin stood there behind the bar with a sawed-off, double-barreled shotgun in his hands. He had a thumb on one of the hammers.

Brad swung his pistol to take aim on Macklin.

"You cock that Greener," Brad said, "and you'll draw your last breath."

Macklin dropped the shotgun onto the bar as if it were red-hot. He threw both hands up in the air in a sign of surrender.

"D-don't sh-shoot," he stammered.

"Step away from that shotgun," Brad said. "Julio, grab it."

Julio holstered his pistol and picked up the shotgun.

Brad walked over to the bar. Macklin was pressed against the wall, his hands held high, bare palms showing. He was shaking like an aspen tree in the wind.

"You saw it all, Macklin," Brad said. "That man went for his gun first. It was a fair fight."

"Yeah, yeah, I did. I saw it all. Abel went for his gun first. I never saw nobody draw as fast as you."

"If you have law in this town, you tell it like it happened."

"Ain't no law here in the Gulch," Macklin said.

They all heard men running out in the street. The footfalls sounded closer.

"Whoever that is out there, you tell 'em it's all over," Brad said.

Joe holstered his pistol and picked up his glass. His eyes were fixed in a blank stare.

"Mister," Macklin said, "I think I know who you are."

"Who am I?" Brad said as he holstered his pistol and walked to his bar stool.

"You're the one they call the Sidewinder, ain't you?"

"Why do you say that?" Brad asked as he picked up his glass and took a swallow.

"I heard of you. Down on the flat. I heard the rattlesnake, only it was you makin' the noise."

Brad smiled as men beat through the bat-wings and came to a halt when they saw the body of Abel on the floor. Abel wheezed and his eyes turned glassy for just a moment as he expelled his last breath and could not draw in another.

"What the hell happened in here?" growled a large man at the head of the small pack behind him.

Todd Sperling was covered in dust. His face bore the ravages of wind and weather. His white hair flowed to his shoulders, and they were wide, brawny shoulders under a checkered shirt. Suspenders held up his heavy-duty duck pants and he smelled of dynamite and crushed limestone, the very earth that covered his work boots.

"Mr. Sperling," Macklin said, "this here's the man they call the Sidewinder and he just put Abel Avery's lamp out. It was a fair fight."

Macklin pointed to Brad.

Brad smiled at Sperling.

"Nice little town you have here, Mr. Sperling," Brad said. "Nice, once you sweep out the trash."

Brad nodded toward the dead man.

Sperling looked at Brad, the faint curl of a smile on his liverish lips.

Flies zizzed around Abel's face and speckled the wound in his belly. For several seconds, that was the only sound.

The sunlight pouring through the windows and the empty places above and below the bat-wing doors was a pale yellow, swirling with dust and striking small sparks off the whirring wings of the sniffing flies.

It was quiet and solemn for several seconds as the men behind Sperling craned their necks to look at the body and at the man known as the Sidewinder.

FIFTEEN

Julio cracked open the shotgun and removed the two shot shells. He put those in his jacket pocket and laid the gun on the bar top behind him.

"Buy you a drink, Sperling," Brad offered.

"No, by gum, I'll buy you a drink, Sidewinder."

Sperling strolled to the bar. Joe got off his stool and offered it to Sperling.

"Thanks," Sperling said.

The men standing in front of the bat-wing doors dispersed and sat down at tables around the body of Avery.

"Looks like we're going to have a busy day. What's your pleasure, Mr. Sperling?" Chet Macklin asked. "The usual?"

"No, I'm working, Chet," he said. "I'll have a beer to wash down the dust."

One of the men at the table got up and walked to the bar after hearing what the others wanted to drink.

"We'll all have beers," the man said. "I'll wait and carry 'em over to the tables."

Joe poured a beer for Sperling, flicked off the excess foam and brought it to him.

"I'll pay for the boys at the tables, too," Sperling said. He laid a pair of twenty-dollar bills on the bar.

Sperling picked up his glass and raised it in a toasting gesture. "I don't know why you killed that jasper, Sidewinder, but I didn't like the cut of his jib."

"It's Brad Storm. You sound like you might have been a sailor once."

"Ah, yes. I sailed the seven seas when I was just a pup. Then, in Rangoon, I saw real gold, and I came back to Coloraddy to dig it out of the ground."

"You bought horses from that dead man and two others?"

"Yeah. They kept me supplied. We wear out horses pretty quick with all the haulin' and road buildin'. They sold 'em to me cheap."

"They're horse thieves," Brad said.

"Well, you know the old sayin', 'Never look a gift horse in the mouth.' I didn't look too hard at the brands, and they had papers on 'em. Gave me bills of sale and all."

"If you look real close at some of those brands, you can see they've been altered, Mr. Sperling."

"Oh, call me Todd, Brad. Everyone else does. Well, some of the brands did look funny, but when I mentioned it to Curly and Nels, they just said they got 'em off'n a ranch in Laramie."

"Were they the men who first offered you horses at a cheap price?" Joe asked.

"Matter of fact, no," Sperling said. "Feller came down here from Cheyenne, name of Jordan Killdeer. He rode a fine horse and told a good story. Said he was overstocked on his ranch up there and was willing to provide us with horses for as long as we were workin' our mines and pannin' the streams. Free delivery and all. I took him up on his offer and next thing I knew, we had horses, good horses, to do the haulin' and draggin'."

"Was that the last time you saw Killdeer?" Brad asked.

"Yep. He never come back. 'Stead, he sent them three: Curly, Abel, and Nels."

"I think those three men raped and murdered my wife,

Todd," Brad said. "And stole a dozen head of horses while I was down in Leadville with my ranch foreman, Julio there."

He nodded toward Julio.

Sperling looked at him and Joe, then swung back around to drink his beer and address Brad.

Macklin was busy filling beer glasses while the man at the bar carried them to the tables two at a time.

"That's tough," Sperling said. "But them three fellers struck me as hard cases right from the start."

"Well, they're gunslingers, all right, and cowards," Brad said. "One of 'em cut my wife's throat with a knife."

Sperling stiffened and squinched his eyes shut as if he had been stabbed himself.

Joe tapped Sperling on the shoulder to get his attention. Todd swung around to face Joe.

"Mr. Sperling, my name's Joe Blaine, and I'm a range detective. Would you be willing to testify in court about your dealings with Jordan Killdeer and those three men?"

"Range detective, eh?" Sperling said. "Well, I don't know. I don't have much truck with the law and courts and such."

"These men are criminals, Mr. Sperling," Joe said. "They deserve to be hanged for their crimes."

"If you served me with a judge's subpoena, I'd show up, of course. Just don't like leavin' the diggin' for too long at a stretch."

"It may not come to that, Todd," Brad said. "Joe is a detective who goes by the book. If I had my way, I'd just catch the thieves and hang them from the nearest cotton-wood."

"Hell, that's my kind of justice, too," Sperling said. "Far as I know, horse thievin' is still a hangin' offense, and if you catch one of 'em, you don't need no trial. Just a good rope and a hangin' tree."

"We're trying to do it right," Joe said, lamely.

"What about the stolen horses?" Sperling asked.

"You'd lose them," Joe said. "Not only are they evidence, but they must be returned to their rightful owners."

"So, no matter what happens with those hard cases and Killdeer, we lose our horses," Sperling said.

"Yep," Brad said. "The horses have to be taken back to their rightful owners."

"Kind of makes us all into criminals, don't it?"

"You wouldn't be prosecuted, Mr. Sperling," Joe said. "Only the outlaws would hang."

"Well, I guess we're between a rock and a hard place, looks like to me. But I reckon you got to do what you got to do." He looked at Brad, a questioning look on his face.

"You ain't a detective, are you?"

"Yes, I am," Brad said. "Julio and I work for the Denver Detective Agency. And right now, so does Joe."

"Hmm, so are you goin' to take our horses away and leave us horseless?"

Joe started to say something, but Brad raised a hand to silence him.

"No, Todd. You can keep the horses you bought in good faith until we wrap up our case against Killdeer and his hirelings. But it's likely you will lose them somewhere down the road."

"Looks to me like we don't have no protection whatsoever," Sperling said.

Brad finished his beer and stood up. "From now on, Todd, you might want to look that gift horse in the mouth and check out the men you deal with in the future."

"You bet I will," Todd said.

"Let's go, boys," Brad said. "I want to track the two men who got away."

"I hope you catch 'em," Sperling said.

Macklin picked up the twenty-dollar bills and left some change in front of Sperling. Sperling looked at it, scooped it up, and stuck it in his pocket without counting it.

"Good luck in finding the gold," Brad said.

"Oh, it's in there. In that big rock out there and glitterin' in the creek." Sperling stuck out a hand and Brad shook it.

"So long," Brad said.

He walked out, followed by Joe and Julio.

"Now there goes a man you'd ride the river with," Sperling said to Macklin.

"I never saw nobody draw a hogleg as fast as he did," Macklin said.

Moments later, Brad, Joe, and Julio were riding out of town.

"We could have wrapped up the case right there, Brad," Joe said. "We had plenty of witnesses and lots of stolen horses as evidence."

"Then who would go after Killdeer and his men? The Denver police?"

"Well, we would, I reckon."

"We have a case on paper, Joe. A few horses with switched brands. We don't have the men to send to the gallows. Just drop it, okay?"

"You ain't much of a detective, Brad. Not in my book."

"You're right, Joe. I'm a cattle rancher and playacting as a real detective. But I've got a stake in this case, too. I lost something I'll never get back, even if a hundred men hang from the gallows tree."

Joe sighed deeply and hung his head.

The tracks of Curly and Nels were easy to follow for some distance. Then they disappeared in the waters of a creek.

"We could split up and see where they come out," Joe said.

"We could," Joe said. "But we'd waste a lot of time. We're heading for Wild Horse Valley. If my hunch is right, we'll find where the thieves keep the stock they stole."

"What good would that do?" Joe said.

"If we find stolen horses there, we'll have what I'm looking for."

"What's that, Brad?"

"An ace in the hole, Joe."

They rode off to the southwest through thick stands of timber. There was no trail. There was only the silence of the high country, the tall peaks with snow on their lofty reaches, and jaybirds squawking whenever crows flew through the trees.

Brad touched the swatch of cloth in his pocket and tears welled up in his eyes.

He felt the presence of Felicity once again as he gazed at the skyline and breathed deeply of the scented thin air.

There was the scent of pines, of course, but there was also the faint aroma of lilacs in bloom.

SIXTEEN

∾

They saw the thin plume of blue-gray smoke before they reached the wide trail leading down into Wild Horse Valley. As the three riders approached the edge of the plain that formed a ridge above the valley, they could smell the faint tang of burning hide and heard the squeal of a horse.

"Looks like we hit pay dirt," Joe said.

"We'll know soon enough when we look down into that valley," Brad said.

They reached the top of the ridge and looked down into the lush valley below. To their amazement, there were hundreds of horses and more grass than they had seen in a long while.

Columbines bloomed on the hillside below them. The light breeze jostled their delicate petals and wafted their aroma to the riders. Yellow-winged butterflies danced on invisible waves and flitted onto flowers and sage. Below, they saw two men around a hot fire. One was holding a haltered horse while the other was wielding a branding iron. Both men looked up at the three riders.

"Uh-oh," Joe said, "they've spotted us. What do we do now?"

"Wave at them," Brad said. "Wave like you were real friendly."

He raised his hand and waved at the two men at the branding fire. Julio waved, too. Joe hesitated and finally gave a desultory wave.

"I don't get it," Joe said.

"A friendly wave puts them at ease. Now we can ride down and talk to them."

"Unless they shoot us first," Joe said.

"They might think we're new blood," Brad said. "Working for Killdeer."

"Sometimes, Brad, it's really hard to follow your thinking."

"Uh-huh. Sometimes it's even hard for me to follow."

Brad urged Ginger forward, and the three of them rode slowly down the steep slope. Brad kept his gaze locked onto the two men, who continued to perform their branding tasks. The horse that was getting the hot iron humped up its back and lashed out with both hind legs. The man holding the rope jerked down on the halter and bowed the horse's head. A small puff of smoke arose from the horse's hip.

"I don't look for gunplay," Brad said, "but be ready in case things go haywire."

"They're both packin' six-guns," Joe said.

"Probably in case they run across a rattler," Brad said.

Joe opened his mouth, but clamped it shut as if he had thought about a retort and decided against it.

"Howdy, fellas," Brad said as the three of them rode up on the two branders.

"Howdy," Wilbur Campbell said in a pleasant tone of voice.

Jack Trask scowled as he buried the business end of the running iron deep into the pulsating bed of glowing coals.

"You come down from Cheyenne?" Campbell asked.

"No, we rode in from Denver," Brad said.

"Denver? Well, I declare," Campbell said.

"Wil, you shut your mouth," Trask said. "We don't know who these fellers are."

Brad shifted his gaze to Trask.

"Who do we have to be?" Brad asked.

"Unless you work for Jordan, you have to be gone from here," Trask said.

He stepped away from the fire ring and spread his legs apart. His right hand floated above the butt of his pistol.

"So, you must work for Jordan Killdeer," Brad said, a faint smile breaking on his face.

"If he sent you, mister, you'd know that," Trask said.

"In a way, Jordan did send us," Brad said.

Trask's hand opened and dipped down closer to his pistol.

"What's that supposed to mean?" Trask asked.

"Oh, Jack, you ask too many questions. They work for Jordan or they wouldn't be here," Campbell said.

"I ain't so sure. You didn't answer my question, mister," Trask said.

"Well, we're looking for horses and it looks like you got plenty here," Brad said.

"We don't sell 'em," Trask said. "We just keep 'em here to graze."

"Are those running irons you got in that fire?" Brad asked.

Trask's hand dipped and his fingers wrapped around the butt of his .45.

Brad drew his pistol in that instant and all could hear the snick of the hammer as he cocked it back.

"Jack," Brad said, "if that iron leaves its holster, your lamp goes out real quick."

Campbell swore under his breath.

Trask stiffened and froze, the pistol fully in his grip but still in its holster.

"What the hell?" Trask said.

Joe and Julio drew their pistols. They cocked them and aimed them at the two men.

"Drop your gun belts," Brad ordered.

"Jesus," Campbell said. He unbuckled his gun belt and dropped the rig to the ground.

Trask twitched, his hand still on the butt of his gun.

"Make it quick, Jack," Brad said. "I got a hair trigger on this Colt."

"Shit," Trask said, but he lifted his hand and began to unbuckle his gun belt.

"What's this all about?" Wilbur asked. "Who are you fellers?"

"Keep your guns on them, Joe," Brad said. He swung out of the saddle and walked over to Trask. He kicked his gun belt a foot away, then turned on Campbell and bent down to pick up his gun belt. He dropped it next to Trask's.

"Step out, Jack, and keep your hands high. You," he said to Campbell, "take that halter off that horse and hand it over."

"Jesus," Campbell said again. But he did as he was told while Trask stepped closer to Joe and Julio.

"Light down, Joe," Brad said. "Julio, you keep them covered."

Joe slipped out of the saddle.

"What are you going to do, Brad?" Joe asked.

"It's what you're going to do, Joe."

"Me?" Joe said.

"Dig out your braces, Joe, and clamp this man's hands behind his back," Brad said.

"Handcuffs?"

"Yeah, handcuffs."

"All right. They're in my saddlebag."

"Cuff him up," Brad said.

"You the law?" Trask asked.

"You might say that," Brad replied. "We're detectives and we work with the law. I'm arresting you for horse stealing."

"I didn't steal none of these horses," Trask said.

Campbell handed the rope and the halter to Brad.

"That's right," Campbell said. "We didn't steal no horses from nobody."

"Tell it to the judge," Joe said as he returned with two pair of handcuffs. He stuck one set in his back pocket, then stepped up to Trask. He spun him around and jerked both arms so that his hands were behind his back. He clamped cuffs on both the man's wrists.

The horse they had just branded whirled and trotted back to the herd.

There was a whicker from somewhere in a nearby clutch of horses.

Brad looked toward the sound and narrowed his eyes.

The horse whickered again, and he saw movement as one of them started toward him.

"Rose," he said. "Come here, girl."

The bay mare broke away from the other horses and walked toward him. Her head swayed from side to side and hung inches from the ground.

"Come on, Rose," he said as he stepped toward the horse.

"That is the horse of Felicity," Julio said.

"His wife's horse?" Joe said, slightly aghast.

"Yes," Julio said.

Rose walked up to Brad. He rubbed her forehead and patted her neck. He spoke to her in baby talk. Then he walked around to her rump and looked at the brand.

Rose neighed softly as he returned and stroked her head with a gentle hand.

"Joe," Brad said, "here's the proof you need. Rose's brand has been switched with a running iron. Looks like you caught the criminals red-handed."

"Me?" Joe said.

"Come over here, Joe. Julio, you watch 'em."

"I will shoot them both if they try to run," Julio said.

Joe walked over as Brad slipped the halter over Rose's head. He patted her topknot as he adjusted it. He handed the end of the rope to Joe.

"You got something on your mind, Brad?" Joe said. "I wish you'd let me in on it."

"I want you to take that feller named Jack back to Denver and lock him up. I want you to take Rose with you as proof. And be sure to pack those running irons with you."

"Just me?" Joe asked.

"Just you, Joe. I'm going to make the other one take me up to Cheyenne to deliver a message to Killdeer."

"What?"

"You heard me. I figure the other feller might be more obliging than Jack there."

"How do you know that other feller won't double-cross you?"

"I don't," Brad said. "But if does, I'll kill him."

"You don't know what he'll do, Brad."

"Oh, I can figure a man pretty close, Joe. Besides, we have a long ride ahead of us and I can be pretty persuasive when I set my mind to it."

"I'll grant you that."

"Meanwhile, when you get to Denver, put all the names down that we know and charge them with horse stealing."

"But . . ."

"Tell the judge we have proof and witnesses. Harry will make sure the charges stick."

"I don't know," Joe said. "It looks pretty ragtag to me."

Brad walked back toward Trask and Campbell. Rose followed as he tugged on the lead rope.

"It'll all work out. Meet me back here in about a week and a half. Julio and I will be waiting for you."

Joe spoke to Campbell.

"What's your full name?" he asked.

"Wilbur Campbell. You going to arrest me, too?"

"No, I'm not going to arrest you, but I'm going to give Brad here a set of handcuffs you can wear when you go with him up north."

Joe slipped the set of handcuffs from his back pocket and handed them to Brad.

"Thanks, Joe," Brad said. "I might not need them. Mr. Campbell here won't want to run away because he knows I'll shoot him dead if he tries it."

Campbell's face went pale as if all the blood had fled to his toes. He gulped a dollop of air.

"Where do you keep your saddles and bridles?" Brad asked.

"Yonder in them trees where the creek runs," Campbell said. "There's a little log shed we put up that's got all our tack."

"And a wagon?" Brad asked.

"We got two wagons," Campbell said. "Same place, where the creek comes in from the bluffs."

"Good," Brad said.

"What's this about ridin' up north?" Campbell asked.

"Why, you and I and Julio are going to Cheyenne and pay Jordan Killdeer a visit. You've been there, haven't you?"

Campbell nodded.

"You know where Killdeer lives, too, don't you, Wilbur?"

"Yeah. I know where he lives, and I know where he works, both on his ranch and his gambling hall."

"Wil, you talk too damned much," Trask said. "Keep your mouth shut."

"Jack, if you open your mouth once more, I'll whop you with the barrel of my gun," Brad said. "What's your full name, by the way?"

"John Trask. People call me Jack."

Brad turned to Julio.

"Julio," he said, "you and Wilbur catch up a couple of horses for these fellers. Put saddles on them and then come back here."

"We got our own horses," Campbell said. "They's in a corral in back of the little cabin where we keep our tack."

"That'll do," Brad said.

"Jordan will kill you if you show up in Cheyenne," Trask said. He watched Julio and Wilbur walk toward the stand of timber below the bluffs where the creek entered the meadow.

"That'll be pretty hard for him to do, Trask," Brad said.

"Oh? Why is that?"

"Because Jordan is never going to see me in Cheyenne. The first time we meet, it'll be right here in Wild Horse Valley."

Joe's mouth dropped.

Trask looked puzzled.

"And, the next time you see me, Trask, I'll be looking up at you standing under a rope on the gallows."

"You won't ever make it back to this valley if you go up to Cheyenne," Trask said.

"I wouldn't bet on it, Trask. Do you know who you're talkin' to?"

"Some no-account detective, I reckon," Trask said.

"Yeah. He's a detective all right. But he's known in these parts as the Sidewinder. Maybe you've heard of him."

Brad slipped a hand inside his shirt and shook his rattles.

Joe and Trask both jumped. Trask's face turned bone white and his knees gave way. He staggered to regain his footing.

Brad smiled and gripped the rattle to silence it. Rose whickered and bobbed her head as she pawed the ground with her right hoof.

SEVENTEEN

෨

Julio and Joe lifted Jack Trask into the saddle of the horse he was to ride into Denver.

"Just to make sure you don't try to escape, Trask," Joe said, "I'm going to make sure."

Trask sat in the saddle with his wrists encased in handcuffs behind his back. He glared at Joe with bitter hatred flashing in his eyes.

Joe cut a length of manila rope and lashed Trask's feet together under the horse's belly. He made sure that the rope was knotted tight. He tugged on it and was satisfied that the rope wasn't so tight as to cut off circulation in Trask's legs.

"There you go, Trask," he said. "Of course if the horse bolts at the sight of a bear or cougar you could break your neck, but you're not going to jump out of the saddle on our ride down to Denver."

"You bastard," Trask snarled.

"Look who's calling who what," Joe said, then turned away before Trask could say anything more.

He walked over to the branding fire and kicked two rocks loose from the ring. He pulled the running irons from the coals and then kicked dirt onto the fire to put it out. He went to his horse and lifted a canteen of water from his saddle horn. He poured water on the hot irons. They hissed and turned black as they cooled.

Brad came over to Joe and took him aside to whisper in his ear.

"If you ride back up here in a week and a half, Joe, and I'm not here, you make camp up on that ridge and wait for me."

"Maybe you better make it two weeks, just in case," Joe said.

"When I finish my business in Cheyenne, I'm going to wear out leather getting back down here. Julio and I will have a lot to do."

"So, a week and a half, you say?"

"Two weeks at the outside," Brad said.

"All right. If I see no sign of you, I'll camp up in the timber at the top of the ridge and wait for you. Where the road comes in."

"Perfect," Brad said. "Good luck in Denver."

Joe picked up the running irons and wrapped them in his bedroll. He secured them behind his cantle and tied the roll down with leather thongs drawn tight to hold it in place.

"It's goin' to take some tall talkin', but I'll see that Jack gets locked up and your horse entered in evidence. I'll also give a deposition and name the witnesses we have so far."

"And see if you can get arrest warrants for Killdeer, Curly, and Nels."

"I can do that, but we don't need 'em," Joe said.

"If you, Julio, and I get killed, the U.S. marshal can execute those warrants," Brad said.

"Hell, I didn't think of that, Brad. Maybe you are a genuine detective at that."

Brad smiled. "I try," he said.

"Well, so long, Brad. I hope your latest plan works."

"If it doesn't, we'll all be in a heck of a fix."

Joe climbed into the saddle and pulled on the lead rope attached to the bridle on Trask's horse. Brad watched the two men ride to the road at the end of the valley. He kept looking at them as they cleared the rim and disappeared from sight.

A few minutes later, Julio and Wilbur emerged from the timber leading a saddled horse.

When they walked up, Brad pulled Campbell aside.

"Maybe you're wondering why I didn't have you locked up, Wilbur," he said.

"I reckon because you still need me to show you where Jordan Killdeer hangs his hat."

"That's part of it."

"What's the rest of it?" Wilbur asked.

"I figure you're just a down-and-out cowboy or horse wrangler. You don't seem to be cut from the same bolt of cloth as Trask, or Abel, Curly, and Nels."

"I ain't. All I was told was that I would be herdin' horses and might have to do some illegal brand changin'. I was flat broke and had worked for Killdeer on his ranch as a wrangler. Job petered out and he asked me if I'd come down here with Trask and tend stock."

Brad gestured to Julio.

Julio walked over to the two men.

"Julio, I want you and Wilbur here to count all the horses in the valley. Take your time and split 'em up if you have to. Julio, look for our horses and tell me how many have their brands altered. Wilbur, you double-check the tally."

"We must do this on the horse," Julio said. "Do you trust this man not to ride away?"

"I'll have my rifle handy, Julio. If Wilbur makes a break for the skyline, we'll have an extra horse in the string."

Julio grinned.

"I won't run off," Wilbur said.

"Get to it. Julio, take my little tablet and make an accurate tally. I need to know how many head are quartered here."

"We will do this," Julio said.

"You betcha," Wilbur said. He climbed into the saddle. Julio caught up his horse after he took the small tablet and a pencil from Brad. He mounted up on Chato, and the two rode off to the far end of the canyon.

Brad nodded in approval. They were doing it right.

He walked to his horse and pulled his rifle from its scabbard.

He sat down and held the rifle in his lap. He watched Wilbur and saw no sign that he would bolt for the timber and try to get away.

It took Julio and Wilbur the better part of two hours to go through the horse herd. When they rode up, Brad was already sitting in his saddle, his rifle back in its sheath.

"What you got, Julio?" Brad asked.

"I did not add them up. I just made the marks."

"I checked 'em," Wilbur said. "It's a good tally."

"Our horses have your brand on them, Brad," Julio said. "All except one."

"Good," Brad said.

Julio handed him the tablet and pencil. There were several pages with four vertical lines and a slanted line going through those for each five head.

"Let me do the count," Brad said, "then we'll ride out of this valley and head for Cheyenne."

The two men waited while Brad counted each jot of five lines. Wilbur rolled a smoke and cocked a leg around his saddle horn. Julio kept his eye on Wilbur, who didn't seem to notice that he was under scrutiny.

"I make it three hundred and two head here," Brad said. "I counted your marks twice, Julio."

"That is a lot of horses," Julio said.

"We must have seen half that number get taken out of here since we come down," Wilbur said.

"So, maybe Killdeer's men have already stolen about seven or eight hundred horses," Brad said.

"I reckon," Wilbur said.

"We could hang them for stealing just one horse. Too bad we can't hang them eight hundred times," Brad said.

Wilbur didn't laugh. He rubbed a hand across his throat with a look of discomfort on his face. He snubbed out his cigarette with two fingers and let the leavings sprinkle down to the ground.

"Let's go," Brad said.

"The horses," Julio said, "they will not run away?"

"Not likely," Wilbur said. "They got graze and water here. We never had none run off."

"There's only one way out of here," Brad said. "Up that road to the ridge. That's why the Utes and Arapahos kept their horses here. And they caught wild ones that wandered down where the road is now and fed on good grass. A horse feels safe here."

"I did, too, until you boys showed up," Wilbur said.

"That's the luck of the draw, Wilbur. Sooner or later, every thief and criminal gets caught."

"I reckon that's so," Wilbur said.

The three rode out of the valley. Several of the horses looked up, then continued to graze. Some were drinking at the creek and a few were lying down in the shade of the pines on both sides. Three sides of the valley were ringed by steep limestone and sandstone bluffs. It was a quiet and peaceful place.

Julio and Brad flanked Wilbur, who showed no sign that he would try to escape.

As they left the road at the top of the ridge, Brad reached into his pocket and felt the soft fabric of the piece of blue flannel that had been part of Felicity's nightgown.

It gave him comfort to stroke it every now and then.

It had become like a talisman, something a knight might carry into battle during medieval times.

And, he knew, he was riding into battle.

EIGHTEEN

❧

Dan Jimson was still mad about what had happened to Abel in Arapaho Gulch. He was so angry that he could think of little else, and he was still shaking over the experience with the Sidewinder.

"Curly," Canby said to him as they sat their horses in a small copse of spruce and juniper, "it ain't the end of the world. You better get ahold of yourself and settle down. I think we shook off them detectives."

They were not far from the creek they had ridden up for at least two miles. Then, it had dropped off into a deep ravine and they could go no farther without riding around the drop-off.

"They was sure as hell a-trackin' us, Nels. I've heard tell that the feller they call Sidewinder is like a damned bulldog. He don't give up real easy."

"He don't give up at all, Curly. But, we got things to do, and I think we lost 'em by ridin' through that crick."

"Well, we're short a man and got us another ranch to raid."

Canby didn't say anything for several seconds. Instead, he filched the makings out of his shirt pocket and plucked a paper from the pack, made a trough of it in between his fingers, and poured tobacco in it. He pulled the string with its tag on it to shut the pouch, then rolled a quirley. He struck a match and lit the end until it flamed, and then drew smoke into his lungs.

"Dan," he said as he blew a plume of bluish smoke through rounded lips, "it's all goin' to work out. Gene Trask is waitin' on us at that saloon in Fort Collins, remember?"

"Yeah. He's got us a ranch all picked out twixt there and Greeley. A lot of horses, he says."

"I like old Gene a whole lot better'n his brother, Jack. Jack's a sourpuss."

Nels laughed.

"Jack's always got somethin' caught in his craw. His big brother is a different sort."

"Gene? Yeah. He's a lot smarter than Abel was. Abel just shook the wrong tree back there in the Gulch."

"You think Gene could have outdrawn that Sidewinder?"

"I dunno. Gene's pretty fast and he's got a cooler head than either Jack or Abel."

"Soon as I finish this smoke, we'll head out for Fort Collins. We might make it by nightfall."

"Lordy, that's a fur piece from where we are right now."

"Well, we'll surely be there at the Prairie Dog Saloon by sunup. At the latest."

"I'm still nervous about what happened in the Gulch," Curly said.

"A shot of red-eye will tame them nerves down right quick," Canby said.

Curly ran a wet tongue over his lips.

"I could use a shot right now, I tell you." He held out his hand. The hand trembled until he balled it up into a fist.

Nels finished his cigarette. He pinched the burning end between his thumb and index finger then rubbed the paper and tobacco into confetti and let it all drop harmlessly to the ground.

"Let's go," he said and ticked his horse's flanks with his spurs.

They rode out of the cluster of trees and headed east

toward the plain. Canby marked the sun's position in the sky and they began to descend to lower elevations along a tabletop between two low ridges.

Canby headed north when they reached a lower level, and the two men rode past Boulder without stopping. They descended to the road and headed for Fort Collins. By late afternoon, they rode into Fort Collins and headed for the Prairie Dog Saloon.

"Is Gene going to meet us here?" Curly asked.

"He has orders to look for us every day from noon until closing," Canby said.

"Then, I guess he'll be there."

"I reckon."

There were horses at the hitch rail in front of the saloon. Some of these had the U.S. brand on their hips and McClellan saddles on their backs. Soldiers walked through the town in pairs and threesomes, and people strolled in and out of shops or examined the vegetables in the outdoor bins. Canby and Jimson dismounted and wrapped their reins around the hitch rails.

Canby walked over to a blue roan that was hitched to the railing.

"This here's Gene's horse," he told Curly. "So, he's inside."

Curly went in first. He was still shaking inside and hoped he could keep his hands still enough to hold a drink between his fingers. The light inside the small saloon was dim. No lanterns were lit, and the only light was from the front windows.

Gene saw him and rose from his table a few feet from the bar. He waved to the two men. Canby squinted to wash the brightness from his eyes and grabbed Curly by the elbow.

"There's old Gene," he said.

Curly saw a shadowy figure and squinted to block the light streaming in through the bat-wing doors.

"I see him," he said.

They walked over to the table. Soldiers sat at the bar and occupied three or four tables.

"About time you boys got in," Gene said.

Eugene Trask was a square-shouldered, lean, and wiry man in his early forties, with a small wizened face and dark hazel eyes that flickered with wedges of gold and green. His mouth was a small slash beneath an elongated nose that bore a deep black scar across the ridge. His beard was sparse on his cheeks and came to a black swirl of wiry hairs on his chin. He looked like, and was, a gunfighter, a drifter, and a cowboy whose bowed legs betrayed his calling.

"We been through a heap of shit, Gene," Curly said. "Whilst you been swillin' down suds ever' day."

"I been workin' my ass off, Curly," Gene said. "Scoutin' out the ranch we're going to hit and sizin' up the spread. Waitin' on you two ain't been real easy, neither."

"Can we get us some drinks?" Canby asked. "Curly's still shakin' in his boots over what happened to us up in 'Rapaho Gulch, and I'm plumb parched."

Gene raised a hand and signaled to a wandering waiter. "You just tell Bohunk what you boys want and I'll take care of it," Gene said. "Goes on the Killdeer expense account."

The waiter known as Bohunk drifted over with a tray and a towel over his arm.

"What's your poison, boys?" he asked.

"Whiskey," Curley said.

"Rye and a beer to chase after it," Nels said.

"I'll have another glass of that sour beer, Bohunk," Gene said.

"Right away," Bohunk said and drifted off to the bar as if he were a man of leisure disguised as a waiter.

"That Bohunk don't seem to be in no hurry," Curly said as he watched the waiter sidle up to the bar.

"He ain't real fast, but he delivers the goods," Gene said. Canby laughed.

Curly scrunched his face up in a sour scowl.

"You boys run into some trouble?" Gene asked. "I see you don't have Abel with you."

"Avery's dead," Canby said. "We sold some horses up in 'Rapaho Gulch and were in the saloon there when three detectives come in and got Abel all riled up."

"Detectives?"

"That's what they said they was," Nels said. "Leastwise that's what we heard. Abel, he got up and braced one of 'em. This'un showed him a scrap of blue flannel and said it was cut off'n his wife's nightgown. Said some men raped his wife and cut her throat. Abel called the man out and got hisself shot. It was so damned quick. Abel hadn't even cleared leather, but he drawed first, or was fixin' to. Curly and I lit a shuck real quick."

"Who was this feller?" Gene asked.

"Don't know his name, but I think the barkeep said he was the Sidewinder. And we heard about him all right."

"Holy Jehoshaphat," Gene exclaimed, "you tangled with the Sidewinder?"

"That's what we figure," Canby said.

"We heard a rattlesnake and it was him," Curly said.

"That's his trademark all right," Gene said.

Bohunk brought their drinks and set them all together in the center of the table.

"Four bucks," he said. "Silver, gold, or paper."

Gene laid a five-dollar bill on the table.

"Keep the change?" Bohunk said.

"If you're that hard up, Bohunk," Gene said.

"I got a wife and kids."

"You got a whore and a jenny mule, Bohunk, that's what you got," Gene said.

"Thank you, Mr. Trask," Bohunk said with mock gravity and gave a little exaggerated bow. Then he answered the call from a trooper at another table.

Curly drank half of his whiskey in one swallow and wiped his lips. His eyes filled with tears as the liquor burned down his throat.

Nels swallowed a mouthful of rye and washed it down with a sip of beer.

"Well, too bad about Avery," Gene said. "You boys ready to work?"

"What you got, Gene?" Canby asked.

"Well, it ain't goin' to be easy, I can tell you. There's a

spread between here and Greeley that's got some mighty
fine horseflesh. Couple of gates on the pasture where two
dozen head graze. We have to go in at night and be real
quiet. They got a nighthawk what makes the rounds ever'
hour checkin' on the corrals and stables."

"You plannin' on catchin' up a dozen head, Gene?"

"Them's the onliest ones that's easy to get."

"You'll have to go with us back up into the mountains.
To Wild Horse Valley," Canby said.

"Plan to. I want to see Jack. How's he doin'?"

"He's doin' fine," Curly said. "He's right handy with
them runnin' irons."

"There's only one hitch to this deal," Gene said.

He drank beer from his glass while Curly and Nels
waited for the other shoe to hit the floor.

"Hitch?" Curly said.

"What hitch?" asked Nels.

"One of us has got to kill that nighthawk and stand guard
at the ranch house."

"Who's in the house?" Nels asked.

"A man and a woman and three sons," Gene said.

Curly sucked in a breath.

The blood drained from Canby's face.

"We could get into a gunfight once them horses start
squealin'," Canby said. "How old are the sons?"

"They're all growed and got hair on their chests. They
all pack pistols out on the range and probably got an arsenal
inside the house."

"You picked a hell of a place to steal horses, Gene,"
Canby said.

"Good horses. If we don't make too much of a racket,
we ought to get away clean. Corral's about a quarter mile
from the house."

"So you want the nighthawk killed?" Curly asked.

"Yup, you're goin' to have to slit his gullet before he
yells out, Curly. With that big knife of yours."

"I don't like it none," Curly said.

"Me, neither," Nels said.

"Well, that's all we got," Gene said. "Tonight's the last night to do it. Old man Rafferty's takin' them horses to auction tomorrow."

"I'm plumb tuckered out," Curly said.

"We rode a fair piece today, Gene." Nels took another swallow of rye, then downed a mouthful of beer.

"Jordan wants us to get these horses," Gene said. "We ain't got no choice. I figger if we go there toward mornin' that nighthawk will be half asleep."

"And we won't be real woke up," Nels said. "Damn it."

"It's goin' to be a long night," Curly said.

"Jordan says if we get these, he'll put a little sugar in your pay next month."

Gene smiled at both men as if he were a kindly mother to them both. He extended his arms and tapped both men on their shoulders.

"As my old man always said, boys, 'everything's goin' to be all right.'"

Curly raised up a fist and shook it at Gene.

"You're a wily bastard, Gene. Killdeer's pet. I got to get some sleep."

"I got rooms waitin' for you at the Bide-a-Wee Boardinghouse. I'll take you there and then roust you out of your bunks a little after midnight."

"Grub?" Nels asked.

"They got a kitchen there, Nels," Gene said.

"You got everything figured out, don't you, Gene?" Canby said. "Hell, we're goin' up against four or five men just for a measly string of horses."

"Good horses," Gene said and finished drinking his beer.

Dusk was settling into the town when the three men left the saloon and walked down the street to the boardinghouse. The sky over the mountains was aglow with gray clouds burnished to a high gold sheen, and golden rays flickered on the snowcapped mountains.

In the distance, a coyote yodeled, and the breeze stiffened and turned chill.

NINETEEN

∾

Black moonless night. Faraway stars twinkled like thousands of prairie campfires. An owl hooted outside the town as three shadowy riders took to the deserted road heading east of town, the leather of their saddles creaking like unoiled door hinges. Slow and steady they rode as dark shapes of sage and cactus floated motionless on an ebony plain.

When they were out of earshot of the town, Gene halted. They could still see the few lights in the distance, but the prairie was pitch-dark.

He pulled the makings out of his pocket and started to roll a cigarette. The moon was up, but it was behind the mountains and shed no light on the plain.

"What're we stoppin' for?" Curly asked.

"To make sure you got your nerves calmed down, Curly," Gene said. "You been a flibbertigibbet since I woke your sorry ass up."

"Hell, I'm just sleepy," Curly said. "My nerves ain't a-janglin'."

"Well, then mine are," Gene said. "I need a smoke before we get to the Rafferty spread."

"I'm just wonderin' why in hell we got to hit this particular ranch, Gene," Nels said. "There's got to be easier ones we can rustle in the daylight."

Gene struck a match and touched the flame to his quirley. He drew smoke through its wrinkled tube and let it out through his nostrils.

"Some time back, Leon Rafferty bested Jordan in a deal up in Cheyenne. It's been ranklin' Jordan ever since. I guess old Leon went behind Jordan's back on some horse deal."

"So, Killdeer wants to get back at Rafferty," Nels said.

"Yeah, it's more than the horses," Gene said. "In fact, he wants to hurt Rafferty real bad. These horses we're after tonight are ones Rafferty raised special and he's right proud of 'em."

"What's the breed?" Curly asked.

"I think they're an Arab mixed with Kentucky thoroughbreds. All sixteen hands high, four white stockings, blaze faces, and flax mane and tail. I've seen 'em. They're grand horses, all right."

"And we're goin' to sell them at bargain prices to miners and loggers," Canby said.

"That's Jordan's idea of revenge," Gene said.

"Kind of a waste of horseflesh, you ask me," Curly said. "If the horses are that good, Jordan should keep 'em hisself."

Gene blew a plume of smoke into the air and it vanished in the darkness.

"Jordan don't want to get caught," Gene said. "He don't want blood showin' on his hands."

"But he gets his revenge against Rafferty," Nels said.

"That's about the size of it," Gene said. He finished his cigarette.

"Now, from here on, you foller me," he said. "Curly, I'll show you where that nighthawk is and you got to get off your horse and sneak up on him. Can you do that?"

"I reckon. You just point him out to me."

The three men rode on over a landscape shrouded in blackness, picking their way across a prairie where the grasses whispered against their horses' hooves and scaled creatures crawled and slithered out of their path. A lone coyote slunk along the outer rim of their vision like some gray ghost, as silent as stone.

Structures loomed up in the distance and Gene reined up, halting his horse. He dismounted and handed his reins to Nels.

"Curly," he whispered, "we go on foot from here. Nels, you wait here until I return."

Curly dismounted. He patted the sheath that held his knife.

"You better pull that out," Gene said. "You're going to need it."

Curly pulled his knife from its sheath. Then he followed Gene, both crouched low, toward the dim outline of a corral. They walked slowly, each footfall as soft as they could manage.

When they drew near to the corral, one of the horses whickered softly and they both froze and hunkered down even lower.

They heard a rustling sound, then the scrape of a boot. The silhouette of a walking man appeared between the stables and the corral. The man reached the corral. He carried something in his hand that he held at his side. It appeared to be either a stick or a shortened rifle or sawed-off shotgun.

"You hear somethin', boys?" the man said in a soft tone of voice. "Coyote?"

One of the horses whickered. Another neighed a longer phrase.

"Settle down," the man said and stepped away from the corral. He disappeared in the deep shadow of the stable barn but did not enter. Curly and Gene heard a board creak.

Gene tapped Curly on the shoulder and pointed to his eyes.

Curly nodded.

With his hands, Gene made a circle and then pointed to the back end of the stable.

His lips formed the word "go."

Curly squatted and duck-walked to the end of the corral, which he circled from about ten feet from the nearest pole. He moved slow and stopped every so often to listen.

Gene watched as Curly moved in a straight line from the edge of the corral until he passed parallel to the back of the stable. Then Curly circled until he disappeared behind it.

Gene waited on his haunches. His calves ached from the strain. His ankles started to hurt. He wriggled his toes inside his boots to restore some circulation to his feet.

It was an agonizing wait. A long wait.

Finally, Gene heard a scuffling noise. Then a rustle of cloth and a deep grunt. Finally he heard a soft thud. Moments later, a man emerged from the rectangular shadow of the stable and walked toward him. Gene recognized both the silhouette and the walk of the approaching man.

He stood up.

Then, he beckoned to Curly and walked slowly back to where Nels waited with their horses. Neither man said a word.

Nels held out the reins for Curly and Gene. They took them and mounted up.

Curly and Nels followed Gene to the corral gate. Gene dismounted and opened the gate. Nels and Curly rode inside. Several of the horses mouthed nickers and some started to circle. Nels rode up to one horse that was standing still and wrapped his arm around its neck. With his other hand he slipped a halter onto the horse and secured it. There was a rope attached to it. He led the horse out of the corral and handed the rope to Gene.

Then Nels rode back in and flanked the farthest horse while Curly pushed his horse to herd the other horses into a bunch. Nels drove his horse into the bunch while Gene rode a few yards away, leading the haltered horse.

The other horses trotted through the gate and followed the horse that Gene led.

The corral was empty.

As Gene rode across the plain with the horse under halter, Nels and Curly made sure that the others followed.

"Good job, boys," Gene said when they were some distance away from the ranch house.

"Now where?" Curly asked.

"Wild Horse Valley," Gene said.

The moon rose over the mountain peaks and silted the prairie with a dull silver. The grasses turned to pewter and the snowy peaks glistened with a soft white glow. Their shadows trailed behind them over gently rustling grasses as the breeze stiffened and washed across their faces.

Curly unsheathed his bloody knife and wiped it on his trousers. The blade glistened in the moonlight, spinning sparks of pure silver.

Nels looked over at him and grinned.

Curly sheathed his knife and gulped in a fresh breezy air.

Gene kept up a steady pace with the lead horse as they headed for the mountains and Wild Horse Valley.

And there was still plenty of night left so that there was little chance anyone would notice the three men and a string of fine tall horses, their hides a bright sheen of brown in the dazzle of the moonlight.

TWENTY

⌐◦

Brad, Julio, and Wilbur Campbell made camp north of Fort Collins near dusk, nearly two days after leaving Wild Horse Valley. They had less than a hundred miles to go before they reached Cheyenne. The horses were tired after wearing their legs out coming down from out of the mountains, and the men were saddle worn and weary, as well.

While Julio gathered dry brush and dung piles for the fire, Campbell picked up rocks and arranged them in a circle around a shallow hole he had dug with his knife and scooped out with his hands.

"I'd say we've got about a two-day ride to Cheyenne," Brad said as he hobbled the horses for the night.

"How come we didn't bunk in Fort Collins when we come through?" Campbell asked. "I don't fancy sleepin' on hard ground tonight."

"Towns have a way of latching onto your ankles and holding you back from your journey," Brad replied. "You got to board your horses, grain 'em, unsaddle and saddle. Eats up time like a hog at the trough."

"You seem more at home in the wild places, Brad," Campbell said. "Maybe you're half wild."

Brad laughed and looked out over the prairie.

"It's true, in a way. Towns are trouble. Civilization is a curse. I feel more at home in the mountains or out here on the prairie."

"But you work for an outfit in Denver. That's a big town."

"I'm just temporary there," Brad said. "I don't live in Denver. I can't live in a town."

Julio lit the fire and the three of them gathered around it with their canteens and frugal grub, beef jerky, hardtack, and dried apples.

"I do not like the towns, neither," Julio said. "You cannot breathe in a town. There is no air."

Brad and Wilbur laughed.

They ate and talked as the sun set behind the Front Range. A brisk chill wind came up suddenly and fanned the fire, blowing sparks into the air and disseminating the smoke. Julio put more wood on the fire.

They laid out their bedrolls and then sat by the fire, each with his own thoughts.

"This place used to be black with buffalo," Brad said. "Indians knew how to live. They followed the herds in late summer and filled their lodges with meat for the winter."

"A hard life," Wilbur commented.

"Hard, yes, but they had the whole sky above them and no landlords or fences. They roamed the plains and they summered in the mountains. It was a good enough life."

"You'd probably make a good Indian, Brad," Campbell said.

"He is a blood brother to the Ute," Julio said.

"Huh?" Campbell seemed surprised.

"Long story," Brad said. "I got bit by a sidewinder, and some Utes took me in and healed me. We traded blood. That made us brothers, in their eyes."

"You are a man full of surprises," Campbell said.

"All men are full of surprises, Wilbur," Brad said. "You just have to look beyond the masks they put on so that they look civilized. Look at the clothes we wear. That's part of the mask. An Indian wears skins and hides for protection, not to impress the ladies."

"You might have a point there. I guess I never thought of the white man that way."

"You could learn a lot from living with Indians," Brad said. "They have a different view of life than we do."

"You stay with them Utes a long time?"

"Long enough to admire them," Brad said. "I don't think they know how to lie. Not like a white man does."

"Aw, I can't believe that," Wilbur said.

"A man who doesn't know how to lie is like a child. Anybody can come up to him and take his candy away. A kid trusts people. When he's growed, he's already learned how to lie and to not trust too many folks."

"Yeah, maybe you're right. Lying comes easy to many a man."

"And one lie begets another lie and still another until nobody knows the truth. It's dead and buried, just like a broken promise."

"I guess all men are fools then," Wilbur said.

"Well, look at the man you work for, Jordan Killdeer. If you work for such a man, you take on his ways. It's as natural as breathing. But sooner or later, you and him have got to pay the piper."

"You believe in sin, then."

"We're all sinners, Wilbur," Brad said. "And you sin a lot more in a town like Fort Collins than you do out here under the eyes of God."

"I'm turnin' in," Wilbur said. "You got me to thinkin' and I ain't much good at it."

Brad laughed. "Good night," he said. "And sin no more."

Wilbur laughed at that and crawled into his bedroll and pulled the blanket up around his neck.

"We go early," Julio said.

"Before sunup, Julio."

"Do you trust this man?" he whispered as he pointed to Campbell a few yards away.

Brad shook his head.

"I trust you, Julio," he said in the same low whisper. "In fact, it's you who is going to deliver my message to Kill-deer."

"Me?"

"Yes. You will be my emissary."

Julio looked puzzled. His face was half in shadow from the firelight.

"What is emissary?" he asked.

"Like a messenger, Julio. *Un mensajero.*"

Julio nodded. "I do not like it," he said. "But I will do it."

The two men said good night to each other in Spanish.

Brad lay down under his blanket and pulled the swatch of Felicity's nightgown from his pocket. He rolled it in the palm of his hand and clutched it to his chest before he fell asleep.

There was no way to bring Felicity back, but the men who were responsible for her death would pay. He was the piper and they would soon have to pay him.

TWENTY-ONE

෨

Brad and his two companions were back on the road before daybreak. All that day there was traffic, including two stages, some freight haulers from the south, a small herd of sheep with two Basque shepherds crossing the road on their passage to the mountains, and they saw grazing cattle and several pronghorn antelope, their hides shining tawny and white in the sun.

They camped one more night and rode into the rail town of Cheyenne the next afternoon.

They rode down the main street of the sprawling town that bustled with activity.

"That there's the Silver Queen," Wilbur said, pointing to a false-fronted saloon in the middle of the block. "Jordan don't go there until after sundown."

"Then show me where his ranch is, Wilbur," Brad said.

"We'll just foller the railroad tracks and then turn east. That's where Jordan hangs his hat. He's got some two thousand acres."

They passed a hotel a few doors down from the Silver Queen. It was in a two-story frame building and looked hospitable. The name on the front read HUNTINGTON HOUSE.

"Is that a good hotel for us to stay at?" Brad asked.

"About the best in town," Wilbur said. "Jordan owns that, too."

"Looks like he's done all right for himself," Brad said. "Who is Huntington?"

"It's just a name Jordan came up with. It ain't nobody, far as I know."

They left the town behind and followed the road along the railroad tracks. They passed Mexicans with carts laden with vegetables and fruits and a few men on horseback riding into town in twos and threes.

"Busy town," Brad remarked.

"Bustlin' and thrivin'," Wilbur said.

Julio waved to the Mexicans who walked alongside the burros pulling their carts. They waved back and then turned their heads away from Brad and Wilbur.

A mile or so west of town, Wilbur turned off on another road. A half mile from there, they came across a large gate connected to a board fence. There was a rustic arch over the gate with the name of the ranch in wooden letters painted red: JK RANCH.

There were horses grazing in the pastures and a small house beyond, with a nearby barn or stable and a long, low building that looked like a bunkhouse. Smoke rose from a chimney on the bunkhouse and there was a white picket fence around the house, with flowers and small trees in the front yard.

"That's where Jordan lives," Wilbur said as they halted in front of the gate.

They saw a lone rider in the distance leading a horse toward a corral near the barn. The horse was a piebald dun and was fighting the rope all the way.

Two saddled horses stood outside the corral, their reins wrapped around a cross pole. On the side of the house, at a hitch rail, there were four saddled horses bearing army saddles.

"It looks like Killdeer has company," Brad said.

"Them two horses at the corral belong to men who work for Jordan. One is Toby Dugan. The other is Cletus Hemphill. Neither one of 'em does ranch work. They're hired guns, and they go everywhere with Jordan."

"Let's mosey back into town," Brad said. "Maybe we'll run into those soldiers later on."

"I wonder why there's soldiers there," Wilbur said.

Brad turned his horse. Julio and Wilbur followed him as they rode away from the ranch.

"Those are cavalry horses," Brad said. "All about the same size and same color. I couldn't see the brands, but I'm sure there's U.S. stamped on the hides of those horses."

"Maybe . . ."

Brad cut Wilbur off with a raised hand.

"Let's not speculate, Wilbur. But we came at the right time. If we run into those soldier boys, we might find out why they're meeting up with Killdeer."

"Yeah. We might," Wilbur said.

They rode back into town. They tied up their horses outside Huntington House.

"We goin' to bunk here tonight?" Wilbur asked.

"No. As soon as Julio delivers my message to Killdeer, we're heading back to Wild Horse Valley."

"Then why are we stoppin' here?" Wilbur asked as Brad swung out of the saddle.

"Information," Brad said. He wrapped his reins around the hitch rail.

"Do we come in with you?" Julio asked.

"Yes. We'll wait in the lobby and talk after I go up to the desk."

Wilbur and Julio slid out of their saddles and hitched their horses to the rail. The three of them entered the hotel. There were divans and chairs set around a large rug. Julio and Wilbur sat down in separate overstuffed chairs. Brad walked up to the counter where the desk clerk was standing.

"Yes, sir, three rooms?" the clerk said.

"Not just yet. I'm wondering if you have some cavalry-men staying here?"

"What is your interest?" the clerk asked, suspicion in his tone.

"I was supposed to meet up with them, but forgot to ask where they were staying. I've, we've come a long way to see them. At their request."

"I see. Well, yes, we have four men from Fort Laramie who checked in early this morning and are staying the night."

"Would that be . . . ?" Brad ventured.

The clerk picked up the ledger, opened it.

"Let's see," he said. "Yes, here we are. There's a Colonel Beacham, a Major Runnels, Captain Dade, and Lieutenant Morris. They the ones you're supposed to meet?"

Brad smiled a disarming smile.

"Yes, they're the ones. Thanks. We'll just wait in the lobby for them, if you don't mind."

"No, go right ahead. If you decide to stay the night, we have several rooms still available."

"Thanks," Brad said and walked away. He sat on a divan and beckoned to Wilbur and Julio to join him.

As they rose from their chairs and walked toward him, Brad took out his tablet and pencil.

Julio and Wilbur sat on the large divan with Brad. They faced the door at an angle and could still see the desk from where they were.

"Wilbur," Brad said. "I'm going to make you an offer. I want you to think long and hard about it, because it has to do with your future."

"Huh?"

"Just listen real hard," Brad said.

"I'm listening."

Brad kept his voice low so that the clerk could not hear him. Julio and Wilbur both leaned toward him so they could listen.

"I was going to send Julio into the saloon with the message I'm about to write. But it would be better if the man the message is for sees you and that you confirm we have all the horses. But if you do anything more than that, you'll probably hang for your part in all this horse thieving."

"What's your offer?" Wilbur asked.

"If you back up Julio and walk out with him, then I'll see to it that you're not prosecuted as a horse thief. You won't even go to jail."

Wilbur took off his hat and wiped a ring of sweat from his forehead.

"Boy, you drive a hard bargain. What do I say to Jordan?"

"You tell him that Trask is in jail and that you're helping with the herd under my orders."

"Hell, he'll probably tell Dugan or Hemphill to shoot me on the spot. Maybe Julio will go down, too."

"Not if you tell him that Julio is just a wrangler who's helping with the herd. You say you rode up with him to deliver my message to him."

Wilbur scratched his head. "Boy, I don't know," he said.

"Think about it. I'm going to write my message now and give it to Julio. Then I'll want an answer. If you don't go with Julio to meet Jordan, you'll be with me and I'll drop you off in the Denver jailhouse."

Wilbur put his hat back on. He looked at Julio, who shrugged and wore a look of innocence on his face.

Brad wrote with careful strokes.

When he was finished, he read the note. Here is what it said:

To Jordan Killdeer

I have all the horses you stole. Three hundred head. I am willing to sell all of them back to you for $5.00 a head. You come down to Wild Horse Valley with $1,500 in cash and you can have all the horses back. Otherwise, I'm *going to sell them myself to the army in Fort Leaven-worth.*

He signed it: "Brad Storm."

He folded the note and handed it to Julio.

"Julio, you tell him that you work for me as a horse wrangler and that we plan to drive the horses from the valley if he doesn't buy them. Will you remember that?"

"I remember. I will tell him we are going to sell the horses if he does not buy them."

Then Brad turned to Wilbur.

"You, Wilbur, if you decide to take me up on my offer, will back up Julio. You tell Killdeer I mean business. You tell him that I'm a horse rancher and have connections with the U.S. Army. Are you willing to do that?"

"What does the note say?" Wilbur asked.

"You don't need to know what it says. You just watch Jordan when he reads it and tell Jordan you're going back down with Julio. You tell him if you and Julio don't show up, that I and my wranglers are going to drive the herd to Kansas."

"Jordan's goin' to be hoppin' mad," Wilbur said.

"You tell him he has a week and a half to come down and buy those horses from me."

"He might know I'm lyin'," Wilbur said.

"He'd better not, Wilbur. You're on a short rope right now. I've got a pair of handcuffs in my saddlebag and I'm ready to haul your ass off to jail and file charges against you for horse thieving."

"I guess I don't have no choice. Except I could tell Jordan that I don't want no part of it and he'll have his men kill Julio."

"You do that, Wilbur, and you won't live long enough to hang."

Wilbur went silent.

Brad and Julio waited for him to decide which side of the fence he was on.

Finally, Wilbur took a deep breath and let it out.

"All right, I'll do it. I think your detective agency is goin' to get Jordan sooner or later, one way or another, so I'd rather throw in with you so I don't do no jail time."

"Or hang," Brad said.

"Or hang."

Four men in cavalry uniforms rode up to the hotel and dismounted. They tied their horses to the hitch rail and walked into the hotel.

They were led by a colonel, and he was followed by a captain, a major, and a lieutenant. They strode into the lobby with satisfied looks on their faces. They stood tall and straight and the dust on their boots told Brad that they had done some traveling that day.

The three top officers stopped in the center of the lobby while the lieutenant walked to the desk to get their room keys.

Brad stood up.

"Colonel Meacham," he said. "I wonder if I can have a few words with you."

The colonel looked surprised.

"Why, certainly, sir. How did you know who I was?"

Brad smiled.

"Your reputation precedes you, sir," he said with his most diplomatic tone of voice.

"Why, of course," Meacham said.

"Perhaps we can talk privately, sir," Brad said. "I won't take up much of your time."

"To be sure. There are two chairs over there. We can converse in private."

Julio and Wilbur watched as the colonel and Brad walked to the two large chairs and sat down. The other officers turned their backs on their colonel and got their keys from the lieutenant. They whispered something to him. Then, they climbed the stairs and left the lieutenant standing there with two sets of keys in their hands.

"Now, sir," Meacham said after he sat down, "what is it you wish to discuss with me?"

"Horses," Brad said.

The colonel smiled. He seemed eager to oblige.

Brad had grabbed his attention with just that one word.

Brad knew he had hooked the colonel and that he would have to say little else to obtain the information he sought.

"Horses," Meacham said, beaming, "yes, the engine of the cavalry. I love 'em."

Brad had to ask only a single question and he was pretty sure the colonel would gladly answer it.

When Meacham crossed his legs and sat back in his chair, Brad was sure of it.

All he had to do was ask one question.

Just one.

TWENTY-TWO

༣

The question perched on the tip of Brad's mind, then flew to his lips.

"Colonel, is the army interested in buying any new mounts for the cavalry?"

Meacham drew himself up straight in his chair. His neatly trimmed sideburns and short-cropped hair seemed to reflect the stiffness of his military bearing. He was broad-chested and square-shouldered, with a ruddy face that seemed chiseled out of the same cloth as his uniform.

"Why, as a matter of fact," he said, "I've just contracted with a rancher here in Cheyenne. Perhaps you know him, Jordan Killdeer. He raises fine horses. I've issued him a purchase order just this morning for two hundred head to be delivered in sixty days time to Fort Laramie, subject to my approval, of course."

"Hmm. That's a sizeable order," Brad said.

"Mr. Killdeer did not seem fazed by my request. Do you know the man?"

"Yes," Brad said.

"You raise horses, do you?"

"A few," Brad said. "Is there any chance you will be needing more?"

"Matter of fact, we may. There is trouble up north with the Sioux and Cheyenne, still, and General Crook may be stepping up the campaigns. So we are prepared to meet the challenges should they develop."

"Well, Colonel, thanks for your time. If I'm in Fort Laramie, I will surely call on you again, with your permission, of course."

"Always glad to talk horses with a breeder," Meacham said.

He rose from his chair. "Good-bye, sir. Sorry we could not do business, but I'm sure you understand."

"I do," Brad said. "Good-bye, Colonel."

The colonel walked over to the lieutenant who gave him his room key. The two left the lobby. Brad went back to the divan.

"I'll wait for you outside the saloon," he told them. "As soon as you come out, we'll leave for Wild Horse Valley."

The setting sun painted shadows on the street and the sides of buildings as Brad looked out the window.

"We'll wait until just after dusk," he said.

"Killdeer will be at the saloon right after sunset," Wilbur said.

An hour later, with a faint glow in the sky, Wilbur and Julio walked out of the hotel and down to the saloon. Brad waited another fifteen minutes, then left the hotel. He unwrapped the reins of their horses and strolled down to the saloon. He tied the reins to the hitch rail, then crossed the street and stood in the shadows between two buildings. He watched men ride up and dismount, then enter the saloon. A few minutes later, he heard musicians tune up their instruments inside the Silver Queen.

He did not see the horses that he had seen at Killdeer's ranch. He reasoned that they were probably in back of the saloon, along with Killdeer's. It didn't matter. He was ready to leave as soon as Wilbur and Julio emerged from the Silver Queen.

The sky darkened and stars began to appear like tiny gems on a charcoal sky.

The waiting seemed an eternity as the evening breeze stiffened and blew through the chimney between the buildings where Brad stood. He buttoned his jacket up tight and tightened his hat's grip on his head.

He waited with his hands in his pockets. One of them stroked the swatch of blue flannel and it gave him some comfort as the minutes crawled along like snails in a torpor.

TWENTY-THREE

꙳

One of the bartenders looked up as Wilbur and Julio came in through the bat-wing doors of the saloon. There were only three men at the bar and two more at a table.

"Why, howdy, Wil," the bartender said. "long time no see."

"Howdy, Ed," Wilbur said. "Jordan back in his office?"

"Sure is. With Dugan and Hemphill. Just holler if you need anything."

"Sure will, Ed," Wilbur said. Then he turned to Julio. "Follow me," he said.

There was a dark hallway beyond the bar leading to a back room and door. Near the end, lamplight cast an ochre glow across the hall and shimmered on the wall. Wilbur walked to the light and turned into the office, with Julio right behind him.

The outer office had a small divan, two chairs, a table, an ashtray, and a lamp. Seated at the table was Cletus Hemphill, a large beer-bellied man with a perpetually frowning mouth, close-set porcine eyes, and a pair of puffy,

wet lips. His hat was off, hanging on a clothes tree in the
corner. He was playing solitaire with a deck of worn cards
that were stained with tobacco, whiskey, beer, and spittle.
Hemphill had a wad of chewing tobacco in his mouth. He
looked up when the two men entered the room. His small
eyes narrowed as he recognized Wilbur.

"What you doin' here, Wilbur?" Hemphill said. "I
thought you was up in the mountains."

"I got a message for Jordan, Clete," Wilbur said. "Can I
see him?"

"What you doin' with a Mex in tow?"

"He's the messenger. I'm just escortin' him. I'd like to
talk with Jordan."

Hemphill put down the cards in his hand, setting them
to the side of the piles of open-faced ones.

"He's in there. Just knock three times and wait for him to
let you in. Him or Toby. Toby's in there with him."

"Thanks, Clete," Wilbur said.

He walked to the door of the inner office and knocked
three times.

"Who is it?" called out a voice that was Toby Dugan's.

"It's Wilbur Campbell."

"It's open. Walk in," Toby said through the door.

Wilbur opened the door. He and Julio walked in to a
large room with a pair of cheap desks, one of them piled
high with receipts and bills of lading. At the other one sat
Jordan Killdeer.

"Wil," Jordan said. "What in hell are you doing down
here? Who in hell's watchin' after the horses?"

Jordan was a short stocky man with coal-black hair that
hung straight down. He had an aquiline nose and bright
brown eyes set symmetrically parallel in a face that looked
hammered out of copper. Toby was a tall, lanky man with a
scarred pair of lips that were fixed in a constant snarl. He
wore a thin muslin shirt stained with unknown substances.
A hand-rolled cigarette dangled from his mouth. He sat in
a chair next to the cluttered desk.

"Nobody's watching the herd, Jordan," Wilbur said. "Jack's in the Denver jail and they let me go so's I could bring Julio down here to give you a message."

"This is some kind of shit," Jordan said. He looked at Julio. "Who in hell are you?" he asked.

"I am Julio Aragon. I got a message for you."

He reached into his jacket pocket and pulled out the folded note. He stepped forward with his hand outstretched and handed the note to Jordan.

Jordan opened the slip of paper and read it. He read it twice. His face did not betray his emotions. His expression was as impassive as stone.

"Who in the hell is this Brad Storm?" he asked Wilbur.

"He's . . ." Wilbur hesitated and looked at Julio. Julio's eyes narrowed and then opened.

"Yeah, go on," Jordan said.

"He's the man who jumped us and another man carted Jack off to jail down in Denver."

"This is a hell of a thing," Jordan said.

"I just brought the messenger down, Jordan. I got to go back with him or that herd's going to be gone."

"Yeah, that's what the note says."

Jordan looked over at Toby.

"We got big trouble, Toby," he said.

"Anything we can't handle?" Toby said.

"I'm thinking about it," Jordan said. "Some sonofabitch has stolen our horses and is holding a gun to my head to buy 'em back."

"Buy 'em back? They're our horses, ain't they?"

"Wil, something smells about this whole deal," Jordan said.

"You know all I know," Wilbur said. "More, because I don't know what the note says."

"Read it," Jordan said and thrust the note at Wilbur.

Wilbur read it.

Jordan turned to Julio.

"Do you know what the note says?" he asked.

"I do not read," Julio said.

"Does that mean you can't read or you just don't read?" Jordan asked Julio.

"I do not know how to read or write," Julio said.

"A hell of a messenger you are, Mex."

Julio said nothing.

Wilbur read the note again. "I guess he's got you by the short hairs, Jordan," he said.

"Who is this man that sent the note? Is he a gunslinger? A rustler? I never heard of him," Jordan said.

"I don't know who he is, Jordan. I never saw him before. But he had men with him and he got the drop on us. One of 'em took Jack off to jail."

"Who was the other man?" Jordan asked.

Wilbur shrugged.

"I don't know," he said. His legs started to shake and he handed the note back to Jordan.

"Was he the law?" Jordan asked.

"I don't know, Jordan. I just know he said he was going to put Jack in jail and if I didn't agree to come down here, I'd probably be in jail now, too."

"This is just shit," Jordan said, his anger rising so that the bronze of his face was turning vermilion.

"You tell this man I'll pay his price," Jordan said. "But if there's anything squirrelly about the deal, me and my men will just blow him clean to hell. You got that?"

"Sure, Jordan. Far as I know, this man just wants to make a little quick money."

"What do you have to say, Mex?" Jordan asked. He glared at Julio.

"This man, this Storm, he just hire me to look after the horses. I don't know nothing."

"No, you sure as hell don't," Jordan said, a look of disgust on his face.

"Sorry, Jordan. I had no choice," Wilbur said.

"Get the hell out of here, Wilbur. Me and the boys will ride to the valley and deal with this Storm feller. Get your ass out of my sight."

Wilbur turned to go.

"Hold on a minute," Jordan said.

Wilbur turned back around. He tried to look meek and wished his legs would stop trembling.

"You tell this Storm I'll pay his price, but he's got to get Jack out of jail and have him there when I come down. You got that?"

"Yeah, I got it, Jordan."

"Now, get a-goin', Wilbur, you sorry sonofabitch."

Wilbur and Julio left the office. He heard Jordan pound the desk with his fist and cringed. He could feel the anger come through the walls and slap him on the back.

Julio and Wilbur walked straight to the bat-wing doors and out into the night.

"Whew," Wilbur said when they were outside. "I thought he was goin' to draw down on us and put out our lamps."

"He wants the horses more than he wants to kill us," Julio said.

They went to their horses. Brad emerged from the shadowy passageway between the two buildings and joined them.

Wilbur started to say something.

"We'll talk about it on the way," Brad said. "We got to light a shuck before Killdeer's had a chance to think about my offer."

The three men mounted up and rode at a brisk pace out of town. Wilbur kept looking back, and so did Julio. Brad stared straight ahead at the empty road. There were no travelers at that time of the night. The stars were out and the moon had not yet risen.

The first part of Brad's plan had been executed. Now he had to think ahead and plan the next stage if he was going to corral Jordan and bring him to justice.

When they were well clear of Cheyenne, Brad slowed his horse so that both men could ride up alongside him.

"Did Jordan accept my offer?" he asked Wilbur.

"He said he would bring the money. He wants you to have Jack Trask there, though."

Brad chuckled.

"Oh, he'll see Jack Trask all right. In jail."

"You're not going to give him all those horses, are you?" Wilbur asked.

"No, those horses will go back to their rightful owners."

"What about Jordan? He'll have some tough men with him. You won't get him as easy as you got me and Jack."

"No, I expect not," Brad said.

And that was all Brad said that night about Jordan Killdeer. His mind was working and he was thinking about Felicity.

He was also thinking about vengeance.

And the two other men who had run away when he killed Abel Avery.

They still had to pay the piper.

He had one thought on his mind as they rode through the night, heading toward Denver.

Revenge.

Revenge for Felicity.

TWENTY-FOUR

❧

It was near dusk when Gene Trask, Curly, and Nels reached the rim of the road leading down into Wild Horse Canyon. Halfway down, Trask slipped the halter off the lead horse and rapped it on the rump with the lead rope. The horse galloped down into the valley. Curly and Nels yelled and slapped a couple of the horses and they all followed the lead horse.

Then, they all rode down into the mass of horses grazing some distance from the corral.

"Funny," Gene said. "I don't see no smoke."

"Ner a fire," Nels said. "And, it ain't dark yet. Wilbur and Jack should still be a-brandin'."

"Ain't no horses in the corral, neither," Curly said.

They rode over to the empty corral. Gene saw the ring of stones and the ashes in the fire pit.

"No runnin' irons here, and the fire's been out for some time," he said.

"What the hell . . . ?" Nels said as he, too, saw the remains of the fire.

Curly looked around at the herd, which was stretched

from one end of the long valley to the other. All he saw were horses.

"They ain't on horseback neither," Curly said.

"This is mighty peculiar," Gene said. Then he cupped his hands together and shouted out his brother's name. "Jack," he yelled.

His voice echoed off the bluffs and died out in a deep silence.

"Let's ride over to where they keep their ridin' horses and lean-tos," Nels said. "Maybe they're both sick."

They all rode over to where the creek curled out of the timber and ran alongside the valley floor. A few horses drank at the stream. These looked up and turned their heads, then dipped their noses back into the water.

It was quiet when they entered the timber. They saw the small log structure that they used as a tack room. There were two lean-tos with bedrolls inside, under the roof of balsam, fir, and spruce.

"Jack," Gene called.

"Hey, Wilbur, where you at?" hollered Curly.

"They ain't here," Nels said. "They ain't been here all day."

Gene dismounted and let his reins fall to the ground. He walked over to the log hut and swung the door open. He looked inside. It was dark and there were some running irons hanging on pegs, some harnesses, a hammer, a keg of nails, old wooden canteens, some halters and bridles dangling from wooden pegs, a pair of small crudely built sawhorses for saddles. These were empty.

He walked over to the corral where there were two horses. Two wagons stood nearby. He looked inside the supply wagon bed. It was empty.

"Strange," he said when he walked back and picked up his reins.

He looked at Nels and Curly for a long moment.

"Looks like they just up and left," he said.

"Why?" asked Curly.

"Damned if I know. Their horses are gone and them two

in the corral ain't had no feed in some days. There's water in the trough. Why in hell would they just leave and keep these draft horses corralled?"

No one said anything for several moments.

"Well, they ain't here," Nels said. "And it looks like they rode off on their own."

"Let's start checkin' the tracks around here," Gene said. "Maybe they'll tell us somethin'."

Nels and Curly dismounted and ground-tied their horses. All three men fanned out and, hunched over, scanned the ground around the lean-tos.

Curly looked inside one of the shelters and then stooped over, picked something up.

"This here's Jack's rifle," he said.

He held up a Spencer carbine.

Nels went to the other lean-to and brought out a rifle and scabbard.

"And here's Wilbur's Remington," he said. "Now, why in hell would they saddle up and ride off somewhere without their rifles?"

Nels looked at footprints. The sky was turning dark as the sun sank below the high peaks.

"There's more tracks here than there should be," he said. "Like someone walked over here with either Jack or Wilbur."

"How many?" Nels asked.

"I see one extry track," Gene said.

Nels and Curly looked at each other.

"You think . . ." Nels said.

"That Sidewinder feller," Curly said.

"What?" Gene said.

"Them detectives we run into," Nels said. "They must have come here and . . ."

"Arrested Jack and Wil?" Gene said.

"Yeah," Nels said. "Bastards."

"This place is giving me goose bumps," Curly said. "It's like a—a ghost camp."

Shadows began to slide into the timber and across the valley.

The three men climbed back on their horses and rode out of the trees and onto the grassy valley.

"There must be better'n two hunnert horses here," Curly said.

"At least," Nels said.

"We better get the hell out of here and ride up to Cheyenne. Jordan's got to know about this."

"He'll be madder'n a wet hen," Curly said.

"Well, I'm mad, too," Gene said. "My brother's probably in jail."

"We could go through Denver and find out," Nels said. "Before we ride up to Cheyenne."

Gene thought about it.

"Yeah, we might better do just that," Gene said. "Then, we can tell Jordan so's he can do something about it."

"It's that Sidewinder," Curly said as they rode up the sloping road to the tabletop.

Neither Nels nor Gene said anything.

The night sky began to form, stealing away the blue, and blackening in the east as a few stars became visible, winking and blinking like tiny diamonds. A breeze flew down from the lofty reaches where the snow chilled it and made them button up their jackets and pull their collars up as they rode toward the gathering darkness in the silence of their separate thoughts.

TWENTY-FIVE

Larimer Street was bustling at that hour of the evening when Brad, Julio, and Wilbur rode into Denver on the third day of riding down from Cheyenne. Gaslights glowed on their standards, music poured from brightly lit taverns and saloons. Horses and riders, pedestrians and drummers prowled the street looking for excitement and pleasure.

They rode on past all the tempting establishments until they spotted a hotel at the dimmer part of the street, where the streetlights were set farther apart. They pulled up at the Hotel Windsor, a two-story clapboard building with lamps burning in the lobby and throwing a rectangle of light onto the hitch rings and boardwalk.

"We stayin' the night here?" Wilbur asked.

"As good as any. I have to get some things here on Larimer Street before we ride back up to Wild Horse Valley. Might be here a day or two."

"I just hope the beds are soft and there ain't no bugs," Wilbur said.

Julio dismounted and untied his rifle and scabbard, then pulled out his bedroll and saddlebags.

They tied their horses to the hitch rings set in concrete.

Brad climbed out of the saddle and pointed down the street where there were no more gaslights.

"There's a livery down yonder," Brad said. "You remember it, don't you, Julio?"

"Yes. Hay and grain, one dollar," he said.

Brad laughed. "Yeah," he said. "Finley's Livery. After we check in, we'll board our horses then walk up Larimer and get some grub. That okay with you, Wil?"

"You bet," Wilbur said. "I could eat porkypine and lizards."

"So, you are a mountain man, then," Brad said.

"I'm just starved," Wilbur said. He took his rifle out of its scabbard, slipped his bedroll from behind the cantle, and slung his saddlebags over his shoulder.

Brad did the same.

The lobby was empty. A clerk rose up from a chair when he heard them come in and stood there with his green eye-shade and garters on his shirtsleeves. He was in his sixties, with a bald spot in the middle of his head and long gray hair hanging straight at the sides.

"Three rooms?" he said to Brad as he stood at the counter.

"Two rooms. One with two beds."

The clerk's eyebrows arched. "Two dollars for the one. Three for the two-bed room."

"Kind of high, isn't it?" Brad said.

"These are lean times, son, and we're well below the rates of the fancier hotels up the way."

"All right," Brad said.

"How many nights?" the clerk asked.

"I'll pay for two nights," Brad said. He dug in his pocket and peeled a sawbuck off the sheaf. He laid the bill on the counter.

"You all got to sign the register," the clerk said.

He pushed an open ledger toward Brad and slid over an inkwell and quill pen. Brad signed his name. Wilbur and Julio stepped up while the clerk was filling out a receipt and both signed the register. Julio wrote down an 'X.'

The clerk handed a receipt to Brad, then turned to the rack of cubbyholes and drew out two keys for adjoining rooms.

"There's a door between these rooms, so you can visit without going out in the hall. No extra charge. My name is Ben Cobbler and I get off at six in the morning. There's no room service, but there's a café up the street, Emmalene's, and further on, there's places where you can eat and drink liquor if that's your pleasure. I don't recommend any of them, however, but they serve beefsteaks, beer, wine, and spirits."

"Thanks, Ben," Brad said. "We'll put our stuff in the rooms, then board our horses and get some grub."

"You have yourselves a fine evening, gentlemen," Ben said.

Brad looked at the numbers on the keys.

"First floor," Ben said. "Straight down the hall. The two beds are in room three and the single bed is in four."

"Thanks," Brad said. He handed the key to room four to Julio. He picked up his gear and the three of them walked down to their rooms. Small lamps lit the corridor, but it was still dim and shadowy. Brad opened the door to his and Wilbur's room.

"How come I got to stay with you, Brad?" Wilbur asked. "Don't you trust me?"

"Not entirely, but you offered to help us, Wil."

He opened the door and went inside. The room was dark, with only a scrap of light leaking through the window. Wilbur dropped his gear and found a table with a lamp and a small box of matches. He lifted the chimney and lit the lamp.

There were two beds side by side. Against one wall there stood a small bureau and next to it a wardrobe with its door open. There was a chamber pot on the floor of the wardrobe. Atop the bureau there were two glasses, a pitcher, and a porcelain bowl. Next to these were small towels, slightly larger than washcloths.

"You take the bed by the window, Wil," Brad said. "I'll

take this one." He dropped his rifle, saddlebags, and bedroll on the bed nearest the door.

"When are you goin' to trust me, Brad?" Wil asked as he walked to the farthest bed with his gear.

"When I've arrested Jordan Killdeer," Brad said.

"So, I'm really a prisoner still," Wil said as he draped his saddlebags over the wooden end of the bedstead. He leaned his rifle against the wall next to a small nightstand with a small lamp. The lamp had a frosted glass with roses painted on it. There was also a small box of matches next to that lamp, as well.

Brad laid his saddlebags under the bed and set his bedroll next to them. Then he leaned his rifle against the flimsy side of his headboard.

"You're not in custody, Wil, but you're kind of on probation for a while."

"I hope you keep your part of our bargain," Wil said.

"If I let you go right now, Wil, where would you go? You can't work for Killdeer. He's going to jail and then to the gallows. You're not a thief. Maybe you can wrangle horses or cowboy for some rancher. This way, you've got room and board."

"But no salary," Wilbur said.

"No. You might collect something when this job is finished. A bonus, or a reward. I'll work on it."

"That gives me some hope."

"Wilbur, there's always hope," Brad said.

He walked to the door adjoining the two rooms. He pulled a bolt and knocked on the other door. Julio opened it.

"Let's leave these unlocked, Julio. Just in case."

"There is a toilet at the end of the hall," Julio said. "With a tub and a water pump."

"Thanks. Maybe I'll shave in the morning."

Julio felt his beard. "I will keep my hair," he said.

"Come on in, Julio. You ready to put up our horses and get something to eat?"

"Oh, yes. I have hunger, Brad." He rubbed his belly and grinned.

They walked their horses to the livery stable, and Brad paid for two days of boarding. Then they strolled up Larimer in the middle of the street.

Wilbur stopped and turned away to look into the window of a smoke shop.

Brad and Julio joined him and they all looked at the boxes of cigars, the stacks of cigarette papers, and sacks of Bull Durham and other brands. There were store-boughts, too, in gaudy packages, matches and tapers.

"I could use some terbacky," Wilbur said. "I run out of the makin's a couple of days ago."

"I'll buy you some tobacco tomorrow," Brad said.

"You don't smoke?"

"No, not anymore," Brad said. "It interferes with my sense of smell. When I'm hunting, I can smell the elk or deer or bear scat. If I smoke, well, my smeller doesn't work as good."

They walked on and finally saw a saloon that served meals. They could smell the cooked beef from outside. There was no music, but there was the buzz of conversation and the clink of glasses.

Brad looked up at the name on the false front.

SAGEBRUSH TAVERN, the sign read, and there was a board outside that listed the fare, but not the prices.

"This looks like a good place to eat," Brad said.

"Fine with me," Wilbur said.

"'Sta bueno conmigo," Julio said.

They went in through the open doorway. There were tables with red and blue checkered cloths, a long bar, and diners eating and drinking at both places.

They found an empty table near the front window where they could look out onto the street and watch the passersby. They sat down and Brad picked up a slate with the menu written in chalk. He read it and passed it to Wilbur, who did the same and passed it to Julio, who only glanced at it.

"I'll order for you, Julio, whatever you want. Unless you want me to read the bill of fare to you."

"Beefsteak," Julio said.

A waiter came over with a blank slate and a piece of chalk.

"What'll it be, gents?" he said. "Something to drink before you give me your order?"

"Whiskey," Wil said rather quickly.

"And two beers," Brad said.

"Comin' right up," the waiter said and stepped toward the bar.

They ordered food as they drank their drinks.

"I never been to this part of Denver before," Wilbur said. "It's lively."

"You can find most anything here on Larimer," Brad said. "In fact, I have some purchases to make tomorrow before we go back up in the mountains."

"Mind if I ask what?" Wilbur said.

Brad shook his head.

"You'll find out tomorrow. But it won't help you much."

"You mean I'm prying again," Wilbur said.

"I guess that's your nature," Brad said.

"Just curious, I guess."

"Curiosity's fine," Brad said. "Just so it doesn't get you killed. Like the cat."

Wilbur sipped his whiskey.

Brad looked out the window. He saw three men ride down the middle of the street. They looked tired and dusty in the misty light of the gas lamp.

They also looked like gunslingers.

And two of them looked familiar enough for him to study them more carefully.

"Well, I'll be damned," he said.

"What is it?" Julio asked. He looked out the window. "Who do you see?"

"Those three men that just rode by. Did you see them, Wil?"

Wilbur shook his head.

"No, I didn't see 'em."

"Well, Julio and I have seen two of them before. Julio, go out there and see where they light. Quick."

Julio scrambled from his seat and went outside. He saw the three horsemen. They were walking their horses slow and looking into windows. They stopped in front of a saloon that was raucous with music from a small band.

Julio crossed the street and held to the shadows. He saw the name of the saloon and memorized the letters.

The three men turned their horses and stopped in front of some hitch rings. They dismounted and walked inside the saloon after securing their reins.

Julio walked down opposite the saloon. Beside the sign there was a painting of a glitter gal with a short skirt, mesh stockings, and a wild look in her eyes. On the other side of the sign there were two girls with their legs up in the air as if kicking something. They, too, were scantily clad.

Julio turned around and went back to the tavern. He sat down.

"Yes, I saw them," he said.

"Curly and Nels?" Brad said.

"And one other I have never seen before," Julio said.

Wil's face turned ashen.

"I know 'em," he said. "They work for Jordan."

"I know. Those two I mentioned are the men who raped and murdered my wife," Brad said.

"What are you going to do?" Wilbur asked, a slight tremor in his voice.

The waiter brought their food on a tray and set down the plates. Then he presented Brad with a bill. Brad paid him, and the waiter thanked him and walked away.

"What do you think I'm going to do, Wil?" Brad asked.

"I wonder who the third man is."

"Well, when we go down there, you can get a good look at him and tell me," Brad said.

"Oh, no," Wilbur said. "I'm not getting into a gunfight. I don't even have a gun on me."

"You can look and then wait outside," Brad said. "With Julio."

"You mean you're goin' in there alone? Those two are killers, Brad. And, you'll be outnumbered."

"Most men can't shoot straight when they're braced," Brad said. "And if the distance is more than ten feet between us, they'll likely miss with the first shot."

"You can't count on that."

Brad patted the butt of his pistol. "No," he said, "but I can count on this."

He dove into his food. He, too, was famished. He ate fast and so did Wilbur and Julio.

"Let's get us an after-dinner drink. What did you say the name of that saloon was, Julio?"

"I did not say. There was picture paintings of the dancing girls and some letters, a 'G,' a 'U,' and a 'Y,' I think, and maybe an 'S.'"

"Guy's Saloon," Wilbur said. "I noticed it when we walked past it."

"Yeah. And, it was crowded," Brad said. He rose from his chair. "Walk with me, boys," he said. "Let's see who opens the ball at Guy's Saloon."

Wilbur's face blanched.

Julio gulped the last of his beer and hitched up his gun belt.

Behind Brad's back, as the three of them were leaving the tavern, Julio crossed himself.

His lips moved in a silent prayer.

TWENTY-SIX

❧

Brad stopped in front of Guy's Saloon and looked at the gaudy paintings of glitter gals. Then he turned to Julio.

"I want you to stay out here, maybe across the street, Julio. Wil and I will go in. He'll stay long enough to tell me who that third man is, then I'll send him out. Both of you wait for me. If you see a policeman or a constable, grab him and send him inside."

"What do you do, Brad?" Julio asked.

"I'm trying now to hold down my anger. I don't know what I'll do once I see those two men who murdered Felicity. I'll try to arrest them, probably."

"And, if you can't arrest them?" Wilbur asked.

"It all depends on what Curly and that Nels does. And if the other man gets in my way . . ."

"As I said before, Brad, you're outnumbered. Three to one."

"Pray for me," he told Wilbur.

"I will pray for you," Julio said. *"Ten cuidado."*

"I'll be careful, Julio. Maybe those two will surrender."

"You don't know Dan Jimson and Nelson Canby the way I do, Brad," Wilbur said. "They're brutal men. Deadly with a gun. They don't back down. That's why Jordan hired them. No tellin' how many notches they've got on their guns."

"I've run into their kind before, Wil."

"I doubt it. These aren't your average killers. They're merciless."

"They killed my wife," Brad said. "I'm merciless, too, when it comes to those two."

"I'm glad I won't be in there to see you shot to pieces by three hired guns," Wilbur said.

"Wish me luck?" Brad asked.

"Luck to you, Brad," Wilbur said.

"*Suerte,*" Julio said. He crossed himself again as Brad and Wilbur headed for the bat-wing doors of Guy's Saloon.

"We'll go to the darkest part of the bar, Wil, so maybe my face won't be seen by those men."

"You lead the way, Brad. I'm shakin' in my boots."

"So am I," Brad said.

But Brad was not shaking. Instead, he felt an inner calm, a state of being that focused on the two men who had murdered Felicity. He knew what kind of men they were. They were the kind of men who had no regard for human life and thought a woman was just something to be plundered and thrown away. Such men never felt the pangs of remorse. They were without conscience. They only thought of themselves and their own well-being. And such men were predators. They fed on the blood of other people. They killed without feeling. They took and never gave. As far as Brad was concerned, they were the lowest form of life on Earth. They were parasites, men who never contributed, never joined the human race, but instead fed off other people, sucking out the blood and then moving on to the next victim.

Brad kept his head lowered as he pushed aside the swinging doors. Out of the corner of his eye, he saw a dark corner at the end of the bar, and the stools there were empty. He made a beeline for that spot with Wilbur close behind him. He sat down on the last stool against the wall at the end of the L-shaped bar and still did not look up.

He patted the stool next to him and Wilbur pulled it out and sat down.

"Don't make it too obvious, Wil, but look around and tell me if you see those three men," Brad said.

It did not take long for Wilbur to scan the tables in the room. While he was at it, he looked up at the second-floor balcony. He saw a number of doors beyond the wooden railing and spotted a man and one of the ladies going into one of them. The band was playing "She'll Be Comin' 'Round the Mountain," and there were a few couples moving around the small dance floor. The tables near the bandstand were all full with three or four men at each table. At one of the near tables, he paused and let his gaze linger over the men seated there.

"I see Nelson Canby at that near table, Brad. He's a-settin' with another man I can't see clearly."

"Just two men?"

"Just two."

"Take your time," Brad said. "Maybe one of 'em's on the dance floor."

Wilbur looked at the men who were dancing. He did not recognize any of them. Then his gaze went back to the table where Nels sat.

"Holy smoke," he said. "I know who the other man is with Canby."

"Is it Curly?"

"No," Wilbur said, "it's Jack Trask's older brother, Eugene. That's Gene Trask sittin' there sure as God made little green apples."

"Where's Curly?"

"I don't know. Maybe he went up to one of them rooms with a dance hall gal."

Brad looked at the all the doors up on the balcony. All were closed.

A bartender startled them when he came up to that end of the bar.

"Gents," he said. "You just gonna gawk, or do you hanker to wet your whistles?"

"One beer," Brad said. "One of us is just leaving."

"Any particular kind of beer? We make our own and that's all we got."

"Just so it's wet," Brad said. He gave the barkeep a scathing look that told him he didn't appreciate his being a smart aleck.

The barkeep walked down to the middle of the bar and lifted a glass, which he put under a spout in a keg below the bartop.

"Go on, Wil," Brad said. "I'll take it from here."

"It's still two against one, Brad."

"If you spot a constable out there, send him in. I'm going to try and arrest Canby."

"Watch out for Gene Trask. He's a fast draw and a quick-tempered sort."

"Go on, Wil."

Wilbur got up and walked quickly to the swinging doors. In seconds he was gone. Brad kept his eyes on Canby the entire time to see if either he or Trask had seen Campbell. They showed no sign that they had even noticed him.

The barkeep brought a beer that was an inch below the rim of the glass.

"A buck," he said.

Brad fished in his pocket and pulled out a silver dollar. He slid it onto the bartop.

"You want company?" the man asked Brad.

"No. I won't be here long."

"Just holler if you do. We got plenty of females who'll dance with you or play housekeeping."

"I'll let you know," Brad said.

He did not drink his beer. Instead, he loosened his pistol in its holster and stood up. He walked slowly toward the table where Canby and Trask sat. They were both talking to each other and did not notice him as he came up and stood next to their table. He looked down at Canby.

Canby looked up.

His eyes widened and his mouth opened in surprise.

"Nelson Canby," Brad said. "You're under arrest for the murder of Felicity Storm."

The words hit Canby like a sledgehammer to the chest.

Trask's head jerked up and back as if he had been slapped with a slab of raw meat.

"What?" Canby said.

"You heard me. You're also wanted for horse stealing, and I'm putting you under arrest."

"Like hell you are," Canby said.

He scooted his chair back and grabbed for his pistol.

Trask pushed away from the table and stood up. He, too, started to drop a hand to the butt of his pistol.

In a flash, Brad drew his pistol and cocked it as the barrel came up to bear on Canby.

Canby's pistol wasn't halfway out of its holster when Brad squeezed the trigger.

Men at the other tables jumped at the sound of the exploding powder.

The bullet from Brad's gun smashed into the juncture between Canby's throat and his breastbone. A black hole appeared. Dust flew from his shirt and was quickly enveloped by a gush of red blood. Canby fell backward in his chair and hit the floor with a loud crash.

Trask drew his pistol and raised it to fire at Brad.

Brad swung his barrel toward Trask and squeezed the trigger.

Such moments take no more than a second or a fraction of a second. That one small increment of time can seem like an hour to a man on the business end of a Colt .45. Time slows down and so, too, does the motion of the shooter.

Trask stared into that dark gulf of time and space like a man under hypnosis. His pistol weighed a ton and his arm moved as if it were gripped in an iron cast.

Brad's pistol spewed lead and orange flame, showered sparks that winked out when they hit Trask's shirt. His right arm sprouted a hole in it that paralyzed him so that time slowed even more.

But Trask bit down on the pain in his shoulder and raised his gun. He thumbed the hammer back and squeezed the trigger.

Brad ducked and sidestepped.

Trask's bullet sizzled over Brad's head and whined over the bar, shattering the glass mirror. The bartenders ducked and so did the patrons seated on the stools. Men at the tables dove under them or pushed them onto their sides as they sought cover.

The band stopped playing and the musicians scrambled off the bandstand.

Brad shot from a crouch and blasted Trask square in his heart. There was a single burst of blood though the hole in his chest and he crumpled and fell to the floor, dead.

The doors on the balcony opened in succession and a man stepped to the rail and looked down. He saw two bodies on the floor that he recognized.

He stared at Canby and Trask in horror, then shifted his gaze to Brad, who stood up out of his crouch and swung his pistol around to cover the room.

"Nobody move," Brad shouted. "It's all over."

On the balcony, Curly turned and ran back into the room. He strapped on his gun belt and pulled on his boots. The girl who was with him cowered on the bed.

"What happened?" she shrieked.

"Shut up, bitch," he said and ran to the window. He pulled it open and stepped onto the roof and slid down it, then dropped to the ground. He ran between the buildings. He drew his pistol before he reached the street and ran to his horse. He crouched over and got to the hitch ring. In seconds he was in his saddle and whipping his horse up Larimer Street.

"Hey, that's Curly," Wil shouted to Julio.

Julio turned and saw the rider as he raced under gas-lit lamps and disappeared into the dark.

"We better go into the saloon," Julio said.

"I heard four shots," Wilbur said.

They started for the saloon, but Brad emerged through the bat-wing doors before they reached the entrance.

"Curly got away," Wilbur said. "We didn't even see him until he was too far away."

"He's the one I want. Which way did he go?"

Julio and Wilbur both pointed toward Sixteenth Street.

"Damn," Brad said and holstered his pistol. "Too bad our horses are stabled for the night."

"We can take Canby's and Trask's horses, try to catch him," Wilbur said. "Julio can borrow one of the others hitched here."

"Good idea," Brad said. He walked to the hitch ring and untied the reins to Canby's horse. Wilbur loosened the reins to one of the horses. Julio untied the reins to a small horse and mounted up.

Brad and Wilbur climbed into the saddles. The horses were skittery, but they brought them both under control.

Without waiting for a reply, Brad dug his spurs into the horse's flanks and galloped up Larimer. He was followed closely by Julio and Wilbur.

Their backs shone under the street lamps, then darkened and lighted again and again. At the intersection of Larimer and Sixteenth, Brad reined up to listen.

There was no way of telling which direction Curly had gone.

They heard the clangs of a police wagon coming down the street.

When they looked back down Larimer, the street was full of people. All seemed to be walking toward the saloon where two men lay dead on the floor.

Brad cursed under his breath. "We lost him," he said to Wilbur.

"We could split up, maybe, and . . ." Wilbur said.

"No. He got away," Brad said.

"What about Canby and Trask?" Wilbur asked.

"They bought the farm," Brad said.

"I heard four shots," Wilbur said.

"Trask fired one of them. It went wild."

"Like you said."

"He had a slug in him when he shot. I was a little off when I shot him the first time."

"You amaze me, Brad."

"Sometimes I amaze myself," Brad said. "Let's ride back to our hotel. I sure as hell can't track at night in town."

"It would be hard," Wilbur said.

They turned their horses and rode slowly back up the street.

A paddy wagon stood in front of Guy's Saloon. There was a flurry of activity inside the saloon. Voices rose and fell as men all related what they had seen and heard.

"I hope the police can sort it all out," Brad said.

"You might wind up a wanted man, Brad," Wilbur said.

"I doubt it. By the time the police finish questioning all the witnesses, they'll have two dozen descriptions of me, and none of them will match what I really look like. It all happened so fast, and after that first shot, everybody in there became moles and started digging holes in the floor."

Wilbur chuckled.

"The Denver police aren't the sharpest knives in the drawer," Wil said. "From my experience with them."

"What's the saying in Spanish, Julio, about tomorrow?" Brad asked.

"Mañana será otro día," Julio said.

"That's right. Tomorrow's another day," Brad said.

Julio dropped his borrowed horse off near the saloon and walked to the hotel.

Brad and Wilbur hitched their horses in front of the hotel and waited for Julio.

Voices floated on the night air and the crowds began to dwindle as people walked back to the various establishments that were still open.

"Two down," Brad thought, "and one to go."

He wanted Curly in the worst way. He wanted him to suffer before he died.

Either with a bullet or the rope.

It didn't matter which.

TWENTY-SEVEN

∽

The next morning when Brad, Julio, and Wilbur went to breakfast at the Yum-Yum Tree on Colfax Avenue, Brad bought a copy of the *Rocky Mountain News* from a newsboy. The headline in large 76-point Bodoni Bold read as follows: "Unknown Gunman Slays Two in Larimer Saloon."

"Read it to us, Brad," Wilbur said.

"It says: 'Two men were shot dead in the early evening last night inside Guy's Saloon on Larimer Street. Witnesses could not identify the gunman. Their descriptions of the shooter varied according to local police.

"'The shooter left the premises before police arrived. Before he left, he told the observers that the two dead men were horse thieves and murderers. Calvin Bostwick, one of the bartenders, said that the killer came in earlier with another man and ordered one beer. The other man left before the shooting occurred.

"'When contacted by a reporter, Mr. Harry Pendergast of the Denver Detective Agency revealed that he was working on a case of horse stealing, but that he did not know who might have killed the two men.

"'Police are baffled and promise a further investigation into the incident.'"

"Is that it?" Wilbur said.

"There's a drawing of a man with a six-gun shooting at two armed men. Smoke is coming out of the barrel, and the two men are clutching their chests," Brad said.

"Let me see," Julio said.

Brad handed the tabloid-sized newspaper to Julio. Julio looked at the picture, then handed it to Wilbur, who read the account again.

Brad finished his coffee. On his plate there were smears of yellow and white from the eggs he had eaten, a portion of rind off a slice of ham, and granules of grits.

"I've got a lot to do," he said. "I'll need you boys to pack some of the items I need. Then we're off to Wild Horse Valley."

"What 'bout Curly Jimson?" Wilbur asked.

"I expect he'll turn up sooner or later," Brad said. "Likely he's wearin' out leather on his way to Cheyenne about now."

"Did you really tell everybody that those two men you shot were horse thieves?" Wil asked.

"And murderers," Brad said. "Yes, I yelled it loud and clear just before I hightailed it out of there."

"Man, I'd liked to have seen that."

~

A few minutes later they were saddling their horses at the livery stable. They rode out into bright sunlight to a Larimer Street humming with activity. Brad led the way and gazed at the shops as they passed. He stopped first at a cabinet maker's.

Inside, they heard the sound of hammering. There was a bell on one of the counters. Displayed on shelves and around the floor were bookcases, small tables, chairs, cabinets, boxes, and various other items made out of wood.

Brad lifted the bell and jiggled it.

The hammering stopped and a man came out of the door leading to a workshop.

"Good morning," the man said. "Need something?"

The man was wearing overalls and a striped railroad cap with a pair of goggles strapped around the crown. His work boots were flecked with sawdust.

"I need a box," Brad said. "A special box, about so big."

He held his arms wide to show the length of the box.

"Special, eh? Well, I'm your man. Name's Hank Chinaski."

"Brad Storm."

"What kind of special box?" he asked as he brushed a strand of gray hair from in front of one lens of his horn-rimmed spectacles.

"I want a spring door that will snap shut after it's opened. I want you to drill the nail holes so that I can pack it flat, and a supply of nails so I can nail it together later."

"That won't be hard," Chinaski said. "What kind of handle or latch do you want on the door?"

"I think a round handle, one I can put a rope or strand of twine through to pull it open."

"One door at the front end?"

"Yes," Brad said as Wilbur and Julio looked at all the various wares in the store.

"Take me about an hour. I'll have the cabinet together so you can test the door and then I'll pull the nails so you can pack it flat."

"You can make the box out of the lightest material," Brad said.

"Pine is what I'd use," Hank said.

"All right. How much?"

"Oh, five dollars ought to do it. You can pay me when you pick it up."

Hank and Brad shook hands.

"See you in about an hour," Chinaski said.

Brad nodded. He and his companions left the store.

"Now where?" Wil asked.

"A hardware store."

"You're very mysterious, Brad," Wil said.

Julio laughed.

At the hardware store, Brad purchased a roll of extra heavy twine, a hammer, and a box of twenty-penny nails.

"That all?" Wil asked when they had packed the hardware items in their saddlebags.

"Next to a feed store," Brad said, and they found one on Curtis Street.

"You can wait out here, boys," Brad said. "I won't be long."

There were wagons and drays parked at the loading dock out front and steps leading up to the warehouse. There was a strong smell of various feeds and dust motes. Brad could smell corn, wheat, rye, sorghum, and hay when he entered the gloomy depths of the store. There was a counter at the back, and it was laden with scales and knives, rolls of twine and, on the shelves, stacks of flour and feed bags.

There, he bought four heavy burlap bags. He paid for them without answering any questions from the curious clerk, a young man with rust-red hair and a bandanna around his neck that he slipped up over his nose to keep from breathing the dust in the store.

Brad handed the bags to Julio.

"Stick these in your saddlebags," he said.

Julio put two sacks in one bag, and one in the other.

"Now, where?" Wil asked.

"Grocery store," Brad said.

At a grocery Brad bought dried beef jerky, cans of apricots, dried prunes and pears, bread, hardtack, ham, coffee, a small bag of salt, and some sugar.

They divided up the foodstuffs and packed the items in their saddlebags.

They rode back to Chinaski's Woodworks and went inside.

Hank had the box on a counter.

Brad could smell the scent of pinewood and there was a black ring screwed into the door. The heavy spring hinges looked brand-new.

"Try it," Hank said.

Brad pulled on the ring. The door opened wide. He

looked inside and then released the ring. The door slammed shut so fast, he jumped back. The door made a loud sound.

"Perfect," Brad said.

"I left the heads of the nails out a little, so I'll just pull 'em for you," Chinaski said.

When he was finished, the box folded up flat and was not too heavy.

"Need something to hold it together?" Chinaski asked.

"We'll pack the pieces under our bedrolls," Brad said.

"Where you going with it? Going to catch rabbits or birds?" Chinaski asked.

"Snakes," Brad said and paid the carpenter five dollars.

They divided up the box panels and secured them under their bedrolls.

"Tighten them down good," Brad said.

"Snakes?" Wilbur said as they rode out of Denver and headed toward Lookout Mountain.

"First, we have to catch 'em," Brad said.

Wilbur's facial features twisted as he grimaced. His mouth opened as if to protest.

"Don't say a word, Wil," Brad said. "I'm not going to explain until the time comes."

"What kind of snakes?" Wilbur asked after a few minutes.

"Rattlers," Brad said.

And they rode on, leaving Denver behind them and heading toward the mountains as if they were on a Sunday ride or a picnic in the country.

Brad fingered the swatch of blue cloth in his pocket and thought about Felicity. He could feel her in the crisp air, in the scent of wildflowers and the columbines.

She was gone, but she was never far away.

TWENTY-EIGHT

～

Dan Jimson was boiling mad when he rode out of Denver before dawn the morning after his friends had been killed. He had brooded all night in a cheap hotel on Curtis Street. It had not taken long for his blind anger to develop into a towering rage. And with that rage came a feral cunning as he thought about how he might kill the object of his rage, the Sidewinder.

During the long night in the Curtis Hotel, Curly had worked out a way to kill the Sidewinder and get away with it. Curly had heard that the day before, Gene had visited his brother Jack in the Denver jail. Word had gotten around about his imprisonment. It had been an interesting meeting.

"Jack was captured up in Wild Horse Valley," Gene had told him and Canby. "It was Brad Storm, the man they call the Sidewinder, and two other men, Joe Blaine, and a Mex named Julio. Blaine hauled Jack down here to Denver and filed charges against him. Jack overheard this Blaine feller sayin' he was meetin' up with Storm somewhere up in the mountains."

There was that, Curly thought, and something else. The

night before, when he had fled from Guy's, he had seen a familiar face when he mounted his horse. Two familiar faces, in fact. One was the Mex, the one named Julio, who had been with Storm at their first encounter up in Arapaho Gulch, and Wilbur Campbell, who had been working with Jack Trask up in Wild Horse Valley.

It took Curly a while to figure it out, but now he was certain that Storm was going to return to Wild Horse Valley. It made sense. He had been hired, evidently, to track down the men involved in stealing horses, and he probably meant to return the stolen horses to their rightful owners.

Yes, it all made sense. When Blaine said he was meeting up with Storm in the mountains, that could only mean one thing. Storm and the other detectives were going back to the valley. And they had Wil Campbell with them. He had seen him plain as day outside Guy's Saloon.

Curly was sure, pretty sure, that Storm was still in Denver. If he could reach Wild Horse Valley before Storm returned, he would have time to scout the valley and pick a perfect spot to pick Storm off when he returned. Maybe, he thought, he could get all three detectives and then Jordan Killdeer would still be in business. There were a lot of horses still up there, money on the hoof. Jordan might even put a little sugar in his pay and give him a bonus for killing three private detectives.

Curly was satisfied that it was a good plan. He rode in the predawn darkness, headed for the foothills. By his reckoning, he should be in Wild Horse Valley before nightfall.

Then all he had to do was find a good place to hide, probably above the bluffs, and wait for Storm and the others to return.

He'd like to kill that traitor, Wil Campbell, too, while he was at it.

The valley was big, and if the men he sought to shoot were scattered, he might be able to take all four of them out with his lever-action Winchester. He could picture it in his mind. Four shots. Four men. No more investigations. No more detectives.

But most of all, he wanted to kill Brad Storm. He hated him as he had hated few men before now. Storm had killed three of his friends, and that made him a permanent enemy. Permanent until he died from a bullet.

Curly made good time, following game trails he knew well. He arrived at the tabletop above Wild Horse Valley late that same afternoon. He circled past the road leading down into the valley and picked his way through the timber above the bluffs. He could hear the horses neighing and snorting down below. The jays squawked at his intrusion, and chipmunks piped their warnings, but otherwise he had the escarpment to himself.

He found a place well beyond the rim and ground-tied his horse to some alder bushes. He slipped his rifle from its scabbard, just in case, and retrieved a pair of binoculars from his saddlebag. He walked to a spot near the top of the bluffs, then crawled the rest of the way until he came to the rim. There, he looked down into the valley. He saw all the horses, including the pintos that were left there long ago by Indians. Some of them had foals they had dropped in the early spring. They cavorted and gamboled through the tall grass.

He raised the binoculars to his eyes and scanned up and down the long valley. He saw no humans and grunted with satisfaction. He also gazed at the road and saw no sign of anyone. No recent horse tracks.

Satisfied, he scooted back away from the rim and stood up, the binoculars dangling from a strap around his neck. He walked back to where he had tied his horse and put the rifle back into the leather sheath. Then he returned to the edge of the timber and walked the length of the bluff and back to the edge nearest the road.

He stepped a few paces from the rim and determined that he could sit on his horse and look down into the valley and see anyone who rode there. He could not see the lean-tos or the wagons or the tack hut from anywhere atop the bluff. But he could see almost all of the entire valley. He recognized some of the horses he, Canby, and Avery had stolen, including those he knew had belonged to Brad Storm.

All he had to do now, he thought, was wait. Sooner or later, Storm would return, along with the Mexican and that traitor, Wilbur.

He would be ready for them.

Curly walked back to where his horse was tied and walked him closer to the rimrock. He saw wolf tracks and cougar tracks in the soft soil, plus some rabbit and squirrel, bird tracks, and one that looked as if it had been made by a crawling snake.

He tied his horse in a copse of pines where there was enough grass. He took off his hat and poured water from his canteen and held the hat up to the horse's nose. The horse dipped into the water and snuffled as it drank.

"That ought to hold you, boy," he said in a low voice.

He left the horse saddled, took out his rifle again and checked it. He jacked a fresh cartridge into the firing chamber and left the hammer on half cock. He walked through the timber and found a game trail leading away from the bluff. Beyond were more hills and beyond them, the high country.

That, he decided, would be his escape path after he had shot Storm and maybe the three other men that might be with him. If he couldn't kill them all, he'd have to get out of there in a hurry, before they chased him down.

He leaned the rifle against a pine when he got back to where his horse was tethered. He sat down at the base of another tree and listened to the sound of birds and the nicker of the horses down in the valley.

He had grub and his bedroll, and he set those out before dusk.

In the morning, he would take another look down into the valley. If necessary, he would wait a week or more to catch sight of Brad Storm.

The thought of killing the Sidewinder warmed his innards, and he dozed with his daydreams until the shadows began to stretch like shadowy fingers across the rimrock.

The sun was setting and he buttoned up his jacket and loosened his pistol in its holster.

"Come on, you bastard," he whispered to himself. "I'm ready for you, Sidewinder."

Gradually, the shadows filled up the bare spots among the trees. Curly buttoned up his jacket and laid out his bedroll between two spruce trees and opened a sack with a sandwich. He got his canteen and sat down again. He looked up at the sky and watched the clouds change colors until they finally turned ashen in the twilight.

TWENTY-NINE

⌒

Joe Blaine had been camped up in the timber bordering the tabletop and road for three days. He had built a crude lean-to in case it rained. It was well away from the road. He had brought some magazines and books to read since he had no idea when Brad would return. Each day, he moved his horse to another location near his makeshift hut and walked the fringe of the timber, stopping often to listen for the sound of hoofbeats or the voices of men.

Harry had been pleased when he brought Jack Trask in and told him of the witnesses they had located at the mining and logging camps. He had helped Blaine when he made his depositions and the charge against Jack Trask. Now, Trask was in jail and they had all those horses as evidence along with Felicity's horse, Rose, whose brand plainly showed that it had been altered.

He had also met with Cliff Jameson and reported on the progress against the ring of horse thieves. He did not tell Cliff that they had located a large number of the stolen horses. If he had, he was sure that Cliff would get together with the other breeders and ride up to Wild Horse Valley to retrieve their stock. Cliff was happy about the arrest of Jack Trask but demanded that all the others in the ring be arrested and brought to trial.

Joe was careful not to mention any names, including that of Jordan Killdeer. The anger among the breeders had risen to such a pitch that Joe was sure that they would all turn into vigilantes and hunt down the thieves and hang them on the spot. So he had walked a tightrope with Jameson who kept trying to pry information out of him. All Joe said, "We're very close to solving this case, Cliff. You just have to be a little more patient."

Now, as the sun was setting, Joe braced himself for another night alone in his lean-to. Just before dusk, he lit a lantern and set it firmly in the ground outside his shelter. Then he took a candle, like the ones he had used every night, walked to the road, and lit it. He set it between two rocks that he had used before. From these two rocks, he had constructed an arrow of other, smaller rocks, that pointed to his shelter.

If Brad and Julio rode up to the road, they would see the lit candle and the arrow.

He chewed on some dried beef and a piece of moldy hardtack and downed the meager meal with water from his canteen. He could hear the neighing of the horses down in the valley, the howls of a timber wolf, and the yapping yodel of a coyote every night before he went to sleep. One night he saw a herd of elk pass nearby on their trek to the high country, and a few times, he had seen mule deer come near his lean-to and stare at him out of curiosity.

And the night before, Joe had killed a pygmy rattler with the butt of his rifle. It had crawled onto his bedroll for warmth, never given him a warning rattle. He was still shivery over that incident and resolved to check every inch of the shelter floor, his bedroll, and his saddle blanket.

He thought about building a fire. He had arranged stones in a circle around a pit for just such an act, but decided against it for the third night in a row. The candle was enough of an indication where he was camped, and the lantern gave off a little heat. It was not that cold during the early evening hours. Toward morning it would get pretty nippy, but he had his blanket and his jacket.

He waited outside his lean-to, listening to the forest sounds, looking up at the stars through the pines, and waiting for the moon to rise.

He pulled out his small pocket watch and held it close to the lantern light. It was nearly eight o'clock, and he could hear deer and elk moving around through the timber. An owl floated overhead on silent pinions and he thought he heard the croak of a frog. Then it was quiet and he listened for any sound coming from the road.

A half hour later he heard the soft scrape of hooves coming from the direction of the road. He sat up and cupped a hand to his right ear. Then he heard a chinking sound as a hoof struck a stone. Minutes later he heard low-pitched voices.

Then, a short silence.

"Looks like Joe left the porch light on for us," he heard Brad say.

Joe smiled.

There was a rustle of cloth and the creak of leather as one of the riders dismounted and picked up the candle.

Joe heard horses coming his way, stepping through the timber, crunching dead pine needles and fallen pinecones. Then, there was no sound at all. As if the horsemen had stopped and were looking at his lantern. He could not see through the darkness beyond the spray of lantern light. He drew his pistol, just in case. But he had heard Brad's voice, hadn't he?

He waited and eased the hammer back as he gently squeezed the trigger so that the mechanism would not make a loud click. A moment later, he heard the muffled shuffle of horses moving toward him.

"You aren't going to shoot me, are you, Joe?" Brad called from the fringe of light. "I know you cocked that hogleg of yours."

"Come on in, Brad. The welcome mat's out. Such as it is."

Three riders moved into the cone of light and Joe stood up, thumbed the hammer of his pistol to half cock, and holstered the weapon.

"Howdy, Joe," Brad said as he eased himself down from the saddle.

"Howdy. I see you still got our prisoner there."

Wilbur dismounted and then Julio hit the ground.

"Maybe an ally more than a prisoner," Brad said. "Been waiting long, Joe?"

"This is my third night. What you got there behind your saddle?"

Then Joe looked around and saw that all three saddles had boards under their bedrolls.

"A little surprise for Jordan Killdeer," Brad said.

"You saw him?"

"Julio and Wilbur saw him. Gave him my message."

"What did he say?"

"Not much he could say. We've got him by the short hairs, Joe."

"So?" Joe stepped in close to Brad so that he could look into his eyes.

"I reckon he wants those three hundred head of horses I offered to sell him for five bucks a head."

"What?"

"It was an offer he could hardly refuse," Brad said.

Julio stepped in close to stand next to the lantern. "Did you hear what happened with Trask and Canby, Joe?" he said.

Joe shook his head. "No. What happened?"

"Brad, he killed them. In Denver."

"Holy smoke. Must have been after I left town."

"It was in the newspaper," Wilbur said.

"Did the police . . ." Joe started to say.

"My name wasn't mentioned, Joe. Curly got away though. He was upstairs in the saloon with one of those dance hall gals."

"Whooeee," Joe said. "That's two less we have to worry about."

"Curly's the one I want."

"Is Jordan coming down here?"

"If he wants to buy the stolen horses back, he'll come," Brad said.

"Then Curly will probably be with him."

"And a couple of hired guns, too, most likely," Brad said. He turned to his horse and untied his bedroll. He set the boards down flat on the ground.

"Stack those boards together," Brad told Julio and Wilbur. "We'll nail them together in the morning."

After the horses were unsaddled and hobbled, the men sat in front of Joe's lean-to. They had set out their bedrolls under the pine branches and the horses were on a patch of grass.

"What's the box for?" Joe asked. "And the gunny sacks?"

"If I tell you now, Joe," Brad said, "you won't sleep too good tonight."

Julio laughed.

Wilbur put a hand in front of his mouth to keep from laughing out loud.

"What's so funny?" Joe asked.

"Nothing," Julio said.

"And, there's a roll of heavy twine," Joe said. "And a hammer and nails to put the box together, I suppose."

Brad didn't explain. "We've got a lot to do come morning," he said. "If you're hungry, Joe, we brought grub."

"I could eat. Want me to build a fire and make us some coffee?"

"Might not be a bad idea," Brad said. "Julio can help you, and Wilbur can start unpacking the grub."

They ate by the campfire and talked about everything except what Brad had planned. But he did say something before they all crawled into their blankets.

"I don't know when Killdeer will get down here," he said. "But I want to be ready for him when he does come."

"I wish you'd tell me your plans, Brad," Joe said.

"When the time comes, Joe."

"Yeah, your time. Not mine."

"Well, you're a detective, Joe. Detect."

Joe walked over to the stack of boards and picked them up and examined them.

"Not a very big box," he said.

"Big enough," Brad said, and then crawled under his blanket after coiling up his gun belt and setting it next to his bedroll.

"Big enough for what?" Joe asked as he stooped to enter his lean-to.

"If I tell you what it's for, will you stop pestering me?"

"I would," Joe said.

"It's going to be a snake box," Brad said.

"A snake box? What in hell's a snake box?"

"Good night, Joe," Brad said. He took off his hat and lay his head down on his rolled-up saddle blanket. In moments, he was asleep and Joe was lying in his blankets, staring up at the thatch of spruce boughs. Through the needles he could see tiny specks of light from the stars.

He dropped off to sleep wondering what a snake box was. He decided then that Brad Storm was more than slightly crazy. He was a full-blown lunatic, for sure.

THIRTY

〜

Toby Dugan and Cletus Hemphill prowled the saloons from Randall Avenue clear to Central and even on Capitol Avenue for the kind of men Jordan had told them to find. Jordan didn't want drunks. He didn't want army deserters. He didn't want weaklings or cardsharps. He wanted tough, rugged men who lived by the gun and did not care how they got their next dollar.

They even bailed a man out of jail that they knew would fit the bill. He had been arrested for fighting and had gotten thirty days for disorderly conduct. This man hailed from Montana where he was still wanted for armed robbery. His name was Terry Wheeler.

It took them three days to find three more men. One of them was a drifter from Kansas who had worked for a stage line and gotten fired for beating up a driver who owed him money. Lenny Holbrook rode shotgun for the Western Freight Company based in Casper and had a big chip on his shoulder. He had beaten the stage driver to a pulp with the butt of his Colt pistol and was known to have been a suspect in a number of robberies around town. He mostly rolled drunks and was just the kind of man who would fit in with Jordan's scheme. He had been a cattle drover and worked on the railroad for a time. He was mean and muscular, just like Cletus and Toby.

On the second day of scouting for gunmen to ride with them down to Colorado, they ran into a man wandering down Randall toward the center of town. He was carrying a worn-out saddle, a bridle, and a blanket and was covered with dust. They stopped and talked to him.

"Where's your horse?" Toby asked.

"Wore him out comin' down from the Badlands," the man said. "Had to shoot him this morning."

"You got money for another horse?" Cletus asked him.

"I can get pretty close, I reckon. Figured to trade my hogleg for a good mount."

"Where you headed?" Toby asked.

"No place in particular. What's it to you?"

"If you trade your pistol for a horse, you'll be ridin' nekkid," Toby said.

"I can always pick up a two-dollar chunk of iron that'll shoot."

"How'd you like a free horse and good pay for a job wranglin' a bunch of horses?"

The man dropped his saddle onto the ground and adjusted the folded saddle blanket on his left shoulder. He squinted up into the Wyoming sun as he looked up at Toby.

"I'd be beholden," the man said. "You makin' such an offer?"

"Maybe. What did you do up north?"

"What I could. I traded my rifle for that horse what foundered just to get this far."

"So, you're a tradin' man," Cletus said.

"Not by choice. It's just the luck of the draw, I reckon. Say, who are you fellas?"

"I'm Toby Dugan and this here's Cletus Hemphill. What's your handle?"

"They call me Jinglebob, but my name's Randy McCall."

"We got a bunkhouse out at the ranch where you can wash up and get some grub. You can pick out a ridin' horse and go on the payroll before sundown."

Jinglebob grinned and held out a hand. Toby shook it.

"Climb up behind me," Cletus said. "You can leave that saddle where it sits. We'll get you a better one."

They found their fourth man on the third day. His name was Jake Fenimore, or at least he said it was, and he had gone through five of the six whores at a crib on Central when Toby and Cletus saw him sitting outside a tobacco shop with a plug in his hand. He was cutting off a chunk with a big bowie knife, and he wore his pistol low on his hip.

"You occupied?" Toby asked him when they rode up.

"What do mean by 'occupied'?" Jake said.

"Gainfully employed," Cletus said.

"I'm a bouncer at a cat house," Jake said.

"Good pay?" Toby asked.

The man shrugged. "I get by. Some of what I earn comes by way of trade."

Cletus laughed.

They introduced themselves and found out that Jake owned a horse and a Sharps carbine and didn't care how he made money. He drank some but wasn't a drunkard. He'd had a few scrapes with the law and was a quick draw. He had robbed a bank with some outlaws who roamed Nebraska, but when two of them were arrested, he headed west with a few dollars in his pocket.

Jake was just the kind of man Jordan would take a liking to once he got to know him.

They paraded the four men in front of Jordan on the fourth day. Jordan looked them over and asked a few questions.

"This could work into a permanent job, boys," he told them. "I need you to help us drive three hundred head of horses from Colorado up here and then to Fort Laramie. Interested?"

They all nodded.

"Thirty a month and found, but maybe a bonus if you happen to plug a certain man when we get down to where the horses are ranged."

"What man?" Jake asked.

"The man I'm buying the horses from," Jordan replied.

"When do we leave?" Jinglebob asked.

"Tomorrow morning," Jordan said. "It's a good three days' ride, some of it up in the hills."

When the men left the house, Jordan spoke to Toby and Cletus.

"You got us some good men there, boys." He reached in his pocket and pulled out a roll of bills. He handed each man a twenty-dollar bill. "I appreciate it."

"We got grub ready to pack and the other men have bedrolls. You have to buy one of them a rifle."

"I've got a rifle I can give him," Jordan said. "He the man who lost his horse?"

"Yeah," Cletus said. "Good man."

"Who doesn't know how to take care of his own horse."

"He bought a broken-down sway-backed nag. I think he was in a hurry to light a shuck," Toby said.

"All right. We're set then. We'll head for Wild Horse Valley at sunup. Bring plenty of ropes and ammunition."

"You figure you can put Storm down?" Toby asked.

"I'm counting on it. The man is a damned thorn in my side. He thinks he's pretty smart, but I think we can outgun him with you, Cleet, and this bunch."

"I think we can, too," Toby said.

After his men left, Jordan opened his safe and took out two thousand dollars in hundred-dollar bills. He put the bills in a small leather case and set it on the table. He went to the gun cabinet, unlocked it and took out one of the rifles, a Remington .30 caliber. He opened a drawer under the cabinet and found a box of cartridges. He set these on the table and then lifted another pistol off a peg. This one he would hang from his saddle horn. It was a Smith & Wesson .38 and didn't weigh as much as his sidearm.

"Just in case," he said to himself.

He walked outside and stood for a long moment gazing at the mountains. They seemed like the backbones of a huge dinosaur in the purple haze of afternoon.

"I'm comin' for you, Brad Storm," he said aloud. "I'll hang your scalp in my lodge, you bastard."

Just saying the words gave Jordan confidence.

He fished a cheroot out of his pocket, bit off the end, and lit it with a wooden match.

The smoke wafted away in the breeze.

He ground up the stub of the cigar, which he had cut off, and scattered the tobacco to the four directions. Just as his Cherokee ancestors had done.

His body was half white, he often thought, but his heart was pure Indian.

It was the Cherokee in him that would make sure that this sale would be Brad Storm's last transaction.

He smiled at the hazy mountains.

He was sure that they smiled back at him.

THIRTY-ONE

By the time the others woke up, Brad was sitting on a log with a knife in his hands. He had started a fire and put the coffeepot on to boil. Stacked on the ground were five or six long sticks, tree branches he had cut down. He had one of these in his hands and was sharpening the forked ends. The branch had been shaved of bark and limbs and was free of leaves.

Joe was the first to walk over. Wilbur and Julio were relieving themselves at trees some distance away.

"What're you doin', Brad?" Joe asked.

"Trimming up this bunch of forked sticks," Brad replied.

"What for?"

"We're going to catch rattlesnakes with these, Joe."

"Rattlesnakes? What in hell for?"

"A surprise for Jordan Killdeer," Brad said.

Joe sat down on the log a few feet from Brad. He rubbed his forehead.

"Brad," he said, "I know you're in charge of this case. And you do a fair job of detective work. Sometimes. But you're way too unorthodox, not only for my tastes but for the police and court system. I don't know why Harry ever hired you, and I sure don't know why he holds you in such high esteem."

"Harry doesn't like to get dirt or mud on his boots," Brad said.

"But he has other detectives who work for him. He has operatives who follow the rules and do their jobs in an orthodox manner."

"I don't know, Joe. Harry doesn't discuss his other agents with me. He just calls on me when he's got some dirty work for me to do."

"Look, Brad, you go about things all wrong. I'm a range detective. That means I dig up evidence and make arrests. Once we had witnesses located, we should have gone to Cheyenne, maybe asked for police help up there and arrested Jordan Killdeer, hauled him back down to Denver and seen to it that he was tried, convicted, and sentenced to hang. A simple, straightforward procedure. Time-tested. Tried and true."

Brad stopped whittling on a forked stick, picked up another one that had not been sharpened, and tossed it to Joe.

"Make those ends real sharp, Joe," Brad said.

"Are you trying to run away from the facts, Brad?"

"No. I'll just ask you this question, Joe. Was your wife raped and murdered? Did you have any horses stolen?"

"That's two questions."

"Just answer either one, Joe."

"So, you think because it's personal, you can just do anything you want, is that it?"

Brad picked up another forked tree limb and began to shave the end of one fork into a point.

"Harry hired me because I get the job done, Joe. In my own way. Orthodox or unorthodox. I solve cases for him. I do what a detective agency is supposed to do. Find the criminals and put them out of business."

"Did you ever bring any criminals into court? Did you ever deliver a live culprit to Harry or anybody else?"

Brad paused and looked up through the pines at the sky. "Not that I recollect," he said.

"See? That's what I mean. You kill whoever you track down. You don't follow the rules."

"Joe, I kill only when I'm forced to. I don't back shoot, and I don't bushwhack."

"He who lives by the gun, dies by the gun, Brad."

Brad began to shave wood with the blade of his knife.

"He who doesn't live by the gun, dies from the gun," Brad said, and his blade went *whick, whick, whick*.

Julio and Wilbur walked up out of the timber and watched Brad and Joe for a few seconds. Brad looked up at them.

"Get your blades out and pick up a couple of these forked sticks," Brad said. "Sharpen the tips of the forks like that one I did."

"What are they for?" Wilbur asked.

"Snakes, Wilbur," Brad said. "We're going to catch us a bunch of live rattlers with these forked sticks."

"Not me," Wilbur said.

"Yes, you. All of us."

Julio sat down first, picked up a stick, and drew his knife.

"I don't want to get bitten by no rattlesnake," Wilbur said.

"I'll show you how to do it, Wil. Now, get to work. I'm going to need a lot of snakes."

"And I don't suppose you're going to tell us what the snakes are for, are you, Brad?" Wilbur said.

"They're for a secret Ute ceremony that will protect us from bullets," Brad said.

Wilbur sat down. "I guess I shouldn't have expected a straight answer," he said. Brad handed him a stick and kept whittling.

Wilbur drew his knife and began to whittle at one of the forks.

"While you boys finish sharpening those forked sticks,

I'll put that snake box together," Brad said. He got up and walked over to the stack of wooden panels. He hammered together the box that wound up being four feet long and two feet wide. The spring-hinged door and its ring worked fine.

When the others had finished sharpening the sticks, they came over to the lean-to and looked at the box.

"How does it work?" Joe asked.

"I'll attach a long length of twine through that round handle so that one of us can pull the door open when the time comes." He demonstrated by pulling the door open and then letting it slam shut.

"You're going to put snakes in there?" Joe said.

"Yes," Brad said.

"Then, what?"

"Oh, there's more to it than that," Brad said. "When the time comes you'll see it all come together." He reached down and picked up the burlap gunny sacks. He handed a bag to each of the men. Then he picked up the roll of heavy twine.

"Each of you cut slits in the open end of each bag about four to six inches apart until you've got holes all the way around."

"What are these for?" Wilbur asked as he held a bag and took his knife out.

"We'll put the snakes we catch in these bags and transfer them to the box when we have enough," Brad said.

"I ain't catchin' no snakes," Wilbur said.

Brad walked back to the log and picked up a forked stick that had been sharpened. He walked to where the others were standing and raised the stick a foot or two off the ground.

"When you spot a snake," he said, "go for a spot just behind its head, then drive the stick down, with the fork straddling its body. Pin the snake firmly to the ground. Then you reach down and grab the snake just behind its head and drop it into your sack. Pull the twine tight and go on to the next rock or cave."

Wilbur recoiled in horror.

"I'll show you how," Brad said. "Each of you string enough twine through those holes and tie the ends so you can pull it tight once you've caught a snake. Do this each time you catch a snake. If you have a snake in your bag and have caught another, shake the bag so that the first snake is on the bottom, then drop the other snake in, tail first, and pull the string so that neither of the snakes can escape."

Brad made slits in one bag and ran twine through the holes to show them how to do it.

"Two of you carry this box out to the road and then stand it on its end with the door at the top," he told them.

When they all had their bags ready and were holding forked sticks, Brad walked toward the road. "We'll spread out," he said when they got to the tabletop. "Kick over flat rocks and be prepared to jab your stick down tight behind the rattler's head."

"This is just scary as hell," Wilbur said.

"I'll catch the first snake to show you how it's done, Wil," Brad said.

They all followed him as he walked up some flat rocks. He moved one or two with his stick. At another, a rattlesnake that was lying under it raised its head and then shook its tail. As it was coiling up, Brad struck.

He jammed the snake between the forks and pushed until he drove the snake flat. It whipped and struggled to free itself. Its rattles shook with alarming rapidity.

Then Brad reached down and grabbed the snake just behind its head with his left hand. He let the stick fall and held the wriggling snake over the open end of his gunny sack. He dropped the snake straight down into the bag, and pulled the looped twine tight and closed the bag.

"Keep the bag away from your legs when you carry it," he said. "And, when you find another snake, just drop the bag on the ground until you need it while you snare the next rattler."

They all stared at him as if he had gone mad. Brad smiled and picked up his forked stick.

"When you have several snakes, you can drop them into

that box back yonder and the lid will close automatically. Then go back and catch more snakes."

"How many do you want, Brad?" Joe asked.

"Fill up the box if you can," Brad said.

"Are you serious?" Joe asked.

"About ten or twenty, Joe. Four or five rattlers apiece."

They all set out in different directions. Brad and Julio paired up and walked well away from the others.

"You are a good snake catcher, Brad," Julio said.

"You've done this before, Julio."

"I have not done it so well as you."

They found a low mound that was surrounded by talus and each took a side and scooted flat rocks away from the hillock.

Julio uncovered a small nest of snakes, and Brad walked around to help him. They managed to get three snakes before the others slithered well away from their hiding place in the rocks.

Brad heard Wilbur yell a couple of times. Joe was searching intently.

Julio chased one rattler that was corkscrewing away, headed for the timber. He jabbed in several inches behind its head.

"Brad," he called, "you come. Give help."

Brad went over and jabbed his stick just behind the snake's head. Julio reached down and grabbed it. He dropped it into his bag and grinned.

"Sometimes it takes two people," Brad said.

They all caught snakes until past noon and dropped them into the upended box. The box resounded with several rattling sounds, and they could hear the snakes squirming and slithering inside.

Wilbur had caught two small pygmy rattlers and a green snake.

"That one's harmless," Brad said, "but we'll keep him."

"Maybe the others will eat him," Julio said.

"Then, we don't have to catch any rats," Brad said.

At the end of the day, when they had finished catching

as many snakes as they could find, Brad told them that they had enough.

"I'm glad that's over," Wilbur said.

"If I never see another rattlesnake, it will be too soon," Joe said.

"They are good to eat," Julio said.

"We're not going to eat any of these, Julio," Brad said. "But they do make good eating."

Wilbur shivered in revulsion.

"Now we ride down to the valley," Brad said.

"For what?" Joe asked.

"We're going to catch up two horses and hitch them to one of those wagons stored in the timber. Then we'll haul the wagon up the road and leave it just below the summit. Won't take long."

They saddled their horses and set out for the road down into the valley.

Just below the rim, Brad stopped and pointed to the side of the road. There was a flat place that sloped at the same angle as the road.

"We'll set the empty wagon here," Brad said. "Tongue pointing upslope. Then we'll attach a long length of that heavy twine to the tailgate. We'll make sure the tailgate is closed, but not secure. We want to be able to pull the twine and open the tailgate."

"More mystery," Joe said.

"Not that much. The snake box will be in the center of the wagon and there will be a long length of twine attached to the round bolt's hole. We'll pull both lines at the same time. The tailgate will drop and the box will open. The snakes will slither out of the wagon and make a hell of a racket as they wriggle all over the place."

"And, when do you do that?" Joe asked.

"The minute that Jordan Killdeer starts coming off the flat and down this road," Brad said. "When he's just slightly past the wagon, we pull the cords and release the snakes."

"A diversion, then," Joe said.

"I get it," Wilbur said. "Then what?"

"Then we ask Killdeer and his men to surrender or we shoot them out of their saddles."

"Where will we be?" Joe asked.

"There's cover on both sides of the road. Two of us will be on one side, two on the other."

"What if he's got a dozen men?" Joe asked.

"Make sure you've got plenty of ammunition for your rifle and pistol. Now, let's go on down, catch two good horses and water ours at the creek."

They rode down into the valley. Joe and Julio shook out their lariats and rode toward some of the grazing horses.

Brad and Wilbur headed for the timber where the wagons were stored.

Up on the rimrock, Curly saw the riders enter the valley.

He put his binoculars to his eyes and looked at each man.

When he saw Brad Storm, he held the glasses still for a long time.

Brad and that traitor, Wilbur Campbell, were heading straight for the bluffs.

He climbed onto his horse and rode to the edge. He jacked a cartridge into the firing chamber as the men walked their horses slowly straight toward where he was waiting.

He made sure the hammer was back in the firing position and sucked in a breath before he brought the gun to his shoulder.

Horses whinnied down in the valley and out of the corner of his eye, he saw the Mexican and another man chasing them with looped lariats.

Somebody, he said to himself, is going to die right soon.

THIRTY-TWO

❧

Curly rested his cheek on the stock of his rifle and pressed the butt against his shoulder. He leveled the front blade sight on Brad Storm, chest high. He lined up the blade with the rear buckhorn sight. He drew a breath with his finger poised to squeeze the trigger.

Just then, he heard a cougar cough. Close by. He had the trigger depressed halfway and could not stop his finger's movement. The horse he was on jerked under him and wheeled. Its shrieking whinny caused the two riders nearest him, Brad and Wilbur, to look up.

Brad heard the explosion from the rifle. It sounded like a bullwhip's lash cracking. A split second later, a bullet whined above his head. He ducked, and so did Wilbur.

Then they heard the delayed sound of the horse atop the bluff. Brad looked up and saw Curly wrestling with the animal as it twisted and bucked, kicked out with his hind legs at empty space.

Brad drew his pistol.

Behind him, Julio and Joe looked up and saw Curly

wrestling with his horse. They had heard the shot and both drew their pistols.

Brad started firing his pistol up at Curly. So, too, did Julio and Joe. Curly brought the horse under control and disappeared from view.

"I'm going after him," Brad shouted to Wil. "You stay here and help Julio and Joe."

He galloped off toward Joe and Julio. He didn't stop.

"Carry out my orders," he told them.

"Where you goin'?" Joe asked.

"That was Curly up there. I'm goin' after him."

And then Brad took off toward the road, the only way out of the valley. He climbed the slope and turned his horse toward the bluff where they had seen Curly.

"Well, he's gone," Joe said to Julio.

"He will catch him," Julio said.

They saw Wilbur riding toward them. His face was nearly the color of white flour.

"Did you see that?" he asked.

"We saw it," Joe said. "Lucky that rifle shot missed Brad."

"It flew right over his head. And mine. A close call."

"Brad said to keep doing what we're doing," Joe said. "When we catch up two horses, we'll lead them to the wagon."

"What if Brad doesn't come back?" Wilbur asked.

"Then we have to do what he would have done," Joe said.

"He will come back," Julio said.

They all heard the sound of hooves striking rock and saw Brad gallop to the spot where Curly had been waiting in ambush. They lost sight of Brad, but could hear his horse thrashing around atop the limestone bluff.

"Brad will track Curly," Julio said. "He is a good tracker."

"Let's get those horses, Julio," Joe said. "We can't worry about Brad anymore."

"That stupid Curly," Wilbur said. "I wonder what made him miss."

"His horse tried to buck him off," Joe said. "Something scared it. A snake, or a bear, maybe just an elk cracking a branch. The horse was spooked just as he fired off his rifle."

"Lucky for Brad," Wilbur said.

"Maybe lucky for you, too, Wilbur," Joe said.

He and Julio trotted their horses after a likely target.

Five horses grazed close together. Two of them were geldings. They appeared to be three- or four-year-olds.

"You rope the sorrel, Julio," Joe said. "I'll put a loop on that other gelding, the chestnut."

Julio nodded and built his loop.

They approached the horses slowly, riding several feet apart. When they were within ten feet, two of the horses looked up at them. They raised their heads and stared at both riders.

Julio closed in on the sorrel gelding and began to swing his loop.

Joe approached the chestnut and twirled his loop over his head.

Both men fired their ropes at almost the same instant.

Julio's loop lazed through the air and dropped over the sorrel's head and settled at the base of his neck at the top of its chest. The horse bolted. Julio wrapped part of the rope around his saddle horn and tugged on his reins. Chato started to back up. The rope tautened and held the sorrel fast.

Joe's rope hit its mark and he pulled it tight and twirled part of it around his saddle horn as well. The chestnut pulled on the rope by jerking its head but did not try to run away.

"We got 'em, Julio," Joe said. "Good ropin'."

"Now we go to the wagon," Julio said.

Wilbur watched the two in amazement. He was impressed by their roping skills.

"Take us to the wagons, Wilbur," Joe said.

"You bet, Joe."

They rode into the timber where once Wilbur and Jack had camped. There were two wagons parked some ways past the shelters and the tack hut.

Joe handed his rope off to Wilbur. Then he lit down and walked to one of the wagons. He checked the side panels and then the tailgate. He opened and closed it. He went to the other wagon and did the same thing. One wagon was slightly larger than the other.

Both tailgates worked well.

"You kept them oiled, Wilbur," Joe said. "Wheels and tongue."

"Yep. Jack was right particular about that. Our supplies depended on them wagons, and he wanted them to be in top shape."

Joe took the rope from Wilbur. "Fetch us the harness, Wilbur," he said. Then he turned to Julio.

Wilbur dismounted and walked toward the tack hut. His horse stood there, hipshot, its reins dropping onto the ground.

"We'll hook 'em up to that short wagon there, Julio. Let's stand our horses on either side of the tongue."

Julio dismounted. He led his horse to the other side of the wagon tongue and backed it up, then held it in position. Joe pushed the chestnut back until it was even with the sorrel, and rubbed the horse's face and worried its nose with his knuckles.

Wilbur came back festooned with leather harnesses. The three of them laid leather across the horses' backs and hooked them up to the wagon. They arranged the reins so that they dropped into the seat well.

"You drive the wagon up the hill to that spot where Brad showed us he wanted it, Wilbur." Joe said. "Julio and I will follow you."

Wilbur climbed up into the wagon and picked up the reins. He released the brake and rattled the reins across the backs of the two horses. They stepped out and he guided them out of the timber.

Joe and Julio followed the wagon to the road.

"Hold it right there," Joe called out to Wilbur when he was close to the spot Brad had pointed out as the place where he wanted the wagon.

Wilbur pulled on the reins and halted the two horses.

"Now, set your brake, Wilbur," Joe said. "That looks to be about right."

Wilbur pulled on the brake until it locked.

"Unhitch 'em," Joe said. "Then, turn 'em loose."

He and Julio watched as Wilbur deftly unhitched the horses from the wagon after slipping them out of their harnesses.

"I guess you'll have to walk back and get your horse, Wilbur," Joe said.

"What's next, Joe?" Wilbur asked.

"We'll lug that snake box down here, set it in the wagon, then pick out spots on both sides of the road to hide in and tie long enough strands of twine to the tailgate and the box."

"Then what?" Wilbur asked.

"Then we wait," Joe said. "We wait for Killdeer to show, or for Brad to come back. We'll hide out in the brush on both sides of the wagon."

"It's goin' to be a hell of a long day," Wilbur said.

"And, a long night, maybe, too. We won't leave here until Killdeer shows. Night or day."

Wilbur swore. Then he walked toward the timber where he had left his horse.

Julio chased the two pulling horses back down into the valley.

He rode back to where Joe waited. "We'll have to hide our horses up in the timber where I have my lean-to," he said.

"Then we carry our canteens back down here," Julio said.

"We'll bring back grub. That roll of twine. We may have a long wait."

"I know," Julio said. He dismounted and handed his reins to Joe.

"After we bring the grub and such, you and I will walk back up and carry that snake box down here and tie on the twine."

"Yes," Julio said.

The two left their canteens under the wagon, in the shade, and rode back up to Joe's camp.

In the valley, Wilbur walked past the bend in the creek and into the timber.

Joe looked back and wondered if Wilbur was going to try to escape.

If so, he had a clear shot, because he and Julio would be in the timber and busy hobbling the horses so that they could graze.

He was betting that Wilbur wouldn't ride out and put distance between him and them.

Somehow, it seemed to him that Wilbur had come over to their side.

Time would tell, he thought.

THIRTY-THREE

∽

Horse tracks.

The imprints of iron horseshoes in the dirt at the top of the bluff were clear and distinct. Brad sat his horse for a few moments as he looked down at the myriad of U-shape impressions and listened for any sign of Curly, any sound that meant he might still be near.

Dead silence.

Brad dismounted and studied each track with a trained set of eyes. He was looking for any blemishes, nicks, distortions in any of the separate impressions of horseshoes.

There was a dimple in one hoof. As he walked by the retreating tracks, he determined that it was in the left high foot of the horse. In another, he saw a V-shaped cut on the right front shoe. It might have been made by a nail, a sliver of sharp flintstone. The other shoes were fairly uniform.

But he had enough now to track Curly.

He ejected the spent hulls from his .45 and inserted fresh cartridges from his gun belt. He spun the cylinder, then eased it to a space between two cylinders and slid the pistol back in his holster.

He mounted Ginger and rode slowly along the line of horse tracks. He rode into the timber where he saw a rumpled bedroll. So, Curly had left his bedroll there. He probably thought he'd kill all of them and have the valley and the bluffs to himself.

The tracks led to a narrow game trail. They continued on and Brad saw that the horse had not been over any of it until this day.

Curly had made his escape along that game trail. The horse tracks were superimposed on the tracks of squirrel, quail, deer, and elk. The tracks were plain to see, and Brad knew they were Curly's tracks.

He rode slowly and noticed that Curly's horse had stopped running after a few hundred yards. In fact, the tracks told him that the horse was on a walk. He looked ahead and saw that the game trail was straight for some distance.

He followed warily, and he stopped every few yards to listen and look around him. There was only the silence of the looming mountains and the hills and ravines in between.

The game trail led across a low hill and down into a swale where grass and bushes grew. It wound through these and continued up another small hill.

Where was Curly headed? Brad wondered.

He also wondered how well Curly knew these mountains since there was no sign that humans had been there. There was no sign of mining or prospecting activity for as far as he could see.

Atop another hill, Brad saw where Curly had reined up his horse. He had probably waited there for a time to look at his back trail.

After that, the tracks led down into a shallow ravine and up a hogback where, at the top of the ridge, the tracks veered off the game trail and the horse Curly was riding clambered over rocks and vegetation. The horse had mashed down the short tufts of grass and moved a few pebbles and stones. The tracks were not as sharply defined as before, but Curly's passage was easy to determine to Brad's trained eye.

Brad looked off to the high peaks from the ridgetop.

They were now well below timberline, but if Curly went higher, he would be crossing in shale and rocky detritus. He would still make tracks, but they would be more difficult to follow if he was on flat stones or harder ground.

The wind rose and turned brisk. Wind could make tracks harder to follow if they smoothed the ridges from the horse's shoes. Still, he kept on and rode down the ridge into a stand of timber. He saw where the horse had scuffed dead pine needles, and every so often there would be the branch of a bush broken or pushed out of place. He saw where Curly's head had struck a low limb and dislodged bark and squaw grass.

The man was going somewhere, he thought. But where?

The tracks veered again. Curly was heading for the high country. After that, the horse tracks were in a wide zigzag pattern that told Brad that Curly was trying to elude anyone who might be pursuing him.

There were trees above the last hill, and above them was timberline, a craggy, barren region above twelve or thirteen thousand feet where no grass grew. No trees, no bushes. Nothing but broken rock, shale, the talus that had tumbled down from the sides of snowcapped peaks.

Brad saw a small cave, just above timberline. But the tracks did not lead there. Instead, they led a zigzag path through timber, over deadfalls and rock outcroppings green with moss and climbing bushes. It was dark inside the timber. The pines were tall and their branches and needles shut out the sun.

It grew colder at that altitude, and Brad buttoned up his jacket as he shivered from the freshets of wind that blew through the pines. He crossed a small spring-fed stream and began to see deer and elk tracks. Once, he saw the faint impressions of a cougar's paws before they left the loamy floor of the timber and as the cat jumped to a long, flat vein of rock. The tracks made Brad somewhat apprehensive. A cougar could be waiting ahead somewhere, atop a boulder or a rocky outcropping, sniffing, looking, its tail flicking like a tabby cat stalking a mouse.

The tracks led out of the timber and headed for higher ground. Just above the timber there was a long, rocky ridge, and he began to see caves where bears might hibernate or mountain lions might sleep during the day.

He found a fresh mule deer kill as he climbed. It had been disemboweled. One haunch had been ripped off and dragged up to one of the caves. There were cougar tracks all around. The deer's neck had been broken. There was a wound at the top of his neck where the cat had pounced and dispatched the mule deer with a single bite of strong jaws, then mangled the hide and flesh as the animal went down and began to die.

Curly's horse tracks led right by the bloody deer, but Brad didn't know if the deer had been killed before he passed that way or afterward.

Brad could smell the fresh blood, the gamy scent of the cougar, and the hide of the deer. All of these aromas were strong in his nostrils as he continued to follow Curly's tracks.

He entered another stand of timber where the trees were dense, grown close together. It seemed a haunted place of deep silence and mystery. There were numerous deadfalls and on banks of soil, large, flat chunks of limestone. It was an eerie place and after riding several yards into this gloomy place, he saw a large outcropping of sandstone embedded in the hillside. In a narrow cleft, there was a large boulder, and beyond, an even larger flat stone that appeared to have markings on it.

Brad rode up to the boulder and behind it to look at the flat rock. Etched in the stone were strange glyphs that he could not decipher. There were what appeared to be stick figures, some with bows and arrows. There was the outline of an animal that looked like a deer. Above these glyphs, there was the outline of a cross and lines scored around it that resembled rays or depicted a shining object.

It was a baffling and puzzling collection of ancient graffiti that made ripples up and down Brad's spine. The shiver he felt was not from the cold, but from seeing something so old that someone had scratched into the stone with flint or some sharp object. A record of people who had roamed the Earth long before the white man came to America.

The sun was setting and still Curly was on the move. Brad left the rocky outcropping and followed the tracks into open grassy swales and over small creeks running with the water from melted snow high in the range that towered above him.

Then he came to a ridge where the tracks followed a straight line. Above the ridge there were more rocks and bigger caves.

Had the people who had carved the glyphs into stone once lived in those caves? Brad wondered.

It grew darker and colder. Shadows began to flow from him and his horse and from rocks and bushes.

The tracks grew dimmer and some were invisible on stone.

Then they took a turn for the rimrock where there were caves peering down at him like hollow dark eyes.

As he turned Ginger, some sixth sense sprouted in his mind.

Brad knew that he was being watched. There was little cover in that place, which was just a hair below timberline.

He looked up at the caves. He looked for one that had a ledge that might support a man on a horse. There was one, and he focused on that as he rode around a pile of boulders.

That sixth sense, that strong hunch, made Brad rein up Ginger and wait behind the boulder for several seconds. He listened intently and looked up at that one cave that was fronted by a wide ledge.

He thought he heard a scraping sound. Or maybe it was gravel slipping down from that high ledge.

The silence around him deepened.

Could a horse fit in that large cave? He looked at it again. The opening was high enough. He could not tell how deep the cave was, but it looked deep from where he sat his horse.

Instinct told him to wait there for a few more minutes, even though he was losing the light.

He heard the soft whicker of a horse and stiffened.

Ginger pawed the ground and let out a soft nicker.

Curly was up there, Brad knew. He was in that cave or one of the others. Or he was hiding behind a rock with his rifle at the ready.

Brad knew it as sure as he knew the day was ending.

He stayed where he was and listened.

He stayed there until the sun fell behind the mountains and the sky was dappled with small tufts of rosy clouds with golden underbellies. Somewhere below, a jay squawked and a pair of crows answered the call with their raucous caws.

Brad shivered in the sudden chill.

He eased Ginger a foot or two from behind the rocks.

He heard the sharp crack of a rifle from somewhere above him and the whoosh of a bullet before it struck one of the rocks and caromed off it with a nasty whine.

"All right, you sonofabitch," Brad said to himself, "I know where you are."

He pulled Ginger back until they were once more hidden by the rocks. Then he dismounted as quietly as he could and stood there as the clouds overhead turned to floating lumps of ash.

The dark came on with a suddenness that seemed to wipe out all traces of the landscape and then there were only the winking stars blossoming in the velvet sky and the rim of the glowing white moon rising slowly behind the highest snow-mantled peak.

The night hid many things. It was hiding Brad, and it was hiding Curly.

But it could not hide the hatred Brad held in his heart for the man he chased.

And hatred, he thought, could move mountains. Just like faith.

THIRTY-FOUR

❧

Pitch-dark and dead quiet.

Brad waited for more than an hour before he quietly sat down and removed his boots and spurs. He stood up and loosened the strap on his knife. Then he lifted his pistol and let it fall back into his holster so that it was not firmly seated.

He heard small shuffling sounds and scraping noises coming from the large cave. He could no longer see the cave, but he marked its location in his mind. He knew where the ledge was, as well.

Still, he waited until the noises diminished, then stopped.

He left Ginger ground-tied to a small bush and slowly stepped out from behind the rocks. He had on heavy socks, and these helped muffle his footfall as he began to climb the slope toward the ledge. The slope was not steep, but he was careful with each step. Before he let his weight fall on one foot, he tested the ground for rocks, pebbles, branches, anything that might make noise and reveal his presence and his path.

It was a slow and painful process just to advance one foot at a time.

The moon seemed to be creeping along the sky behind the mountain peaks. It did not rise but floated just below the jagged rim of the world, with only a small portion of it rising above the highest peak every so often.

Brad saw the ledge off to his left. He climbed up even with it, careful not to shake loose any talus. He crawled part of the way and had to use his knees for balance and keep his feet off the ground. He reached the ledge and slowly stood up, masking his mouth with cupped hands as he panted for breath.

Carefully, he picked his way across the ledge until he felt the edge of the cave with his outstretched fingers. He paused there for a long moment.

Then Brad reached down inside his jacket and shirt and touched the thong that encircled his neck. Slowly, he pulled the set of rattles up, squeezed them in his hand and then let them dangle silently on the outside of his jacket.

He listened at the cave and could hear the sound of breathing from both the horse and Curly. The sounds were very faint, but he sensed that Curly was dozing, and the horse was lying down, breathing through its rubbery nostrils.

He held on to the leather thong with his left hand and drew his pistol. He squeezed the trigger slightly and thumbed the hammer back to full cock. The action made a soft snick as the sear engaged. Brad held his breath and waited.

When he was calm and ready, he shook the rattles.

There was a stirring from inside the cave. The horse snorted. Curly, roused from sleep, screeched.

Brad moved the pistol just inside the cave and tilted its barrel upward. Then he squeezed the trigger.

The explosion, amplified by the hollow cave, sounded like the roar of a cannon.

A split second later, the horse came bounding out of the cave.

Curly shouted a loud curse that took the name of the Lord in vain.

The horse leaped off the ledge and fell through darkness. It landed with a clatter. Brad could hear the thump of its body as it fell. It kept tumbling downward, releasing a small avalanche of rocks, crashing through bushes and tearing limbs from trees. The horse screamed in agony.

Curly stepped up to the entrance, his gun drawn.

Brad saw only his bulky silhouette, his outstretched hand and arm with the pistol a black blob in his hand.

Brad stepped close and brought his gun down on Curly's arm.

Curly screamed in pain and the pistol in his hand fell onto the hard surface of the ledge. He whirled to face Brad and drew his knife.

"You bastard," he grunted. He lashed out with his left hand and knocked Brad's Colt from his hand. The pistol struck the ledge and lay still, silent, and useless.

Brad saw the faint gleam of Curly's knife blade. He drew his own knife and went into a fighting crouch.

Curly lunged with his knife and swiped a half-circle arc with the blade, inches from Brad's body.

Brad sucked in his belly and lunged toward Curly.

Curly backed up a foot and his blade swished at Brad. Brad rushed in, reaching for Curly's arm. Curly pulled his arm back. His bald head gleamed in the dark like some ghostly overturned bowl.

Brad whipped his knife downward as he closed the gap between him and Curly. He felt the blade slice through the fabric of Curly's jacket and strike flesh.

Curly yelled.

"Damn you," he shouted and backed off. Brad had struck his left arm, but Curly didn't appear to be disabled. He roared and charged Brad, swinging his blade back and forth as if it were a sword.

Brad stepped back in retreat and heard the shish-swoosh of Curly's blade as it sliced through the air in two directions. At the end of one sweep, Brad charged forward and crashed into Curly's unprotected gut. The air flew out of Curly's lungs.

Brad jabbed with his knife, straight into Curly's exposed side. He felt the blade strike leather and metal as it penetrated Curly's gun belt with its loop of pistol cartridges. Then the blade struck flabby flesh, and hot blood spurted from the wound.

Curly whirled and grunted in pain. He raised his right arm and struck downward with his blade, straight at Brad's shoulder.

Brad dropped to his knees and grabbed Curly's leg. He struck again with his knife, driving the blade into Curly's calf. Then he pushed with his shoulder and felt Curly's leg give way, then buckle.

Curly screamed in pain. He fell backward and hit the ledge with a loud thud. Brad scrambled to his feet and stomped on Curly's arm with his stockinged foot. Curly tried to bring up his knife, but his arm was pinned under Brad's foot.

Brad stepped over him and straddled his body. He pressed downward with his foot.

Curly's hand opened. His knife slipped from his fingers, clattering on the limestone ledge.

Brad dropped to his knees, then crushed into Curly's chest. He leaned down and grabbed Curly's left arm at the elbow. He twisted the limb until Curly screamed as a bone cracked.

Brad felt Curly's breath on his face as he brought it down close to the man.

"Was it like this for my wife when you were on top of her, Curly?" Brad husked.

"You bastard," Curly growled.

"You know, Curly, when you shoot somebody, they still have a chance to live. They don't die real quick sometimes."

"Who gives a damn," Curly snarled, inches from Brad's face.

"But," Brad said, "when you cut a person's throat, that ends it right there. One deep slice and there is no more life."

"Go hump yourself, Storm," Curly snapped.

"One quick slice and you take away a person's life just like that."

"Go to hell, Storm," Curly husked, the pain creeping into his voice like drifting sand.

"Was that how it was with Felicity? You took your knife and cut across her tender throat and opened it up so that she could not breathe, could not scream, could not ever live another moment."

Curly did not reply. He cringed as Brad brought his blade up so that it floated right in front of Curly's eyes.

He could sense Curly's eyes widen.

Curly turned his head as if to escape the blade.

"See how you like it, Curly," Brad said.

He brought the knife down and swiped the blade across Curly's throat from his left ear, around to his right.

Blood spurted from the wound. Curly gurgled on the blood as he released his last breath. His head dropped to the ledge and his body went limp.

Brad sat there for a long time, breathing heavily. He closed his eyes and thought about that terrible moment when Felicity had her throat cut and the last thing she saw was that bald-headed bastard's ugly face looming over her.

"That was for you, Felicity," Brad breathed. "Now maybe you can rest in peace, my darling."

Brad wiped his blood-soaked blade on Curly's jacket and sheathed his knife. He stood up and walked to where his pistol lay. He picked it up and opened the gate to eject the empty shell with the sliding rod. He pushed another bullet into the cylinder and slid the pistol back in its holster.

The moon finally rose above the mountains and shone down on the gory ledge with a pale, ghostly light. Curly's corpse lay there, still in death, washed to a ghastly luminosity, the bright red blood turning black and shiny, frosting over in the moonlight.

"Rot in hell, Curly," Brad whispered and bowed his head in memory of Felicity.

THIRTY-FIVE

Brad unbuckled Curly's gun belt. He picked up his pistol and holstered it. Then he searched the cave. He lit matches to see what was inside. The cave was deep and had a high ceiling. There were dark smudges on the walls that told him the cave had been used by ancient peoples, Indians most likely. There was evidence of a very old fire on the cave floor, as well. He found what he was looking for, Curly's Winchester, and he picked that up. He wrapped the gun belt into a ball and walked back down to where he had tied Ginger.

The horse whickered when he walked up in his stockinged feet. He patted the horse's withers and spoke soothing words to him. He put Curly's pistol and gun belt into one of his saddlebags and attached his rifle behind the cantle with tightly knotted leather thongs that were used to hold his bedroll in place.

Then he sat down and brushed all the sand and twigs and leaves off of his socks and slipped on his boots and spurs.

He untied Ginger's reins and mounted up. He had no idea what time it was, but he knew that the night had not yet seen midnight. He made his way slowly downward, using dead reckoning to find the game trail where he had first begun to track Curly. There were no landmarks, except for the rocky outcroppings and the big boulder in front of the rock where he had seen the glyphs. But it was easy going after that, with the moon high and beaming down light that bounced off his and Curly's tracks.

It was after midnight when he took his final bearings and then emerged on the rimrock above the valley. He could see the dark shapes of horses, some of them lying down, others nibbling grass or just huddled together against the brunt of the chill breeze that blew across the grassland.

He rode back to the road and found his way to the lean-to where Joe was sleeping. He saw the bedrolls of Julio and Wil, lumpy blankets pewtered with moonlight, and his own bedroll, still laid out, inviting and dappled with leafy shadows and the tiny fingers of pine needles still on the trees.

He unsaddled Ginger and hobbled him with the other horses and walked back to his bedroll with Curly's rifle and gun belt. He laid them next to his blankets and sat down, suddenly tired and very sleepy.

"Brad, that you?" Joe whispered from his shelter.

"Yeah. Just got back."

"Bring Curly with you?" Joe climbed out of his bedroll and walked over to sit on the ground next to Brad's bed.

"Left him to the wolves," Brad said. "That's his rifle and pistol there." He pointed to the dark lumps near where he had rolled up his saddle blanket to use for a pillow a few moments before.

"Did you have to kill him, Brad?"

"Yes. I had to kill him."

"Why?" Joe asked.

"For Felicity. For me."

"You couldn't arrest him?"

"I could have, maybe. But, his horse is dead. Broken neck. I would have had to ride back double, with Curly wrapped up like a Christmas turkey in rope and handcuffs."

Wil sat silently and Brad didn't elaborate on what had happened up on the ledge in front of the cave.

"Well, get some rest, Brad. We got the wagon set and the snake box is in it. Will they live long enough to do what you want 'em to do?"

"I reckon. I don't care. Good night, Joe."

"Good night, Brad."

Brad watched Joe tiptoe back to his shelter. He unbuckled his gun and knife, rolled the rig up, and set them next to him, within easy reach. He crawled into his bedroll and pulled the blanket up to his chin.

He heard a soft snore from Julio's blankets and then it stopped.

He gazed up at the moon until his eyelids grew heavy. He closed his eyes and soon dropped off into a deep sleep.

He had the swatch of cloth from Felicity's nightgown in his hand. Slowly, his fist relaxed and he was gone from the world, locked into a dream of caves and horses, shadowy men with spears and lances, huge battle-axes. He saw strange symbols in the stars of the dreamscape and they made no sense to him, but he knew they were messages from another time, another existence.

Beyond his hearing, a wolf howled mournfully and an owl flapped over the campsite on silent wings.

Later, it perched on a limb and hooted. But nobody there heard it, and if they had, none would have understood its mysterious message.

THIRTY-SIX

❧

Seven men rode hard toward Longview, Colorado. Their faces and their clothing were covered with dust and their faces, hands and wrists were tanned by the sun. At the head of the column rode Jordan Killdeer on a tall black horse. His saddle was studded with silver, and sun glinted off each strip, buckle, and reinforcement band that lined the cantle, horn, and stirrup.

"We gonna stop in town?" Toby asked as he rode up alongside Jordan.

"No, Toby. No towns. Not yet."

"We're gonna stop somewhere, though, right?"

"We'll rest the horses and have a smoke by and by," Jordan said.

They did stop, on a lonely square of prairie just before they rode past Longview. Jordan led them well off the road. In the distance, coming from Denver, they could see the spools of dust kicked up by the Cheyenne stage with four horses pulling it.

The men dismounted and relieved themselves. They gathered in a circle around Jordan who filled a pipe and lit it. It was a meerschaum, and he had bought it from Aber-crombie & Fitch in New York out of a catalog. Some of the men rolled quirleys and a couple had ready-mades that they shook out of square packs.

"How much further?" Terry Wheeler asked. "My butt's plumb achin' and I got saddle sores."

"Another day to Denver, maybe," Jordan said. "Most of it anyway."

"We goin' to Denver?" Jinglebob asked.

Jordan gave him a withering look.

"We'll skirt Denver, ride along the foothills," Jordan said. "Then we head into the mountains. Be most of another day getting up to the valley."

"So, two more days of blisterin' sun and prairie winds," Jake Fenimore said as he puffed on a store-bought.

"We want to get there in daylight," Jordan said. "It's better'n a hundred miles from Cheyenne to Denver and the miles after that are all uphill."

"Your saddle sores will have saddle sores," Cletus said. "Maybe we'll find some horse liniment up in the valley we can swab on your butt."

The others laughed.

"How many men we goin' up against?" Terry asked.

Jordan seemed to think for a moment before he answered.

"Hard to tell," he said. "Maybe only two or three. Or half a dozen. It don't make no difference."

"It makes a hell of a lot of difference to me," Terry said. "I want to know what I'm getting into up yonder."

Jordan fixed him a scornful look.

"When we get there," he said, "they may think we're going to do some horse trading. But there ain't a man up there right now what's goin' to get out alive."

"You aim to kill 'em all?" Jinglebob said.

"Every last one of those bastards," Jordan said.

Cletus and Toby laughed. The others looked worried.

"How come?" Terry asked. "How come we got to kill 'em all?"

"We don't want no detectives doggin' us and we sure as hell don't want no witnesses," Jordan said.

"That's right," Toby said. "There's a man there what's tryin' to pull a fast one on us. We aim to snuff out his lamp."

"I guess we all knew that from the start," Jinglebob said. "I mean, you boys told us there'd be gunplay."

"That's right," Cletus said. "You were hired to do a job. Your guns are on the payroll, too."

"I reckon we can handle it all right," Jake said. "I don't like detectives no way."

"Me, neither," Lenny Holbrook said. He had a wad of tobacco in his mouth and a rolled cigarette dangled from his lips.

"You got enough terbacky to last you, Lenny?" Clete said. "Seems like you're burnin' the candle at both ends."

"I likes to chew and I likes to smoke," Lenny said. "What's wrong with that?"

"Nothin'," Clete said. "You just might die of terbacky pizenin', that's all."

All of the men laughed. Even Jordan.

"When you finish your smokes and your chaws," Jordan said, "let's get back to it. I gave us three days to get to that valley and we're burnin' daylight without makin' no progress."

There were grumblings among the hired men, but they all put out their smokes and mounted up.

They passed through Longview and kept riding all afternoon. In the distance, toward late afternoon, they saw the outlines of Denver on the horizon. Some of the men licked their lips and a couple made motions of tipping a glass with their hands.

Jordan kept on and they rode past Denver and into the dark of evening.

"No use ridin' up there at night," Jordan said. "We'll camp out below Lookout Mountain and get an early start in the morning."

"How early?" Terry asked.

"Before sunup," Jordan said.

"So, sleep fast, Terry," Toby said.

Some of the men laughed as they rode a brown ribbon of road up to the nearest foothill. The lights of Denver looked inviting to some of them, but they stopped when Jordan stopped and started untying their bedrolls. They were well off the road and behind a small hill where they could not be seen from the road should anyone pass at that hour of the day.

They kept their horses saddled, but hobbled them so that they wouldn't stray. There was plenty of grass, but no water.

"I can't wait to get that sonofabitch Storm in my sights," Jordan said to Toby as he pulled off his boots and laid them next to his bedroll.

"You don't even know what he looks like, Jordan," Toby said.

"He'll be the one with his dirty hand out," Jordan said.

"He might be tricky. He makes a noise like a rattlesnake."

"Yeah, I know. A sidewinder."

"Well, there's one sidewinder, Jordan, you got to admit that."

"Yeah, Toby. Brad Storm. But you know what we do with rattlesnakes, don't you?"

"Shoot 'em," Toby said as Jordan crawled under his blanket.

"We cut their heads off," Jordan said and pulled the blanket over his head.

Toby walked away.

"That'd be a neat trick," he said, more to himself than to Jordan. "But I sure like the idea."

They slept until just before first light and then took the hobbles off their horses and mounted up after finishing their calls to nature. It was still dark, but the road glistened under the moon. It snaked up the mountain like the track of a serpent. Gradually, as the eastern sky burst into a foamy cream, they began to see bushes and rocks. The horses were jittery and some of them fought their reins.

Then they rode past the blunt top of Lookout Mountain, and the newly hired men looked up at the high peaks and at the phalanxes of pines rising in rows ahead of them and felt very small. They were nervous as they entered a strange and silent land where they had only their wits to rely on, and there were shadows around every rock and tree. Menacing shadows not yet burned away by the light of the sun.

None of them knew what awaited them in Wild Horse Valley. It was the mystery that made them nervous and tense. Most of them had never faced down an armed man in daylight before.

But all of them had killed men.

Some were strangers, some were not.

Their bellies quivered in anticipation, and their lips turned dry and cracked into open fissures that had the pink taint of blood.

They rode in silence, following a half-breed Cherokee, whose veins ran with ice from what they'd seen of him.

A damned half-breed, and he was looking to collect scalps.

THIRTY-SEVEN

&

Brad woke up before any of the others. His dreams had disturbed him, set him to thinking about Curly and the other men he had killed. It made him think about his character and how it would be changed by his actions.

Revenge was not sweet, as they said, but bitter and cloying, like an unknown and unseen disease. The men he had killed were evil, but he wondered if his own actions were not equally as bad. Yes, those men would have killed him if he had not defended himself, but did that make it right?

What would Felicity say if she were alive? What did Julio and the other men who worked for him think of him? Was he just another killer in a different guise? Was he justified in taking a life, even though his actions were in self-defense?

He lay there in his bedroll, looking up at the silent stars, and felt humbled and small. Was he some Cain who had slain his brother Abel? Was he some kind of vigilante who disregarded the law, or took the law into his own hands? How would civilized society view him? How would the world see him after what he had done?

Brad agonized over the questions and could not come up with any useful answers. Curly had tried to kill him. So had the others. But he had gone after them. He had forced them into corners where there was no escape. Was he really a hired detective, or just another hired killer?

The sky began to lighten in the east. Brad crawled out of his bedroll. He slipped on his boots and spurs, strapped on his gun belt. He walked deeper into the timber and relieved himself. He rubbed the bristles on his face and walked back to camp. He picked up Curly's rifle and gun belt, then strode to Wilbur's bedroll.

The man was still asleep. So were all the others. He walked back and dropped the rifle and rig on his blanket. Then he stepped to the fire ring and picked up a stick that they were using for kindling. He stirred the coals and then started laying on squaw grass and small branches. He let the coals start the fire, then added light pine logs.

Joe stirred in his lean-to, then cocked himself up on one elbow.

"You're up mighty early, Brad," he said.

"Sun's coming up, Joe. Time to rise and shine."

Joe groaned. Every muscle in his body ached at that moment. He sat up and rubbed his arms and legs. Julio woke up and then Wilbur. Joe looked at them through rheumy, sleep-clogged eyes. He rubbed away the grit.

"I'll make us coffee," he said. "After I heed nature's call."

It was cold. Brad warmed his hands over the blazing fire. He watched Joe and the others walk away and stepped back from the fire as his pants began to heat his calves. The flames waved and lashed. Sparks flew up in a dizzying spiral, then winked out like fireflies.

Joe put the coffeepot on. Wilbur and Julio returned and stood by the fire opposite Brad.

Brad walked back to his bedroll and picked up the rifle and pistol rig. He carried them to the fire and held them out to Wilbur.

"These are yours now, Wil," he said.

"I recognize that gun belt," he said. "Curly's?"

"The rifle, too."

Wilbur took them and looked at Brad.

"You trust me?" he asked.

"You've earned the right to pack iron," Brad said. "When Killdeer comes down, you might need them."

"I'm no gunfighter," Wil said.

"You know how to shoot, don't you?"

"Yes. I can shoot. I'm a pretty fair shot. At tin cans, stumps, and rocks."

"Well, that's a start," Brad said.

"I don't know if I could shoot a man, much less kill anybody." Wilbur still held the gun belt in one hand, the rifle in the other.

"Strap it on. It'll need reloading, maybe. I'll give you some cartridges for both the Colt and the Winchester."

Wil set the rifle down and unfurled the gun belt. He wrapped the gun belt around his waist, then buckled it. It slipped down from his waist.

"You'll have to put a couple more holes in that belt so that it rides high and tight," Joe said as he jiggled the coffeepot so that the water swirled inside.

"Yeah, Curly was bigger around the waist," Wil said.

"He was fat," Julio said. "Like pig."

The others laughed.

"Yeah, he had a gut on him," Brad said.

Joe passed out cups and when the coffee boiled, he filled them. He put more wood on the fire and sat down.

The sun rose above the horizon and sprayed beams through the pines, gilded the spruce and fir trees, set the junipers ablaze with bright light.

They sat on the log and drank their coffee. Wil, Joe, and Julio got hardtack and jerky and chewed on their food as the sun began to warm them.

"You ain't eatin', Brad?" Joe asked.

"I never eat before I go hunting," Brad said.

"You're going hunting?"

"We all are, in a way. Killdeer could get here anytime. I want to be ready for him."

"Well, we've rigged the twine, and the snake box is in the wagon bed," Joe said.

"I can't wait to see what you've done."

"One thing I was thinkin'," Joe said. "You can just leave that tailgate down. You wouldn't have to pull it open when Killdeer passes by the wagon. Be one less strand of twine to worry about."

"Yeah, we could do that," Brad said. "But, I plan to pull the gate open so that it makes a noise. If I figure right, Killdeer and his men will look over at the wagon. Then, when we open the snake box, they'll scatter, maybe be a mite confused."

"I see," Joe said. "I think you're right. When that tailgate slams down, they'll sure hear it."

"What happens when the snakes start crawlin' out of the wagon?" Wilbur asked. He was using his knife to make holes in Curly's gun belt. He put the tip of the blade on the leather at a spot where he wanted a hole, then worked it in a circular motion to puncture the belt.

"I have no idea," Brad said, and sipped his coffee.

"I think what he means, Brad," Joe said, "is what do we do when Killdeer and his men are distracted? Do we yell at them to surrender, or do we start shootin'?"

"Good question, Joe," Brad said.

There was a long pause and a long silence.

"Well, you gonna answer that, Brad?" Joe asked.

"Do you think a bunch of hard cases are just going to surrender?" Brad asked.

"Well, if we all stood up and pointed our rifles at them, they might," Joe said.

"Have you been readin' those dime novels, Joe?"

"That would be the way I would call it," Joe said. "Speaking as a detective, duly sworn to uphold the law."

Brad waved an arm in a half circle in front of him.

"Look around, Joe. Do you see any law out here? Anywhere out here?"

"You know what I mean," Joe said.

"Yeah, I know what you mean, Joe. You want everything smooth and steady. The bad men ride up, see us, see our rifles aimed at them, and then they throw up their hands and surrender. Never mind that if they did that, they'd know they were going to jail or prison and might just hang for stealing horses."

Joe didn't speak for several seconds. Julio and Wil looked at him, wondering what he would say.

"No, I guess they wouldn't just give up without a fight," Joe said. "But, you still have to make the offer. I think, anyway."

"What offer is that, Joe?"

"Why, tell them they're all under arrest and they should give up."

"We could do that," Brad said. "Might be interested to see what they would do."

Julio's face twisted into a wry grimace. "You give them warning," he said, "you ask them to shoot you. That is what I think."

"I dunno," Wil said. "It's right scary, you ask me."

He cut three holes in the gun belt, stood up, and strapped it on. He had a hole to spare as he tightened the buckle on the next-to-last new hole. The belt fit tight.

"You look like a regular gunfighter," Joe said.

"Well, I ain't," Wil said.

"You will shoot?" Julio asked.

"I reckon," Wil said. "If somebody's shootin' at me."

"Don't close your eyes when you pull that trigger," Joe said.

"I hope I don't have to pull no trigger," Wil said.

"Let's get to it, boys," Brad said. He stood up, shook out the drops of coffee still in his cup, and tossed it into Joe's lean-to.

The others finished eating and drinking their coffee.

"Bring your canteens," Brad said. "It might be a long, hot day. And carry your rifles with you."

They filed out of camp and headed for the road. The sun

was high in the sky and the breeze had dropped off to a whisper.

They looked like men on a death march, all in single file and silent, their heads bowed to shield their faces from the sun.

A quail piped its plaintive call from somewhere on the tabletop, and a hawk floated over the road, its head turning from side to side. A chipmunk squeaked and ran to a hole as they passed.

In the valley, a few of the horses whickered at the sight of the men walking toward them.

The only sound was the crunch of their boots on the gravel of the road.

THIRTY-EIGHT

❧

Harry Pendergast was tired and sore from sitting in the saddle. He was in a sullen mood and not very good company for the other men who rode with him. Harry kept wiping his face with a sodden handkerchief and guzzling water from his canteen. The canteen clanked against his leg where it hung from his saddle horn, and that was another irritation.

"This blamed heat," he said to Peter Farnsworth, who rode alongside him.

"It's a hot one, all right," Farnsworth said. He was one of Harry's detectives and had been a big help when the two men interrogated Jack Trask in the Denver jail. Trask had been reluctant to give out any information until Harry made him an offer.

"If you tell us who's behind this horse thieving ring, Trask, I promise you won't hang."

"Can you guarantee I won't swing?" Trask had said.

"He can and I can," Farnsworth had said. "We've already talked to the judge. If you tell us who's the big boss, you'll get a short sentence in jail, that's all."

"I got to see it in writing," Trask said. "From the judge hisself."

"You've got a deal, Jack," Harry said. "We'll have it here first thing in the morning."

"I ain't sayin' a word until I see that judge's signature on his official letterhead."

"Tomorrow," Harry said.

He and Pete had gone to see Judge Phillip Wormser that very afternoon. They were ushered into Wormser's office by his court clerk, Timothy Evans.

Harry knew Judge Wormser well, but he had never asked him for a favor. After he and Pete were seated, the judge entered his office and sat behind his desk. He was in court at the time, which was in recess, and still wore the black robe of his office. Pete felt a trifle intimidated because Wormser was a tall man with a ruddy face and a shock of flowing gray hair. He wore expensive spectacles and was, indeed, a commanding presence.

"Make it short, Harry," Wormser had said. "I've got a full docket and this is a very brief recess."

"We are investigating a ring of horse thieves," Harry said. "They're very organized. We have one of the thieves in custody at the jail. But he's a small fry and I'm after the big fish. This man knows who the boss is. We have solid evidence against him and his gang, but we've only managed to capture this one man."

"So?" Wormser said, his gray-blue eyes piercing through the glass of his spectacles.

"He's booked on a hanging offense, Your Honor," Harry said. "He won't talk unless we offer him a chance to live."

"You mean you want to have him tried on reduced charges?"

"Yes. But I need a letter from you to take to this man guaranteeing that he won't face hanging in court."

Wormser doubled up his fists and glared at Pete and Harry.

"The court views horse thieves as among the lowest of

the low," he said. "The court has dealt harshly with horse thieves in this country and sees no reason to change its attitude toward such criminals at this point."

"Judge," Harry said, "I know I'm asking a lot, but this man has valuable information that would result in the arrest of the entire gang. They are not only horse thieves but have murdered the wife of one of my agents. I want them all to hang, but this one man is the key to my uncovering the identity of their leader and perhaps all of the culprits."

"I see," Wormser said. "But can't your agents find the ringleader without granting a lesser penalty to the man we have in custody?"

"They are trying, Your Honor. I have two agents out in the field, but I have not heard from them in some time. And time is precious. This involves a number of honest ranchers who have lost valuable horses to these thieves."

The judge pulled out his watch and glanced at it. The watch was gold and so was the chain. He tucked it back in his watch pocket.

"I am reluctant to grant favors to criminals. Especially before they are deemed guilty in my court. I am further reluctant to put such a guarantee in writing."

Wormser seemed adamant.

Tim, the judge's secretary, came into the office.

"Five minutes, Judge," he said, and then left.

"Your Honor," Pendergast said, "if we don't get the information from this man that we need, we may very well be unable to solve the case and bring the rest of the gang to justice. It is essential that we get this man's cooperation. A great deal of money is at stake. The horse breeders are up in arms, and they wield a great deal of influence in these parts."

Wormser leaned back in his chair. He took off his spectacles and pinched the bridge of his nose. Then he put the glasses back on.

"I see the importance of your case, Harry," Wormser said. "I also see that losing the case, not breaking into the inner circles of the ring could have far-reaching consequences. What would the lesser charges be for this prisoner you have in custody?"

"Possession of stolen property, Judge," Harry said quickly.

Wormser harrumphed and drew a sheet of paper out of a desk drawer. The paper bore the imprint of the court and the judge's name. He picked up a pen from the well on his desk and began writing rapidly. When he finished signing the document, he raised it in both hands, held it level, and blew the ink dry.

"Here you are, Harry," Wormser said. "I hope it helps you in your investigation."

"Thank you, Judge," Harry said. He took the paper and handled it as if were a delicate treasure. He and Pete left the office, went to the Brown Palace and had a drink in celebration.

The following morning, Harry, Pete, and Cliff Jameson rode out of town.

"This map that Trask drew for us, Harry," Pete said, "do you think it's accurate, or is he just sending us on a wild-goose chase?"

"I told Trask that if we did not find this ranch and this Jordan Killdeer, that the judge would rescind his order and he would hang."

Pete looked back over his shoulder. Then he leaned over and whispered his question to Harry so the man riding behind them would not hear what he had to say.

"Did we have to bring Jameson along?" Pete said.

"Cliff might be a big help. He's got a lot at stake in this case."

"But he might want to take revenge when we arrest Killdeer."

"No chance of that. Cliff wants to see that gang stand up on the gallows with ropes around their necks. I want him with us so he can look over the horses at Killdeer's ranch and see if he recognizes any of them as being stolen from him or the members of the association."

"All right," Pete said. "You're the boss, Harry."

They rode into Cheyenne and passed the nightclub owned by Kildeer.

"Trask said he doesn't go there until evening," Harry said.

"I know. I heard him."

"Let me take a look at that map that Trask drew for us, Pete."

Farnsworth slipped the folded map from his pocket and handed it to Harry.

Cliff rode up alongside Harry.

"That the map?" he asked.

"Yes."

"I ain't been to Cheyenne in some time, but I know about where that ranch is," Cliff said.

"You take a look at it then, Cliff. See if we're on the right road."

He handed the map to Jameson.

Cliff looked at it and then at the buildings they passed, and as soon as they had reached the outskirts of Cheyenne, he nodded and handed the map back to Harry.

"This is the right way," Cliff said.

They reached the ranch gate and halted their horses.

"Check your guns," Harry said.

"It looks deserted," Pete said. "I don't see no riders, nobody tendin' to the horses."

"What do you think, Cliff?" Harry asked.

"It does look awful quiet."

He saw that there were no horses in the corral. A few were grazing in a couple of pastures.

"Shall we go in?" Harry asked. "Do you recognize any of the horses, Cliff?"

"Too far away," Cliff said.

"Well, we'll just ride up and knock on Killdeer's door. If he answers, we'll arrest him."

"I'm all for that," Pete said. He rode up to the gate and opened it.

They rode up to the silent house. Cliff rode around the house to the stables, but he did not dismount or go in. He sat there for a few moments and listened, his right hand resting on the butt of his pistol.

"I'll knock on the door, Pete. You be ready if he makes a move."

Harry dismounted and walked up to the door. He rapped on it loudly.

There was no answer. He knocked again.

"Either he's not home or he's hiding," Harry said.

"Man don't have no maid, no hands out workin'. I'd say he ain't here."

"I think you're right, Pete."

Harry walked to his horse and stepped into the stirrup as he gripped the saddle horn. He pulled himself up into the saddle. Then he and Pete rode around to where Cliff was waiting.

"Anybody home?" Cliff said.

"Nope," Pete said.

"Let's ride out and look over those horses in those two pastures," Harry said. "But keep your eyes open in case somebody was in that house and decides to chase us off."

They rode out and opened the gate to the first pasture. Harry and Pete waited outside the fence while Cliff rode up to look at the horses and check their brands.

"Nothing here," he said. "Horses have the Killdeer brand on 'em. And they ain't been altered with a runnin' iron neither."

Cliff checked the horses in the other pasture with the same results. No altered brands, no stolen horses.

"Well, I'm disappointed that Killdeer isn't here," Harry said. "I wonder if he's at the Silver Queen."

"We could find out real easy," Pete said. "And wet our whistles at the same time."

"A wasted trip," Harry said.

"Looks like," Pete said.

"Well, you found out something anyway," Cliff said. "He ain't keepin' any of the stolen horses on this spread."

"I wonder what he does, or did, with all the horses he stole," Harry said.

Pete shrugged and Cliff said, "When we find out, we'll have him where we want him."

But Harry was dejected. He realized now that he had made a bad bargain with Jack Trask. Jack had directed them to Killdeer's ranch, but Killdeer was gone.

He wondered, as they rode back into Cheyenne, if Joe Blaine and Brad Storm might have lured Killdeer away from his ranch. Maybe, he thought, they might even have him in custody by now, along with the rest of his gang.

Then there was the alternative, which he did not want to think about.

Brad and Joe might both be dead.

He pushed the thought aside, but it nestled in the back of his mind like a rat in its hole just waiting to sneak into a kitchen after dark.

THIRTY-NINE

∽

As Jordan Killdeer led his men into the mountains, past Lookout, he felt as if he were coming home. He felt that same strong tug he had known as a young boy, when he had lived there with the Arapaho. He had been captured in Oklahoma by Cheyenne and Arapaho warriors when he was ten years old.

He had been told by his parents and the elders of his tribe that if he was captured, he would be tortured and made into a slave. Neither had happened to him. When the tribes returned to the north, with many ponies, he had been adopted into the Arapaho tribe and they had made him into one of their own. He rode and hunted with young boys his own age and they had given him the name of Kills Deer because of his prowess with a bow and arrow. When he had rejoined the white race, he kept his given name, Jordan, and shortened his Arapaho name from Kills Deer to Killdeer.

He had kept his childhood a secret from all, and had listened to the patois of cowboys so that he could imitate their speech until it became second nature to him. The Arapaho had taught him much, but the main inheritance he had gained from them was the value they had put on horses. That stayed with him, so he had learned from the white man how to acquire and breed good horses. This love of horses had shaped his life to the point where he sought wealth not only in the breeding of fine horses but also in illegal ways to acquire them and sell them to miners, prospectors, and lumberjacks for a quick profit. He saw nothing wrong in this practice because he had been on many raids with both the Arapaho and Cheyenne when they raided other tribes and white men for horses and ponies.

While he lived with the Arapaho, he discovered that they used Wild Horse Valley to keep their wealth away from other tribes, including the Ute.

When Jordan was sixteen, he stole away in the night with the three horses he owned, horses he had captured himself on a Kiowa raid with the Arapaho. He wandered around until he met a rancher who agreed to hire him on and let him keep and breed his horses. Jordan left with a stallion and two mares. The rancher had been impressed with Jordan's knowledge of horses, and when he died, he left his ranch to Jordan, when Jordan was in his mid-twenties.

Now in his thirties, Jordan owned a successful horse ranch but wanted more. He wanted more land and more horses. And he had found a way to raise the cash the way he had been brought up by the Arapaho. By stealing horses.

"You ain't takin' the usual way up to the valley," Toby said as they rode through a thick stand of timber where the elk were bedded down.

"No. This is the old way up there," Jordan said. "You can't see it, but there's a wide trail here. It's all growed over now."

Toby looked around him at the ground. All he could see were rotting deadfalls, craggy rock outcroppings, and plenty of pine and spruce. There was a juniper tree that looked as if it had been blasted with dynamite, a tree that a bull elk had rubbed the previous fall, to sharpen its antlers, mark its territory, and attract a mate.

"I don't see sign of no trail in here," Toby said.

"Ain't been used in years, like I said, Toby."

Toby snorted and continued to look for anything that resembled a trail. He shook his head after a few minutes and gave up.

They climbed ever higher and it did seem to Toby that Jordan knew where he was going. There were a lot of fallen pines, and he detected the scent of bear scat near one log that had been ripped open in the bear's search for grubs. The bear smell made the horses nervous, and Toby rode on with one hand on the butt of his pistol.

They left the timber and crossed a swale of grass before Jordan spurred his horse to jump across a small creek and then they were in the timber again. It seemed to Toby that they were climbing straight up and the horses were straining to climb the steep slopes that were sparsely dotted with all kinds of trees, including a few firs, a blue spruce, smaller pines that had been stunted by the wind, and a few more junipers that had been ravaged by bull elk.

"Figured out when we should get to that valley?" Clete asked. His horse was streaked with sweat and panting from the exertion of the climb.

"Yeah," Jordan said. "Noon or shortly after. And it looks like we'll have clear weather all day."

"Seems like we used to ride up there on a more round-about way," Cletus said. "Warn't so steep."

"This is the shortest and quickest way."

"If we was bein' chased, maybe," Clete said, half under his breath.

Jordan said nothing. When the Arapaho had used the trail before, they were being chased and it was the quickest way to get to the valley and leave their pursuers behind. It had not seemed so steep then, but he was much younger in those days. Some of the Arapaho braves were bleeding from wounds, and some had arrows in their legs or backs and wanted only to lie in the valley next to the creek where they could tend to their wounds.

The men riding behind Jordan, Cletus, and Toby were

cursing the brush and the flies, batting at the insects with their hands, and slapping their horses' necks to kill the deer flies.

Jordan rode a black Arabian, fourteen and a half hands high, with a small star blaze on its forehead. The small hoofs made it more sure-footed in mountain terrain, and the horse did not struggle like those ridden by the others in Jordan's band. He called the horse Sugarfoot and spoiled it by feeding it apples and sugar lumps when the animal was at pasture.

The sun climbed higher in the sky as the earth turned in its orbit, blazing down through the trees and heating up the thin mountain air.

Jordan looked up and marked the sun's position in the sky. On a narrow strip of grassy plain, he raised his hand and called a halt.

"We'll rest here for a few minutes," he said. "We're about two miles from the mesa. From there, we follow a road to the valley. I want the horses rested before we make the last climb and we'll halt again once we hit the tabletop."

"The horses are plumb tuckered from all that climbin'," Jinglebob said. "That's for sure."

"It's good for their lungs," Jordan said. "You do that once or twice a week, you got yourself a champion runner."

"I don't want a champion runner," Jinglebob said. "I just want a horse that'll carry me from sunrise to sunset without founderin'."

"You'd have that, too, Jinglebob," Toby said. "Jordan knows horses. Look at that Arab he's ridin'. It ain't hardly broke into a sweat."

The men stepped down from their saddles, rolled smokes, or bit off chews, and urinated into the brush. The horses shook themselves off, their tails switching at deer flies. They, too, urinated and dropped apples onto the turf.

Jordan felt the muscles in Sugarfoot's chest, squeezing them and kneading them with his supple fingers. He patted the horse on its rump and Sugarfoot tossed its head, making a waving shawl of its mane.

The men slapped at flies on their necks and blew smoke at others that zizzed past their sweat-streaked faces.

Then Jordan called for them to resume their trek up the mountain.

The going was rough the rest of the way, and the horses doubled up their legs and propelled themselves up the steep incline like mountain goats. When they reached the table-top, Jordan called another halt.

"No smokes. Stay mounted," he said. "It ain't but a half mile or so to the rim of the valley."

"About damned time," Terry grumbled.

"Just a stretch of the legs," Lenny said, as he worried a gob of tobacco back and forth in his brown-stained mouth.

"Be quiet from here on in," Jordan said. "Startin' now."

The men snuffled and closed their mouths.

One of the horses snorted, and Jordan gave the rider a sharp look of disapproval. Then he raised his hand and pointed down the road. "Stay sharp," he said in a low tone of voice.

They rode slowly toward the lip of the tabletop. When they reached the edge at the drop-off, Jordan stopped. The other riders rode up and lined up alongside him.

They all looked down at the grassy valley and the dark shapes of horses grazing. One or two of the men sucked in their breaths at the sight of so many horses in one place. Their gazes roamed from side to side.

Jordan looked down at the wagon cocked at an angle on the side of the road.

"What the hell's that wagon doin' there?" he said to no one.

"It's probably broke down," Toby said.

"Anything in it?" Jordan asked.

"Not that I can see," Cletus said.

Jordan listened in silence for a long time. Some tic of suspicion began to twitch in his mind.

It was very quiet. Too damned quiet.

He saw no men anywhere he looked. He saw only a valley full of his horses.

Where in hell was this Brad Storm?

"I don't like it," he muttered.

"Looks like there ain't nobody here," Toby said.

"No, and there should be. You watch your p's and q's," he said. "Somethin' sure as hell ain't right."

Nobody said a word.

Jordan eased Sugarfoot onto the down slope of the road. He kept his eyes focused on the empty wagon. He looked at both sides of the road where there was thick brush. He looked for any sign that he might be riding into an ambush.

He walked his horse very slowly, and his right hand dropped to the butt of his pistol.

Some of the men held on to the stocks of their rifles.

It seemed to Jordan that none of his men were breathing.

He, too, was holding his breath, his nerves tingling like a dark cave full of jiggling beads on long strands of electrified wire.

And the sun stood directly overhead, burning down onto hat brims and sweat-oiled faces.

Even the horses in the valley were silent. The whole world was silent in those first few moments when all the riders began their descent into the peaceful valley that seemed rife with danger.

FORTY

∾

Brad directed Wil and Joe to take up their hiding places on the side of the road opposite the wagon.

"Julio and I will be on the other side. I'll handle the twine to open the tailgate and snake box," he said. "Lay low and stay quiet."

"It's gonna be a long day," Wil said.

"Probably the longest day of your life," Brad said.

"We can handle it," Joe said.

"You probably won't need your rifles, but keep them handy." Brad hefted his Winchester for emphasis.

"Yeah, when they come down the road and pass by the wagon, they'll be real close," Joe said.

"And, when they get their wits back, they'll be shooting right and left," Brad said.

"But we're going to ask them surrender first, aren't we?" Joe asked.

Brad looked at him in the dim light of morning.

"If you want it by the book, you can politely ask them, Joe."

"You know what I mean," Joe said.

"Yeah, I know. Go ahead and demand their surrender. But you better be ducked down when you do. Unless I miss my guess, Jordan's men won't throw up their hands and throw their guns down."

"No, I expect not," Joe said.

"Play it any way you like. But be ready to return fire if they start shooting," Brad said.

"We will," Wil said. "I swear."

Brad watched the two men cross the road. Then he and Julio went to the wagon side and climbed into the brush. A cottontail jumped up and ran out as they entered the thicket.

"Pow," Julio said and squeezed a mock trigger with his right hand. "Supper," he said.

"Let's just hope all the rattlers are in that box, Julio. Stomp around here to make sure."

Both of them made a racket as they burrowed out a place for them to sit and wait. It was a spot where they could both sit and stand up with an unobstructed view of the road and the wagon. The two strands of heavy twine lay a half foot away. Brad reached over and picked them both up. He sat down and pulled them almost tight. A quick jerk would drop the tailgate first and another jerk on the second strand would open the snake box and release the rattlers.

He hoped the snakes would wriggle out the back of the wagon and start streaming toward the road. If any came their way, they could be in trouble.

The men in hiding drank from their canteens at frequent intervals. They sweated under the hot sun, and wiped their sweaty hands frequently on their trousers. The morning wore on and the sun continued to climb the heavens.

Then, at around noon, all of them heard the faint sound of hoofbeats up on the road. The riders were advancing very slowly.

Brad hoped that Wil and Joe would resist the urge to stretch their necks to see who was coming down the road.

He hunkered down and drew his pistol.

He nodded to Julio who also drew his weapon.

They waited.

From his hiding place, Brad could see the top of the road as it dipped off the tabletop. In a few moments, the road filled with riders. A man on a black Arabian halted and the others crowded around him.

Brad saw them all scan the valley with their eyes slitted.

It seemed an eternity before any of the men on horse-back moved.

Then they all slowly began to descend the road.

Brad figured the man on the black Arab was Jordan Kill-deer. As the men rode down the road, he noticed that Jordan let them pass him as he continued to look in all directions. Jordan's gaze was fixed on the wagon as they all approached it. He heard the low murmur of voices as the men in front of Jordan expressed their opinions on what they were see-ing and not seeing, what they were not hearing, as well.

Then, Jordan halted as the others rode on down toward the valley.

"Storm," Jordan called in a loud voice. "We're here. Show yourself."

The men halted for a moment and turned to look back at their leader.

"Storm, I've got your money. Come out, wherever you are." Killdeer's voice was even louder as he cupped his hands around his mouth to amplify his voice as if he had a megaphone.

Brad set his pistol down in front of him and picked up both strands of twine.

The men in front of Killdeer resumed their descent into the valley. When they were just below the back end of the wagon, Brad pulled the cord attached to the tailgate.

The tailgate opened and dropped. Wood slammed against wood.

All of the men halted and stared at the wagon.

A second later, Brad pulled the other cord and the snake box opened. He held the door open and watched for the snakes to wriggle toward the tail of the wagon.

A second or two later, the first snake reached the edge of the wagon bed. The snakes began to shake their tails. Then the entire bunch of them steamed off the back of the wagon and dropped to the ground.

The rattling of the snakes startled the horses and the men riding them.

Snakes began to streak toward the road. The horses neighed in terror and a couple of them reared up and the riders had to force them back down on four legs.

"Snakes," one of the men shouted.

"Rattlers," cried another, and the riders began to fight for control of their mounts as the horses milled in confusion.

Across the road, Joe shouted.

"Drop your guns. You're all under arrest."

Jinglebob was the first to draw his pistol. He cocked it and fired at the sound of Joe's voice.

The bullet sizzled over his and Wil's heads, and caromed off a rock and spun off with an angry whine.

Then all of the riders drew their pistols.

Brad stood up and shot Jinglebob out of the saddle. The bullet from Brad's .45 smashed into his left side and crushed ribs, mangled his left lung and smashed a hole though his stomach.

Jinglebob doubled over and tried to turn his horse and raise his pistol. Instead, he dropped from the saddle and hit the ground, gushing blood from two wounds.

All of the men started firing their weapons, both in Brad's direction and at Joe and Wil.

The blast of gunfire from several weapons thundered from different explosions.

Julio stood up and picked out a target, shot a man in the upper chest.

Lenny's horse spun around in a half circle and he grabbed his saddle horn, mortally wounded.

Joe and Wil shot at the milling riders as fast as they could pull the triggers on their guns. A horse was hit and fell forward as its knees buckled.

Smoke filled the air. Sparks and flame flew from pistols.

As Brad watched, Killdeer turned his horse and galloped

up the road. He fired a quick shot at Killdeer, but the man topped the rise and disappeared in a drumbeat of hooves.

"Drop your guns," Joe shouted again.

He and Wil stood up, rifles in their hands.

"Now," Wil shouted as he levered a cartridge into the firing chamber of his rifle.

The remaining men dropped their pistols.

Brad and Julio scrambled out of the thicket and approached the men on horseback.

"Raise your hands," Brad said. "Grab some sky."

The men raised their hands high as Wil and Joe came up on them with leveled rifles.

Brad ran to Jinglebob's horse and grabbed the reins. He pulled himself into the saddle.

"Tie 'em up," he told Joe.

"Where you goin'?" Joe asked.

"Killdeer got away. I'm going after him."

Two men lay dead on the ground. Joe ordered the other riders to dismount.

Snakes swarmed the road, their rattles frantically knocking together.

Will kicked one away and stomped on another. The snakes wriggled into the brush on the other side of the road where he and Joe had been. They continued to rattle until they were out of sight.

The riders dismounted and Joe made them all line up and turn their backs to him.

Brad galloped off on the blue roan that had belonged to Jinglebob. A Winchester jutted from its scabbard. He disappeared over the rim of the tabletop.

"Wil," Joe ordered, "cut me a up a bunch of that twine. Julio, you shoot any man who turns around." He began to kick the fallen pistols off the road while Wil dashed to the wagon and picked up one of the strands of twine.

"You damned traitor," Toby said to Wil.

"Shut your mouth," Joe commanded.

Wil cut several lengths of twine and brought them to Joe.

"Keep 'em covered, Wilbur," Joe said.

To the prisoners, he said: "Put your hands behind your back. Any funny moves and you get a bullet."

The men put their hands behind their backs. Joe tied Cletus's hands together first and pulled the twine tight before he knotted it.

"That hurts," Cletus said.

"It's supposed to hurt," Joe said.

"You ain't the law," Toby growled.

"Yes, I am," Joe said, "and I told you to keep your damned mouth shut."

He went from man to man and tied their hands behind their backs. When he was finished, he, Wil and Julio marched them up the road as their horses ran down the road and onto the grass of the valley.

All of the rattlesnakes had disappeared.

When Joe looked back, he saw Brad up on the rimrock, following tracks.

The tracks of Jordan Killdeer.

"I hope he catches that sonofabitch," Joe said.

"I do, too," Wil said. "I truly do."

"He will catch him," Julio said.

Joe herded his prisoners into the timber toward his lean-to and their camp.

"Sit down," he ordered, "five feet apart. Make a circle and turn your backs to each other."

The outlaws did as he ordered.

"Wil," Joe said, "if any of them try to get up or run, you shoot 'em down. Can you do that?"

"I sure can," Wil said.

Then Joe turned to Julio.

"Julio," he said, "do you think you can go down on your horse and round up their horses, bring them back here?"

"Yes, I can do that," Julio said. "Then what will you do, Joe?"

"We'll wait for Brad. But I want to have their horses up here and hobbled. Ready to go."

"To Denver?" Wil said.

"Yes, to Denver and to jail."

Some of the prisoners cursed under their breaths.

Julio went to his horse and saddled up. In fifteen minutes, he rode away toward the road.

"Now," Joe said to Wil, "we wait."

He looked at the men sitting in a circle on the ground, their backs to one another.

He wondered if Wil would back him if there was trouble.

"Do you know any of these men, Wil?" he asked.

"I know two of 'em," Wil said. He pointed to Toby. "That's Toby Dugan." He pointed to another man. "And that's Cletus Hemphill. I don't know who these others are."

"Friends of yours?" Joe asked.

Wil shook his head.

"Nope. They work for Jordan is all. On his ranch. But they're horse thieves all right."

"You may have to kill them, Wil. Could you do that?"

"I could shoot 'em down like the dogs they are," Wil said.

"Good," Joe said. "I just wanted to make sure."

Wil tapped the receiver of his rifle. Curly's rifle.

Joe smiled at him and patted his rifle.

He had no idea how long they would have to wait for Brad to return, but he hoped he'd bring Killdeer back alive.

He wanted to see Killdeer, along with the men he had in custody, hang from the gallows.

Joe walked to where he had his lariats coiled and picked up one of them. When he returned, he cut lengths of three feet each. Then he squatted and began to tie the rope around the booted ankles of the prisoners. Each man glared at him as he tied their feet together.

Then he picked up his rifle and sat down on the log, the rifle in his lap.

The sun began to slide on its downward arc. Beams of yellow light streamed through the pine boughs. Wil sat down on the log and laid his rifle across his legs, his finger inside the trigger guard.

Joe nodded in approval. He knew he could count on Wilbur.

The man was reformed, for sure.

FORTY-ONE

೧

The tracks Brad saw were small and easy to follow. The horse that had left the tracks moved at a gallop for some distance, so the ground was chewed up where its hooves had landed. The horse seemed to have been recently shod, as well, so the impressions were especially sharp and well defined. In between the tracks, there were small clumps and clods of dirt kicked up so that the trail seemed to have arrows pointing in the direction the rider was traveling.

For some distance, Killdeer's horse climbed almost straight up the small hills toward ever higher ones. Brad followed the tracks across small gullies and shallow ravines, and then, as the hills grew in size, he noticed the tracks were in parallel zigzags to the summits.

The tracking became more difficult as the terrain became steeper and more broken. None of the country looked familiar to Brad and he realized he had never been there before. At one point, the tracks followed a game trail for a mile or so, then Kildeer doubled back into a gully where the tracks were harder to see.

After that, he crisscrossed through ever deeper ravines,

only to climb out at a low point and head for higher ground. Then Brad lost the tracks for a brief spell when the horse hit a rocky plateau where it left no visible tracks. He was able to pick up the trail again by studying the dislodged stones and the overturned pebbles that revealed their wet or damp undersides.

He knows I'm tracking him, Brad thought as he picked up the trail again in an expected area beyond the plateau.

After that, he strained to follow the thread of the tracks as Kildeer backtracked and sidestepped, or rode back over hard ground where the impressions were faint. And in one small stretch, the horse was backed for several yards, then turned around and headed in a different direction.

"This guy knows what he's doing," Brad muttered to himself as he rode through a brush ravine and into a canyon that was open on both ends.

As the afternoon wore on, the chore of tracking became more taxing on Brad. Killdeer seemed to enjoy leading his pursuer onto consistently more difficult paths through thick timber, grassy swales, brush-choked gullies, and difficult, rock-infested ravines. Yet, there was no avoiding it. If he was to catch Killdeer, he had to keep after him.

He was somewhat encouraged by the age of the tracks. It seemed to Brad that he was closing the gap. Yet, at other times, he sensed that Killdeer had gained time on him. Perhaps he was becoming disoriented and confused by the winding trail he followed, the up and down path that Killdeer was forging in the rugged mountains.

Then suddenly, Brad noticed a new pattern. From the high hills, the tracks led downward; although still in a zigzag, they were descending to another level. The tracks led him into heavy timber, older pines with many deadfalls and elk beds. He jumped a pair of muleys and began to smell bear scat.

On a lower level, he began to see where Killdeer had ridden his horse over rotted deadfalls as if to thumb his nose at his tracker. The logs were mashed down in the center and leaked crumbling pulp from the innards. Not hard to track, but disconcerting, because a man usually made his horse jump deadfalls, not step and walk on top of them.

He began to see rocky outcroppings on small hillsides that were heavily thicketed with brush and pines. By then, Killdeer was riding in a straight line toward some unknown destination, staying at the same level on the hillsides. And he was moving faster. That told Brad that Killdeer either knew the country, or he was betting on his horse not stumbling into a burrow or sinkhole. The tracks were straight, and the stride of the horse indicated its faster speed.

Toward late afternoon when the light in the timber began to lessen, Brad saw another set of tracks that he recognized. Curly's tracks from the day before. To his surprise, he passed the large boulder that guarded the depression in the hillside where he had seen the stone with the ancient glyphs etched in its surface.

His heart quickened as he saw Killdeer's tracks blot out or mar some of the tracks that Curly's horse had made the previous day.

He suddenly realized that Curly had not found that cave by accident. He had known where he was going all the time.

And now it seemed clear to Brad that Killdeer was heading in the same direction, over the same path.

His hunch was verified later when he saw the caves and, when he looked closely at the ground, there were the tracks of Killdeer's horse heading up to the cave where he would have a commanding view of the terrain below the ledge. This gave Brad a sudden chill. In the distance, he saw the bare rim of the ledge and the large cave. As he rode to higher ground, he even saw Curly's corpse, lying there on the ledge where he had left it.

He reined up and rested the roan while he thought of his next moves.

Was Killdeer in the cave, the same cave where Curly had hidden out yesterday? Was his horse inside with him as Curly's had been?

He looked at the pile of stones where he had hidden

below the ledge. He did not want to go there again. If Kill-deer was up there in that same cave, he would know that Brad had concealed himself there. His tracks would be plain to see.

Brad now knew that he was following a very crafty man.

Should he wait him out? Or try to sneak up to the cave on foot as he had done before?

He breathed and rested. He patted the horse's withers and thought about what he should do.

Finally, he turned the horse until he could no longer see the ledge and the large cave. He slipped out of the saddle and ground-tied the reins to a sturdy juniper bush. Then he pulled Jinglebob's rifle from its scabbard. He eased the lever down and saw that there was a fresh cartridge in the chamber. He seated the lever.

He waited there for several minutes, listening for any sound coming from the cave, the scrape of a boot, the nicker of a horse. Anything.

Then he walked upslope until he was about even with the ledge. He walked toward the ledge and found a shallow depression where he could sit and see the cave opening as a black blot on the face of the limestone bluff.

He waited and listened as the sun began to descend toward the snow-flocked peaks. The air turned chill, and he felt the whisper of a breeze on his face.

The silence was excruciating.

The silence was deep and ominous.

FORTY-TWO

⁓

When Jordan first got a look at the rider who was following him, he thought it was that new man, Randy McCall, the one they called Jinglebob. When he had a chance to look again a half hour later, he saw that the rider was not Jinglebob. Instead, it was a man he had never seen before.

Who was he?

Jordan wondered. Was he a hired tracker? A detective? A U.S. marshal?

It didn't dawn on him until later that the man he caught a glimpse of whose pursuit was relentless, might be the man who had made him the offer to sell his horses back to him—Brad Storm.

When he spotted the man again, he was sure that it was the one they called the Sidewinder. Brad Storm. The man was a superb tracker. No matter where Jordan led him, the Sidewinder picked up his trail. He waited for an opportunity to draw his rifle and pick off the tracker, but each time he stopped and tried to get a fix on Storm, the man seemed to know he was being watched and did not present a clear target.

The man was uncanny, Jordan thought. Storm seemed to know when Jordan was waiting in ambush, and he would blend into cover and turn invisible. It was maddening to have a man like that on his trail. Even when he did see Storm in the open, he could never see all of him. Storm either hunched low over his saddle, or rode into a copse of thick trees, or just halted his horse and waited a few seconds. At such times, all Jordan could see was the switch of the roan's tail, or a leg or two, perhaps the horse's rump, or the boots of the rider.

After two or three hours, Jordan knew that he would not lose his tracker with any of the tricks he had learned from the Cheyenne and Arapaho. He had tried everything he knew and remembered from when they were being pursued by Kiowa or Utes from whom they had stolen horses.

Storm seemed to possess a sixth sense that warned him of danger. Jordan had no doubt that the Sidewinder could read tracks like some people could read books. He seemed to unravel every deception, every doubling back, every trail through thick brush or over trackless stone.

Jordan and Sugarfoot climbed ever higher. He stopped just below timberline and realized that he dared not go farther. Up on the barren slope he saw a large mule deer standing like a sentinel looking down on him. If he ventured to that open space below the snowcapped peak, he would be an easy target for a rifleman.

He turned his horse and headed back down. He knew now where he had to go if he was to make a stand and shoot the man who tracked him like a dog on the scent or a cougar stalking a wandering deer. He rode straight down into the thick timber that he knew. He still tried to throw Storm off his track, but after a time, he knew that he would never shake him. The man was as good a tracker as any Arapaho or Cheyenne brave. He was relentless, and he was not misled by any of Jordan's backtrackings or tricks.

He rode now with a purpose. He knew where he could go and have a chance to shoot Storm and kill him. He passed a place he knew well, where a large stone guarded the cavity in the hill where there was an ancient stone that the Arapaho had told him contained messages from their ancestors. He knew the stone well, for he had looked at it many times as a boy. And, more than once, his Arapaho companions had gone there to speak of the days before the white men, the days when their people talked with gods and believed that they had been created as special people to inhabit the Earth.

He passed by there, and pangs of memory trickled through his mind like waves in a pool startled by a thrown stone.

The ancient ones left records of themselves on many stones throughout the Rockies, and some of the elders in the Arapaho tribe remembered the stories they had been told, about a frozen world of ice and snow and a terrible deluge that had covered the Earth, except that one man and his kindred had escaped on the back of a giant turtle and repopulated the Earth.

Jordan rode to the place of the caves and spotted the wide ledge where he could ride Sugarfoot and both of them disappear into a very large cave. A cave where he had heard the ancestors of the Arapaho once lived after the rains that nearly drowned the entire world.

He rode up to the edge of the ledge and urged Sugarfoot onto it. He rode toward the cave and saw something he never expected to see.

There, lying flat on his back with his throat cut deep from ear to ear, was one of his men. He recognized Dan Jimson, the baldheaded gunslinger the boys had all called Curly. He had been stripped of his gun belt and had already begun to decompose.

Sugarfoot shied away from the dead man, and Jordan reined him in so hard the horse's head bowed. He looked down over the edge of the ledge and saw a dark lump lying in a pile of brush and boulders. Curly's horse. It must have leaped off the ledge and fallen to its death, Jordan thought.

The shadows below the ledge began to deepen when he rode inside the cave and dismounted.

He led Sugarfoot deeper into the cave and patted his neck. He pulled his rifle from its scabbard and walked back toward the entrance. He leaned the rifle against the cave wall next to the entrance and then dropped to his knees.

He drew his pistol and checked that all the cylinders were full. Then he laid the pistol in front of him on the cave floor as he knelt and waited, listening for any sign that Storm was closing in on him.

Jordan knew that this was his last stand. He had to either kill Storm or Storm would kill him.

He knelt there and listened until he heard the soft sound of a horse moving toward the pile of rocks that were below the bluff and the ledge.

The horse moved close to the rock pile and then Jordan heard the footfalls retreat. It was quiet for a time. Then he thought he heard the sounds of a man on foot. And the man was climbing up the slope beyond the edge of the ledge off to his left.

Storm would reach the ledge in a few minutes, Jordan knew. If he had been the one to kill Curly, then he would know that he and his horse were in the cave.

He heard the scrape of a boot on stone.

Jordan began to chant the Arapaho death song in a low voice that gradually grew louder. He knew the words, and he knew what they meant.

"It is a good day to die," he sang in the Arapaho language. "I do not fear death. Death is my friend who comes for me. It is a good day to die."

He sang and waited, his rifle close at hand, his pistol lying ready just in front of him.

The footsteps grew louder and louder.

Storm was approaching.

Soon, Jordan knew, he would be in a fight to the death.

It was a good day to die for either one of them.

FORTY-THREE

~

Shadows crawled up the cliff face and burrowed into the hollows beneath the ledge. They shrouded the face of the bluff and slid into the cave where Jordan Killdeer knelt and chanted his death song.

He stopped and listened for the scrape of a boot or the crunch of stone underfoot. Instead, he heard what sounded like a faint whisper, a swishing sound as if someone had stroked an eagle feather with a pair of fingers.

Brad Storm hugged the cliff face and heard the same sound, as if someone had breathed out a lungful of air, or brushed the seat of a chair with a feather duster.

Swish, swish.

Then, a silence for a few seconds.

A soft scraping sound.

It sounded like coiling scales.

The brittle rattle from the edge of the cave broke the silence.

Brad heard another series of sounds and a soft grunt.

"I know your tricks, Storm," Jordan yelled from inside the cave. "You don't fool me."

"That's not my rattle," Brad said.

The rattling grew louder.

Brad heard the sound of boots striking the cave floor.

"It's a snake," shrieked Jordan.

Brad moved then, through the shadows and into the dark of the cave. He slid around the lip of the entrance and saw a dim figure stomping the ground. He heard the rattles become more frantic and looked down. There was a three-foot rattler coiled up and moving its head. Its forked tongue twitched as its eyes followed Jordan's movements.

Jordan had a pistol in his hand and was backing toward the wall.

Brad ducked his head and charged straight at the man. He jumped over the coiled rattler and slammed into Jordan's midsection with the force of a pile driver.

Jordan grunted in pain and tried to club Brad with the butt of his pistol.

Brad swung his gun hand in a wide arc and cracked into Jordan's arm. The pistol flew from Jordan's hand and clattered on the cave floor.

The rattler uncoiled and slithered from the cave, its rattles clattering together like hollow dice.

"Bastard," Jordan growled and stooped to pick up his pistol.

Brad rammed his gun barrel into Jordan's gut and knocked the air out of his lungs.

Sugarfoot neighed his fear and displeasure from the back of the cave.

Jordan grappled with Brad. He lashed out with both arms, and his hands grabbed Brad's arms as the half-breed tried to edge away toward the cave entrance.

Brad shoved his pistol back in its holster and spread his arm to break Jordan's grip. Jordan's hands flew off Brad's arms as Brad drove him backward and slammed his body into the hard rock wall.

Jordan cursed and brought his arms up. His made fists and lashed out at Brad with his right hand.

The blow landed on Brad's jaw and staggered him. He

doubled up a fist and drove it straight into Jordan's belly. Jordan cried out in pain and doubled over for a second or two. He came out of his crouch swinging. He punched with a right and a left, trying to drive Brad backward.

Brad fended off the blows with his arms and elbows, but stepped backward, out of range of Jordan's fists.

"I'll get you, you sonofabitch," Jordan snarled, and he waded toward Brad, both fists cocked to deliver blows once he had his attacker in range.

Brad sidestepped Jordan's charge and landed a glancing blow on his face with a roundhouse right. Jordan cried out in pain and fell toward the back of the cave.

Brad went after him. Both men panted hard as they grappled again, each trying to land fists on the other's body and face.

Jordan was strong. Brad could feel the corded muscles in his arms, the power of his legs as Jordan pushed against him and tried to encircle him with his arms.

Brad stepped a half pace backward and escaped the lethal grip of Jordan's hands. He lashed out with a left hook and caught Jordan on his right ear with a stinging blow.

"Owwww," Jordan erupted and staggered sideways. Then he recovered and swung a right at Brad's head.

Brad threw his head back and felt the air rush past his chin. He reached up and grabbed Jordan's wrist. He dug in his nails and squeezed the wrist hard.

With an extra effort, Jordan broke the hold and tried to knee Brad in the crotch. He came close.

Brad brought a fist down and cracked the knuckles into Jordan's upper leg. He was so close he could see the pain etched on Jordan's face.

But Jordan danced away, limping slightly from the pain in his leg.

Brad pressed his advantage and strode close. He hammered Jordan with a quick left and then a right, landing both blows on either side of Jordan's jaw. Jordan winced and retaliated with a flurry of fists that drove Brad backward toward the cave entrance.

Both men could hear each other's labored breaths.

Jordan pursued Brad with flailing fists. He was fast. Brad stepped slightly to one side and Jordan threw himself off balance for a split second. Brad rammed a fist into his side. Jordan staggered and grunted in pain.

But Jordan was still standing. He whirled to attack Brad again from a better angle.

Brad was ready for him.

As Jordan charged him with his fists doubled up, Brad stood his ground. He jutted his elbows out, and Jordan's blows stung both of them with tremendous force.

Brad saw his opportunity. Both of Jordan's fists were low and he had not yet drawn them back toward him to strike out again.

Jordan cursed him in Arapaho.

Brad drove an uppercut between Jordan's arms and bashed him on the point of his chin.

Jordan's head snapped backward. His arms went slack. His eyes rolled in their sockets and he had to widen his stance to keep his balance.

Brad followed up with a savage left hook that slammed into Jordan's jaw with hammering force. Jordan spun around, dazed, and struggled to keep from falling.

"Give it up, Jordan," Brad panted.

"Not until you're dead," Jordan said. His voiced sounded as if he had a mouthful of mush. Blood leaked over his lips and when his mouth opened his teeth were covered with blood.

Brad's fist had cracked one side of Jordan's lips, drawing blood, splitting the tender skin.

Jordan tried to recover. His dark eyes seemed to have a light of their own as he charged Brad with swinging fists.

Brad tucked in his belly, and one of Jordan's fists missed its mark. The other one caught Brad high in the chest. It was a skin-tightening blow that filled his lungs with a sudden heat.

Brad grabbed one of Jordan's arms and twisted it. Jordan cried out in pain and swiveled around until he dropped to one knee.

"Damn you, Storm," Jordan yelled, and there was pain in his voice.

Brad continued to twist until he heard something snap in Jordan's elbow.

Jordan screamed and dropped to his knees.

Brad released his grip on Jordan's arm and saw the forearm dangle uselessly, swinging back and forth in a slow motion, like a broken pendulum.

Jordan tried to rise to his feet.

Brad stepped closed to him and drove a straight right hand into Jordan's temple. He heard a sound like a cracking pane of glass. Jordan slumped over and collapsed in a heap. He was out cold.

Gasping for breath, Brad stood over the fallen man and gulped in air to drench the fire in his lungs. After a few moments, Brad walked back to where Jordan's horse was stomping its feet and pawing the stone floor of the cave. He loosened the leather ties on one of the lariats attached to the saddle. He patted the horse's neck and spoke a few soothing words to it.

"It's all over, boy," he said to the horse as he walked back toward Jordan.

Brad knelt down next to the unconscious man and drew his knife. He stretched out a length of rope and cut it, then used that piece to measure three others and cut them all to the same size, quickly, deftly. He sheathed his knife and let the remainder of uncut rope lie where it had fallen.

He pushed Jordan onto his stomach and drew his arms backward until both hands were behind him. Then he lashed Jordan's hands together and tightened the rope before tying knots. He pulled on the rope to test its hold.

Satisfied, Brad stood up. He pulled Jordan to his feet. Jordan was slowly regaining consciousness. He tried to pull one arm free of the rope bond, but gave up while Brad watched. The other arm was useless and Jordan could not move it or his hand.

"You won this one, Storm. But it ain't over yet." Jordan,

obviously in pain, slurred the words out and appeared to be in a daze.

"No, it's not over yet, Killdeer," Brad said. "There's one more rope I don't have on me at the moment."

"Huh? You got ropes in your hand."

"Not the one I really want," Brad said.

"You talk like a crazy man. What rope?"

"The rope they're going to put around your neck up on the gallows. The rope that's going to break your damned thieving neck."

Brad shoved Jordan back toward his horse. He dropped the extra lengths of rope and grabbed Jordan. He forced him onto the saddle, pushed him until he lay on it, belly down. His legs dangled on one side.

Brad wrapped rope around Jordan's ankles, then walked to the other side. He attached the other end of the rope to a D-ring and secured it firmly. Then he tied another rope to another ring and walked to the other side where he wrapped the rope around Jordan's knees and tied it tight. With the last strand of rope, he ran it under Jordan's belt and wrapped the other end around the saddle horn and tied it.

Then he unbuckled Jordan's gun belt and rolled the rig into a ball, which he put into one of the saddlebags.

"I can't breathe," Jordan said.

"You can breathe," Brad said.

He picked up the dangling reins and led the horse toward the cave entrance and into the dark.

"Where you takin' me, Storm?" Jordan asked as the night air washed across his face.

"Why, back to Wild Horse Valley where you can take one last look at all the pretty horses," Brad said.

"You are one mean and devilish sonofabitch," Jordan snarled.

"It takes one to know one," Brad said as he led the horse along the ledge.

The dwindling moon peeked over the rim of the mountains and cast a glimmer of light on the two of them as they cleared the ledge and headed down the slope to where Jinglebob's horse was tied.

The horse whickered as they approached.

Jordan's horse replied with a rippling nicker.

"I ain't real comfortable hogtied like this," Jordan said as Brad pulled himself into the saddle and pulled on the reins of Jordan's horse.

"You'll get used to it, Killdeer," Brad said. "Just think about all those horses you're going to see one last time."

"I ain't through with you, Storm. I got friends."

"If you do have friends, you'll have some company when you go to the gallows."

"I don't buy it," Jordan said.

"It's free, Killdeer. You don't have to buy it."

Brad touched spurs to Jinglebob's horse, and they rode out of the small clearing and headed down into the timber. Moonlight painted streaks of silvery light through the needles and branches of the pines. The beams looked like misty lances of fairy lights as they wound their way over and past deadfalls.

Brad knew the way back to Wild Horse Valley. And so did Jordan.

Brad could hear him wheezing as they descended through the shadows of night along unseen pathways where ancient men had hunted and left strange markings on stone to mark their brief days in a time most men had forgotten, when the West was young and unmarked and un-owned by anyone.

FORTY-FOUR

❧

The prisoners lay asleep in their bedrolls when Brad rode up with Jordan and his horse in tow. Firelight flickered on the blankets of the sleepers. Joe was sitting on the log near the fire with a rifle across his lap. Brad saw that Julio and Wilbur were also asleep, and their blankets danced with black shadows, orange and blue tongues of light.

Joe looked up as Brad approached.

"Is that Jordan's body on his horse?" he asked as he stood up, his voice pitched low.

Flames from the fire scrawled arabesques of color across his face, glanced off the metal and wood of his rifle like living wraiths of multicolored light.

"No, Joe," Brad said as he swung out of the saddle, "he's alive. Got a busted arm and a few bruises and welts is all."

Joe swore in disbelief.

He walked to the side of Sugarfoot and looked at Jordan's swollen face. He was out cold. There were puffy lumps under his eyes and one of his earlobes was the size of a small peach.

"You got him trussed up like a sack of meal," Joe whispered.

"I wanted him alive," Brad said. "I want to see him hang for his crimes."

"I'll lay out his bedroll and help you get him down," Joe said. "Tired?"

"Beyond tired," Brad said. "My muscles are locked up tight, and every bone in my body is screaming. I could use a cup of strong coffee and a few hours of sleep."

"Maybe some oil for your joints, too," Joe said.

He walked back and untied Jordan's bedroll and laid it near the lumps of prisoners. He and Brad lifted the limp body of Jordan out of the saddle after Brad loosened the ropes under the horse's belly and the one attached the saddle horn.

They carried Jordan to his tarp and lay him down.

"He's still breathing, anyway," Joe whispered as he pulled the blanket over Jordan.

"Get me one of those lengths of rope I left back there," Brad said. "I'm going to tie his feet together."

"Sure," Joe said. He went quickly to where Brad had dropped the ropes and picked up one of them. When he got back, Brad was kneeling at the feet of Jordan. Joe handed him the rope.

Brad lifted Jordan's boots and wrapped rope around the ankles. He tied them tight. Jordan did not awaken.

"That ought to hold him," Brad said. He stood up.

"He ain't goin' nowhere soon, that's for sure," Joe said. "There's still coffee left in the pot. Probably cold by now. I'll set the pot on the fire and stoke it up."

The two men walked to the fire ring. Joe put more wood on the hot coals, then set the coffeepot where the flames could reach the bottom. They sat down while the horses stood hipshot, staring at the fire.

"Well, Brad," Joe said, "we got almost all we need. As soon it gets light, I'll take Wilbur down to the valley with me and I'll start writin' down brands to take to court."

"You trust Wilbur?" Brad asked as he rubbed his hands together over the fire to warm them.

"I think he's a changed man," Joe said. "What about you?"

"Pendergast might want to hire him," Brad said.

"You'd recommend him?"

"Yeah, I would. I think Wil might make a good detective. There's nothing like a reformed criminal to track down others of his kind."

"You may be right. He'll be a big help to me in the morning when I check those brands."

"Oh?"

"The ones that are changed. He can tell me what they were, or what kind of running iron he and Trask used so I can figure it out."

"Big job," Brad said.

"With Wilbur's help, we can go through the horses pretty fast," Joe said.

They drank coffee and talked in low tones. Then Brad and Joe unsaddled the two horses and hobbled them with the others. Brad said good night and went to his bedroll. He was surprised to see his rifle lying half under it.

"Julio got your rifle," Joe said, "and your canteens after the fight. He chased out a couple of rattlers where you was hidin'."

Brad chuckled as he pulled the blanket over him. "I can take the watch when you get tired, Joe."

"I'll wake Julio in a couple of hours. You get some sleep. You got to be worn to a frazzle."

"I am," Brad said and closed his eyes as Joe walked back toward the fire. He heard him drop more wood on the fire. The wood crackled as it released gases and sparks into the night air.

One of the prisoners droned on in a soft snore and Brad fell into a deep sleep.

When he woke up, Joe and Wilbur were gone. Pale light illuminated the eastern sky and shafts of light filtered through the pines. Julio sat by the fire and Brad smelled the enticing aroma of coffee.

He threw off his blanket and stretched. He strapped on his gun belt and walked over to the fire.

"Morning, Julio."

"Morning."

"All the prisoners are still asleep."

"They are tired from the wrestling," Julio said.

"The wrestling?"

"They still think they can untie themselves and run away."

Brad sat down. Julio poured him a cup of coffee.

"They are no trouble," Julio said. "They have the ropes on the hands and the feet. You caught Jordan, eh?"

"You saw him?"

Julio nodded.

"He give out the moans when I wake up. I give him some water and he go back to sleep. His face look like he in a big fight."

"He was in a fight," Brad said.

"You did not kill him," Julio said.

"The rope will kill him," Brad said.

Julio grinned wide. He poured himself some coffee.

"We get our horses back, no?" Julio said.

"When we finish up with putting these rascals in jail, we can get our horses and go back home."

"That is good," Julio said.

Later, Julio and Brad rousted the outlaws out of their sleep and sat them up in a circle where Julio indicated they should sit.

"We will feed them now," Julio said. "You feed two. I feed two."

"We have enough grub?" Brad asked.

"They have grub in the saddlebags. There is much food."

Brad sipped his coffee. Then he got up and walked over to where Jordan was still curled up in his bedroll. He knelt down and shook him.

"Wake up, Killdeer," he said. "Get something to eat. Are you thirsty?"

"Yeah, I'm thirsty and I hurt all over."

"You'll live," Brad said. "For a while, anyway."

"You bastard. You ain't seen the last of me yet. I still got an ace or two to play."

"You're finished, Killdeer. Your thieving days are over."

"We'll see," Jordan said.

Brad helped him sit and then get to his feet. He forced Jordan to hop over to the circle of men and sat him down hard.

"Howdy, Boss," Cletus said. "Sorry you got caught up with the rest of us."

Jordan huffed up with a lungful of air and just glared at Brad.

"He beat you up pretty bad, looks like," Toby said. "We didn't do too good, either. Them boys plumb snookered us."

"CJ will fix this," Jordan said.

"Yeah," Toby said.

Brad was kneeling down and picked up hardtack and jerky from a flour sack. He half heard what the men were saying, but put no importance on any of it.

He took food to the prisoners. Julio was already feeding Lenny and Terry by hand. He gave them both sips of coffee when they finished chewing.

Brad fed Toby and Cletus. He looked at Jordan.

"You hungry, Killdeer?" he said.

"I can't eat just now. My lips are all swolled, and I got so much pain I don't know if I could chew."

"Coffee, then?" Brad asked.

"Maybe. A little."

Brad picked up the same cup he'd used to serve Cletus and Toby in between bites. He held it to Jordan's lips and tilted it slightly.

Jordan's mouth filled with a tablespoon of coffee. He winced at the pain in his lips, but swallowed the coffee.

"More," he said.

Brad gave him more coffee as Toby and Cletus looked at their boss.

"Better eat, Jordan," Cletus said.

"Later," Jordan said.

Inside of an hour, Julio and Brad had finished feeding the prisoners. All except Jordan, who looked like a battered prizefighter with a broken arm.

"We got to piss," Toby said.

"Piss your pants," Brad said. "You're staying right where you are. All of you."

The prisoners cursed Brad. Jordan merely glared at him with a burning hatred sparking in his slitted eyes.

Joe and Wilbur returned in late afternoon. Joe had a tablet in his hand when he dismounted.

"Get all of them?" Brad asked.

"I think so. Most of 'em are brands I know from my work with the breeders association."

"Is this good evidence to take into court?" Brad asked.

"It's all we need. We can bring some of the horses down when we need them as evidence. I'll get the judge to issue subpoenas once he sets a court date, and then I'll round up the witnesses we talked to at Arapaho Gulch and the lumber camp."

"Will you need my help with those subpoenas?"

"Nope, Brad. I know where to go and who to give 'em to. Your job is just about finished, I reckon."

"Good. Julio and I want to get our own horses and head back to Leadville. Unless you need them?"

"I don't need 'em," Joe said.

Wilbur sat down after he finished unsaddling the horses and hobbling them in the timber with the others. He looked at Jordan for a long time.

"Traitor," Jordan hissed.

Wilbur turned his back on him and joined Brad and Joe. He wiped his forehead with the back of his hand. It came away wet with sweat.

"A lot of horses they stole hadn't had their brands changed yet, including yours, Brad. So, they wouldn't work as evidence."

"Good. I'm anxious to get back to my own ranch, and Julio's wife is probably throwing plates at the wall by now."

Julio laughed.

"She does not throw the plates," he said. "She pulls hard on the cow's teats."

Wilbur and Joe laughed.

Later, Brad walked into the timber with Joe.

"We could start down toward Denver any time now," Joe said. "I got all I need."

"Let's ride, then," Brad said. "It might be slow going and we have to make sure none of those boys get the itch to run."

"Once we get moving, we can keep a close eye on them."

"Okay, let's saddle up and start loading bodies into saddles," Brad said.

"Boy, CJ will be pleased," Joe said as they walked to where they had stored their saddles and bridles.

"What did you say?" Brad asked.

"I said Cliff will be right happy to see we broke up the gang," Joe said.

"No, you didn't say that," Brad said. "You said something like CJ."

"Yeah. Cliff Jameson. Some call him CJ."

"Well, I'll be damned," Brad said as he leaned over to pick up his bridle.

"What?" Joe asked.

"Nothing, Joe. I'll let you know if there's anything to it."

"When?"

"After we put these bastards in jail."

It took more than an hour to saddle up all the horses and another half hour or so to get the prisoners in their saddles. Brad tied Jordan to his saddle the same way he had lashed him to his horse before.

The lights of Denver glistened in the early dusk as the procession dipped below Lookout Mountain on their way back to the city.

Brad was leading Jordan's horse well behind the others, who had moved at a fair pace all the way to the foothills.

All during the ride down, Brad's mind had raced as he went over the conversation he had overheard. Something

Jordan had said about having an ace in the hole. And, more than once, Jordan had said that it was not over yet. He had some plan in his mind, or he did, indeed, have an ace in the hole.

Then, when Joe had mentioned that CJ would be pleased, it jarred loose the buried conversation between Jordan and his men.

Jordan had mentioned CJ.

Then Joe had said that some people called Cliff by his initials.

This was either an odd coincidence or it meant something.

Brad knew what he had to do when he got to Denver. Just the thought of it made the bile stir in his stomach. Something was wrong if Jordan Killdeer thought he could beat the charges and beat the hangman.

The prairie disappeared in shadow and the lights of Denver wavered in the pale light of dusk as if it were a sunken town just drifting below the dark waters of a calm sea.

And the knot in Brad's stomach grew hard as a balled-up fist.

FORTY-FIVE

Joe booked his and Brad's prisoners into the Denver jail. Jordan Killdeer was taken to the infirmary where a doctor set his broken arm and put it in a plaster cast.

Afterward, Joe, Brad, Wilbur, and Julio put all the outlaws' horses into the livery stable near the stockyards. Then the four of them rode back to the Brown Palace Hotel and entered the dining room.

After a waiter took their orders, Brad turned to Joe.

"Let me have a look at those brands, Joe, the ones you wrote down on a tablet."

"Sure," Joe said. He reached inside his jacket and pulled the folded notepapers from his pocket.

He handed them to Brad while Wilbur and Julio drank from their water glasses.

Brad scanned the list once, then read the brands again more slowly.

"What's Cliff's brand, Joe?" Brad asked.

"It's CJ. That's what he calls his ranch and that's the brand he puts on his horses."

"Well, there's no CJ brand listed here," Brad said.

Joe's face mirrored his surprise.

"What? Let me take a look." Joe took the notepapers from Brad and read them over twice.

"I'm dumbfounded," he said. "I was sure that Cliff had horses stolen from him. Maybe they were sold and just weren't there."

"Don't try to make excuses for Cliff Jameson," Brad said. "I think he's in this thing up to his neck."

"Maybe," Joe said, "but how do you prove it?"

"I have a hunch," Brad said.

"A hunch? There you go again, Brad. What's your hunch?"

"You'll see. Let's get some grub in our bellies and then I'm going to the telegraph office."

Joe looked at Wilbur.

"You remember seeing the CJ brand on any of the horses you and Trask put to the running iron?" Joe asked.

"Nope. Don't recall," Wilbur said. "And that would have been a hard one to change."

"How would you change it?" Brad asked.

Wilbur thought about it for a minute or two.

"Well, it'd be tricky, but it could be done, I s'pose."

"That's what I thought," Brad said. "Cliff never had any horses stolen by Killdeer."

"He's the president of the breeders association, for God's sake," Joe said.

"Seems he's playing both sides of the field," Brad said.

"I can't believe it," Joe said.

"We'll see," Brad said.

After they finished their supper, all of them followed Brad to the telegraph office. There, he sent a telegram, which he showed to the others before he had the clerk send it.

The telegram read:

COLONEL BEACHAM
FORT LARAMIE, WYOMING

SIR: CAN YOU TELL ME THE NAME OF THE PERSON
WHO DIRECTED YOU TO PURCHASE HORSES FROM
JORDAN KILLDEER? IMPORTANT.

HARRY PENDERGAST
DENVER DETECTIVE AGENCY
BROWN PALACE HOTEL
DENVER, COLORADO

"What do you expect to learn from the colonel?" Joe
asked.

"We'll see," Brad said.

They walked to the Brown Palace and checked in at the
desk, taking four rooms and charging them to the Denver
Detective Agency.

"We'll see Harry in the morning," Brad said. "Wilbur,
I'm going to trust you to stay in your room."

"I ain't goin' nowhere," Wil said. "This whole mess is
getting real interestin'."

Joe laughed.

"Wait'll you meet Pendergast, Wil. He might offer you a
job. On my recommendation, of course."

"I—I don't know what to say," Wil said.

"Say good night," Brad said. "I'll see you all the morning, say eight o'clock? For breakfast."

The others assented as they took their keys and walked
upstairs to find their rooms.

They all carried their bedrolls, saddlebags, and rifles
with them. Brad stayed at the desk for a few more moments.

Brad told the clerk to put their horses up for the night at
the nearest livery.

As he ascended the stairs, Brad glanced down the mezzanine. The detective agency's offices were dark. He went
to his room on the second floor, the one Harry always re-
tained for him when he was on a case. He went inside and
dropped his rifle and gear on the table. Then he pulled out
the swatch of blue flannel cloth that had been part of Felicity's nightgown.

He sat down and stroked the cloth in the palm of his hand.

Tears welled up in his eyes and flowed down his cheeks.

"I haven't forgotten you, darling," he whispered.

Then he got up, lit the lamp with the matches and box beside it.

His tears dried on his face when he lay down, and he had the faint taste of salt in his mouth as he dropped off to sleep.

He dreamed of Felicity, but in the landscape of his mind, she was a small girl skipping rope and playing with a doll that resembled him. She spoke to the doll in a strange language that he could not understand, and there was a rope around the doll's neck. She pulled on the rope to make the boy doll dance and then the face of the doll changed and became an Indian's face. The Indian's face was covered with war paint and the doll brandished a rifle that turned into a buzzing rattlesnake.

Someone in the dream screamed.

It was his own scream that Brad heard, deep in the dark and shadowy world of the dream where everything seemed real, but in truth, none of it was.

FORTY-SIX

❧

When Byron Lomax ushered Brad, Joe, Wil, and Julio into Pendergast's office after breakfast the following morning, Harry was seated behind his desk with a telegram in his hand.

"Thank you, Byron," Pendergast said. "That will be all for now."

"Yes, sir," Lomax said. He left the office and closed the door behind him.

"Please be seated, gentlemen," Harry said. The four visitors sat down in comfortable leather chairs.

Harry waved the telegram at Joe and Brad.

"Maybe one of you might explain this to me. It's a telegram from a Colonel Samuel O. Beacham at Fort Laramie. I didn't send him a request, but I have a feeling one of you did."

"I did," Brad said. "Last night."

"Maybe you'd like to explain why you conducted such an enquiry, Brad."

"Harry, I think Cliff Jameson is behind the horse thieving. A half-breed named Jordan Killdeer ran the operation from his ranch in Cheyenne, but it's my strong hunch that he was, in Joe's words at breakfast this morning, aiding and abetting Killdeer. Recently, I uncovered a deal between Killdeer and Colonel Beacham to buy two hundred head of horses. Stolen horses. Killdeer and his gunmen are all in jail."

"I know," Harry said. "I was informed by the Denver police last night that you had brought in several suspected horse thieves and murderers. I have their names right here."

He picked up a sheet of paper and flourished it as he had the telegram. He put both down and made a steeple out of his fingers. He looked long and thoughtfully at Brad. Then he picked up several sheets of paper that appeared to be covered with typed text.

"It might interest you, Brad, that I had my own suspicions about Cliff Jameson. I'll tell you what I discovered before I read the colonel's reply to your enquiry."

"Go ahead, Harry," Brad said. "I'm all ears."

Harry cleared his throat and set the papers down in front of him. He glanced over them before he spoke.

"Clifford Jameson served in the army. He was cashiered out of the Seventh Cavalry by General Custer himself. It appears that he was selling horses to the Sioux and the Cheyenne. Army horses. He reported them stolen in midnight raids, but an undercover officer caught him in the act.

"Jameson came down here from South Dakota and started a ranch. He wormed his way into the horse breeders association by falsifying his government records. So he attained the high office there through deceit and subterfuge. I was about to send Pete Farnsworth out to his ranch to question him after I got the telegram early this morning."

"What did Colonel Beacham have to say?" Joe asked.

"I'll read what he put in his telegram," Harry said.

He picked up the telegram and read the message.

"'Most esteemed gentlemen of the Denver Detective Agency,' it begins. 'Per your request, I offer the following. STOP. I was contacted by a Mr. Clifford Jameson about purchasing horses. STOP. He recommended one Jordan

Killdeer, of Cheyenne, Wyoming. STOP. I subsequently purchased two hundred head of horses to be delivered to me at Fort Laramie. STOP. I trust you will inform me of the reason for this inquiry. I am at your service. STOP.'"

Harry set the telegram down on the desk.

"It is signed by the colonel and I do owe him an explanation. I assume you have spoken to him before, Brad."

"Yes, I met him in Cheyenne, briefly, but did not tell him anything about this case."

"Good. You make a pretty good detective, Brad."

"I'm not cut out for such work," Brad said. "But you hired me, so I do my best."

"How do you plan to proceed, may I ask?"

Brad looked at Joe, then back at Harry.

"I thought Joe and I would ride out to the CJ ranch and have a little talk with Cliff. Joe has a list of the horses and their brands that have been grazing up in Wild Horse Valley. Over three hundred head. Not a one of them carries the CJ brand and none of the ones that were sold to miners and lumberjacks carried that brand. We have witnesses who will testify that Killdeer made the deals and his men carried out his orders."

"I wrote out a full report for you last night, Harry," Joe said. "It tells of our investigations, the outlaws we uncovered, and a list of those who will never go to trial."

"Why is that, Joe?" Harry asked.

"They're all dead, Harry. Brad killed the men who raped and murdered his wife. As you know, we have Killdeer in jail, along with the remainder of his hirelings."

Harry rose from his chair behind his desk and walked around to the front. He sat on the edge.

"I want you to arrest Cliff Jameson," he said. "I think we have enough evidence to convict him. As for the stolen horses, we might contact the rightful owners and see if they are willing to sell two hundred head to the colonel."

He paused and looked at Wilbur.

"And, who, pray tell, is this man who is with you?"

"Harry," Brad said, "this is Wilbur Campbell. He worked

with Jack Trask with the running irons. He stole no horses and he's been a big help to both Joe and me."

"So, you're one of the Killdeer gang, are you, Mr. Campbell?" Harry said.

"No, sir," Wil said, "not no more. I been reformed. Least that's what Brad said."

"He might make a good detective," Joe said.

"We'll see about that," Harry said.

"Sometimes, Harry," Brad said, "it takes one to catch one."

"What, a thief? You said Wilbur wasn't a thief."

"A criminal then. He was just a working hand for Killdeer. He's not a real criminal," Brad said.

"Humph. Well, I'll think about it. Now, you two go out there to the CJ ranch. Bring Jameson back in handcuffs. I want him brought in alive. Do you understand me, Brad?"

"He'll be alive," Brad said. "Unless . . ."

Harry waved his hands in the air as if to shake off the rest of Brad's sentence.

"Alive," Harry said. "Or fairly alive. I won't mind it if he comes here with a bruise or two."

Brad and Joe got up. They started to leave.

"Julio's got his orders from me, Harry. But I'm setting Wilbur here loose. He's in your hands now."

Before Harry could protest, Joe and Brad left the room, swinging the heavy door open and stalking past Lomax and the secretary at their desks.

"You'll need some training if you're going to work for me as a detective, Wilbur," Harry said.

"Oh, I'm willin', sir. More than willin'."

"Do you have any money?"

"Nary a cent, sir," Wilbur said. He patted both pockets.

"Tell my man Byron Lomax to send in Miss Fitzgerald and I'll see that you have some spending money. You're staying here in the hotel?"

"Yes, sir. Brad got us all rooms."

"So, he trusts you," Harry said.

"I reckon. Some."

"He trusts you, Wilbur, and so will I. But if you ever go back to your sinful ways, I'll have you in the hoosegow so fast your head will spin."

"Yes, sir," Wilbur said, "I'm goin' to toe the line."

Harry turned to Julio.

"Need any money, Julio?"

"Sir, I do not need no money. You have already paid me enough," Julio said.

"Thanks for your help, then. You and Brad did a good job on this case."

"And, Joe, he did a good job, too," Julio said.

Harry ushered them out of the office.

He went back to his desk and looked over the list of brands and number of horses still up in Wild Horse Valley. Joe had left the list on his desk.

He smiled before the door opened and Byron entered with Velma Fitzgerald.

He thought about Brad. He knew he would lose him as soon as he and Joe brought Jameson in. He hated to lose him.

Brad was the best detective he'd ever had working for him. Unconventional, yes, but he brought the criminals in, dead or alive.

And, now that he thought about it, mostly dead.

But few detectives were willing to risk their lives in the pursuit of criminals.

Brad was one who was not afraid to put his own life on the line.

And Brad Storm always got his man.

FORTY-SEVEN

～

The CJ ranch was north of Denver. Joe had been to it many times since hiring on as a range detective. There was a winding road to the ranch house, a creek lined with trees and horses grazing on lush prairie grass.

"Nice little spread," Brad said as they rode through the arched gateway with its gates swung open.

"He has better'n two thousand acres," Joe said.

"Is that Cliff out there by the corral?" Brad asked.

"Yeah, he just forked some hay into the feeding trough. Looks like he came from the barn yonder."

"Well, let's say good morning to the squire," Brad said, a sarcastic tone to his voice.

"He sure does look like the country squire," Joe said. "Polished Justins and all."

"He's not wearing a gun belt," Brad said.

"No reason out here. He's got some goats what keeps the snakes out of his yard."

Brad saw goats roaming around the frame ranch house, nibbling on grass, flowers, and what looked like spilled corn meal.

"Howdy, boys," Cliff said as Joe and Brad rode up. He set the pitchfork down and leaned against the pole corral. There were three horses inside the square arena, all of them at the hay trough.

"Mornin', Cliff," Joe said.

Brad said nothing.

"Light down. You got news for me, Joe?"

"Yeah, I do," Joe said. He and Brad dismounted.

Cliff walked over to them and shook Brad's hand.

"I know you got a man in jail," Cliff said. "You boys want some coffee, sweet tea?"

"No, we won't be here long, Cliff," Joe said.

"That Trask. You caught him with the running irons, right?"

"We caught all of them," Brad said.

"What?" Jameson seemed surprised.

Brad wondered if it was an act, part of the same act he used to deceive his fellow members in the breeders association.

"Yeah, Cliff," Joe said, "we caught every one of the horse thieves, including Jordan Killdeer."

Both men watched Cliff's face for any sign of recognition.

"He the boss?" Cliff asked.

"We thought so," Joe said.

"And now?" Cliff said.

"We know he wasn't the real boss," Brad said. "Just the straw boss."

"I don't get you, Storm," Cliff said.

"I'll make it short then, Cliff," Brad said. "I'm arresting you. Joe and I are arresting you."

"What for?"

"For murder, horse thieving, and maybe a whole lot more," Joe said.

"You're joking, right?"

Cliff looked genuinely puzzled.

Joe reached into his back pocket and pulled out a pair of handcuffs.

Brad grabbed Cliff's arms and pinned them to his side.

"Put your hands behind your back, Cliff," Joe ordered as he opened both cuffs.

"Damn you. Are you crazy? I ain't done a damned thing. You're making one hell of a mistake, Joe."

Brad twisted one arm to turn Cliff around. Then he grabbed both wrists and jerked them back, crossed them, and held on tight.

Joe slapped the cuffs on Cliff and closed them tight.

"You got a horse saddled, Cliff?" Brad asked.

"Hell no, I ain't goin' nowhere."

"He keeps a couple of riding horses in the barn there, Brad," Joe said.

"Well, we'll just have to saddle a horse for you, Cliff," Brad said.

He walked off toward the barn while Cliff cursed Joe.

He returned some ten minutes later with a horse that was saddled and ready to ride.

"Help me boost him up into the saddle, will you, Brad?" Joe said as he pushed an unwilling Cliff toward the horse, an old sway-backed mare with healed saddle sores and scars where saddles had worn down the hide and the open wounds had become infected.

"I don't ride this horse no more," Cliff said. "She's twelve years old if she's a day."

"You'll ride her to the Denver jail," Joe said.

Joe and Brad mounted up. Joe picked up the trailing reins to the bay mare and they headed for town.

"You're a traitor to the association," Cliff said as they rode through the gate. "The members will have me out of jail as soon as they find out what you've done."

"The breeders will be right happy to get their horses back, Cliff," Joe said. "And the only way you'll get out of jail will be when you're carried out in a pine box."

"You miserable, no-good bastard," Cliff snarled.

But he said no more until they booked him into jail when he again protested his innocence.

Later, at the hotel, Brad and Julio came down from their

rooms. They carried their saddlebags, bedrolls, and rifles and went into Harry's offices. They set their belongings down. Lomax was not there, but Velma looked up when they approached her desk.

"I'm heading home, Velma," Brad said. "Is Harry in? I'd like to say good-bye."

"Oh, you just missed him. He and Byron are making the rounds of the horse breeders to tell them the case is solved and they can get their horses back."

"Julio and I are riding up to the valley where all the horses are to drive ours back to my ranch in Leadville."

"Well, maybe you'll run into Mr. Pendergast up there. He planned to take as many of the ranchers up there that he can. I think Pete Farnsworth is with him and said he knows where that valley is."

"Maybe we'll see him, then," Brad said. "If not, tell him I said good-bye."

"I will surely do that, Mr. Storm. You take care now."

~

Julio and Brad rode up to Wild Horse Valley just before dusk.

"We get our horses now, Brad?" Julio asked as they both gazed down at the horses from the top of the road.

"Tomorrow, Julio. Early. One more night up here won't kill us."

"No. Nothing will kill us," Julio said.

"That lean-to Joe made is still up. You can bunk in there for the night."

"You can sleep there, Brad."

"Make a fire. I'll sleep close to it."

"You were born in the trees, I think," Julio said.

"If I wasn't, I should have been."

They talked around the campfire that night. There was no sign of Harry or any of the ranchers. It didn't matter.

Brad was finished with the Denver Detective Agency and he didn't fancy listening to Harry try to talk him out of it.

He was a cattle rancher and soon he'd have his horses back. Then there were the Brahman cattle. He was anxious to see how the breeding program worked out.

Julio was pining for Pilar, and Brad was still broken-hearted over the death of Felicity.

He would never get over it, he knew. There was just a vacant spot where she had been, a spot that could never be filled by any other woman.

That night, he slept with the patch of blue cloth in his hand. He was sure that one of the stars was winking at him wisely.

That star was either Felicity or her spirit twin.

Just before he closed his eyes to go to sleep, Brad gazed at that one bright star for a long moment.

Then, he winked back.